CURSES, BOILED AGAIN!

Shari Randall

St. Martin's Paperbacks

This is a work of fiction. All of the characters, organizations, and events portrayed in this novel are either products of the author's imagination or are used fictitiously.

CURSES, BOILED AGAIN!

Copyright © 2018 by Shari Randall.
Excerpt from *Against the Claw* copyright © 2018 by Shari Randall.

For information address St. Martin's Press, 175 Fifth Avenue, New York, NY 10010.

ISBN: 978-1-250-11670-3

Our books may be purchased in bulk for promotional, educational, or business use. Please contact your local bookseller or the Macmillan Corporate and Premium Sales Department at 1-800-221-7945, ext. 5442, or by email at MacmillanSpecialMarkets@macmillan.com.

Printed in the United States of America

St. Martin's Paperbacks edition / February 2018

St. Martin's Paperbacks are published by St. Martin's Press, 175 Fifth Avenue, New York, NY 10010.

10 9 8 7 6 5 4 3 2 1

For Mom and Dad

Acknowledgments

This book wouldn't exist without the encouragement, love, and support of so many friends and family members. I'm afraid I'll leave someone out if I start listing names, but I send a special thank you to my Chessie Sisters in Crime. Barb and Sherry, I miss our plotting parties. And I'm tremendously thankful to the artists of the Boston Ballet, especially Elizabeth Olds and Dawn Atkins, for the peek into the dancer's world.

The cure for anything is salt water:
sweat, tears, or the sea.
—ISAK DINESEN, 1934

Chapter 1

"What could go wrong?" Aunt Gully said.

My sister, Lorel, shot me a look as we drove into Mystic Bay's historic district. Aunt Gully sat in the backseat cooing to the pot next to her as plumes of black smoke sputtered from her van's tailpipe.

What could go wrong? What hadn't already gone wrong? This morning we'd discovered Aunt Gully's van had a flat tire. After I'd put on the spare, she'd forgotten her lucky apron and we had to go back home for it. When we'd swung down to the dock behind her Lazy Mermaid lobster shack to pick up fresh lobsters, her supplier was late. We were seriously behind schedule.

Aunt Gully hadn't even mentioned the mysterious letters we'd received this week. Threatening, anonymous letters.

I rubbed a smudge of grease from my chin and willed my heart rate to slow.

Though our most important task today was to feed a grand total of four lobster rolls to the judges in the Mystic Bay Food Festival Best Lobster Roll contest, Aunt Gully insisted that we provide free samples for all festival visitors. Aunt Gully was a Larkin, an old New England family that hadn't exactly come over on the *Mayflower*—maybe one of the later ships—but she had the soul of an Italian mama who had to feed everyone. Everyone. That's why I struggled to find a comfortable position in the shotgun seat of her jam-packed little gray van, trying to keep stacks of paper plates, napkins, rolls, and ceramic mermaids and nautical flags (because our samples booth has to look nice) off the soft boot covering my almost-healed broken ankle.

I caught sight of my bleary blue eyes in the visor mirror and snapped it up. An early riser I am not. As a dancer with New England Ballet Theater, I'm used to working matinee and evening performances. Since I'd broken my ankle in a tumble down some stairs, I'd returned home to heal and help get Aunt Gully's new business running. Now I rose before dawn to do prep work at the Lazy Mermaid.

Why hadn't Aunt Gully opened a nightclub instead?

Aunt Gully hummed as Lorel drove at exactly the speed limit into town where red-white-and-blue bunting draped storefronts and sea captains' homes.

Every Memorial Day weekend, Mystic Bay hosted the food festival on the town green, one block from the harbor. Foodies jammed the narrow streets to sample the best New England cooking. That Aunt Gully, the new kid on the block, had been chosen to compete in the Best Lobster Roll competition was quite a coup.

Food prep took place in the kitchen of the Mystic Bay Congregational Church and in overflow tents on the green. At the church, Lorel eased the van past large television and news trucks. The largest had YUM NETWORK painted on the side, the letters formed by photos of happy people eating various delicious foods.

A food fest volunteer waved us into the lot behind the

church. All the volunteers wore black T-shirts, making them easy to spot.

Lorel squeezed the van into the space between a Dumpster and an oversized food truck with KAHUNA'S blazed on the truck's side panel in neon orange over a swirling Hawaiian print.

"Ernie Moss went to Hawaii when he was in the navy and never got over it," Aunt Gully said. "Now where did I put my glasses?"

"Top of your head, Aunt Gully," Lorel and I chorused.

A surprisingly cool breeze carried the scent of salt water, baking—ah, cinnamon rolls—and coffee. I looped a soft lamb's wool scarf around my neck and carefully placed my walking boot on the pavement. A three-foot-tall lobster painted on the food truck loomed over me.

The lobster sported a black fedora and brandished a fork as if it were a tommy gun. HOME OF THE GOD-LOBSTER. NEW ENGLAND'S BEST LOBSTER ROLL.

"We'll see about that," I said.

The side door of the van rumbled open.

"It would be great to get a food truck," Aunt Gully said as she unbuckled a large pot. The lobsters inside scraped their claws against its battered metal sides.

"One step at a time, Aunt Gully," Lorel said.

Aunt Gully dreamed big, and I loved her for it. My older sister, the MBA, was the practical one. The careful one.

The pretty one. While Lorel's auburn hair gleamed with gold highlights, mine was the deep red that came with freckles and sunburns.

Lorel slid her pricey sunglasses onto her golden, unfreckled nose. We wore matching pink Lazy Mermaid Lobster Shack T-shirts, with strategically placed red clamshells on the chest—Aunt Gully's design. Lorel's was tucked into her khaki skirt. Mine was somewhat less visible, tucked into my faded jeans and topped with my scarf. The back of our tees read NO FUSS FINE FOOD.

Aunt Gully's Lazy Mermaid lobster rolls were New England traditional all the way. Fresh-as-could-be lobster, piled high in a buttery toasted roll topped with Aunt Gully's secret-recipe lobster sauce. That's it. It's almost too simple, but the flavor is sublime.

A crew of food fest volunteers pushed a cart toward us. We unpacked the van and rolled toward the large white tent on the green. Aunt Gully hugged us and hurried to join the other contestants in the church kitchen. Lorel and I would supervise lobster roll and coleslaw samples for food festival visitors.

Lorel scanned the area. "I hope the lobster libbers aren't here," she whispered.

For the past week, letters signed "Lobster Liberation Group" had been pushed under the door at the Lazy Mermaid. Inside a plain white envelope was a short message typed on plain paper: "Save the lobsters! Close or else!" Aunt Gully had tossed the letters in the trash. "Silly practical jokes!"

I'd examined the envelope—I don't watch *CSI* for nothing—but there were no postmarks, helpful fingerprint smudges, bloodstains, or distinctive handwriting. Plain paper. Plain envelope. No clues.

But why was it so hard to forget those stupid letters? Were they from someone we knew? Someone out there didn't like us, or at the very least, got a kick sending threatening letters. Aunt Gully didn't want to report the letters, but I was determined to find out who sent them.

Still, I tried to channel some of Aunt Gully's calm. "Lorel, you worry too much."

We went into high gear, unpacking dozens of rolls, made mini-sized for the lobster roll samples we'd hand out to hundreds of hungry foodies. We'd also brought Aunt Gully's tangy secret-recipe coleslaw to go alongside.

"Allie, do you think we should be with Aunt Gully?" Lorel twisted her hands, a sure sign she was nervous.

"You know how she is." I shouldered a bag of decorations for our free-samples booth. "She's in her happy place with her lobsters."

Aunt Gully loved lobsters. She said they made the ultimate sacrifice for our happiness and that we had to treat them with respect. Aunt Gully went a few steps beyond respect with her lobsters, but that was fine with me. In the rest of her life, she was a normal person. Well, fairly normal.

"Winning this competition would raise the profile of the Lazy Mermaid beyond anything else we could do," Lorel said.

We hurried to the free-samples-booth area on the green. The green sat right at the top of Harbor Street, overlooking dozens of touristy shops that, I had to admit, oozed charm. Trees were in bright green leaf, the hard winter forgotten in the sparkling spring day.

Still, my stomach knotted as I worked and greeted passersby. Could one of these smiling people be the anonymous letter writer? Would Aunt Gully win? Aunt Gully's lobster rolls were the very essence of New England traditional cooking, but what if the judges didn't like them? I shook my head. Preshow jitters were normal. I coped with stage fright before every performance. Every dancer learns to use adrenaline to their advantage when the curtain rises.

My nerves settled as Lorel and I chatted with the group from the Happy Farmer Organic Farm in the next booth. Friends and neighbors stopped by to wish us luck.

A woman with long white-blond hair picked up a mermaid bobblehead and held it at arm's length. "Ha! Your aunt is so cute."

"Hello, Finella." Inside I seethed. Finella Farraday owned She Sells Chic, a pricey resort wear and gift shop right across from the green. She was Aunt Gully's archenemy. Well, that's how I thought of her. Finella had wanted to open an outlet in the building that became the Lazy Mermaid lobster shack, but Aunt Gully'd prevailed despite some shady real estate maneuvers on Finella's part.

"Those T-shirts." She looked me up and down over her Chanel sunglasses. "Cute." Her pursed lips said otherwise. She set the bobblehead down as if it were radioactive. "Here to help your aunt win the contest?"

"I'd do anything to help Aunt Gully." As I said the words, I felt nothing could be more true.

It had been only nine months since Aunt Gully's husband, Uncle Rocco, passed away and she'd thrown herself into opening the Lazy Mermaid. People smarter than I am probably saw that opening the restaurant was her coping mechanism, a place to pour all the energy she'd put into her loving marriage. Still, she'd made so many changes so fast. She'd left her longtime job as a cook at the elementary school to take a chance on this business.

"Ta." Finella waved a red-tipped hand and left. Lorel and I shared a look.

"You can always count on Finella to spread good cheer," I said.

Lorel laughed and her shoulders relaxed.

"Let's see how Aunt Gully's doing. We'll just peek," she said.

"Let's just finish up with the mermaid stuff."

We set out Aunt Gully's "mermaidabilia," a collection of ceramic mermaids, seashells, and fishnet tchotchkes that would give our booth Aunt Gully's signature boatyard-meets-yard-sale look.

Then we hurried past the broad white pillars into the church, showing our badges to volunteers at the door.

"Since when is there all this security at the food festival?" I said.

"With all the celebrities they have to do it." Lorel nodded at a rotund man wearing a lobster-print tie. "Look, there's Keats Packer."

"Mayor Packer's hardly a celebrity." He walked over to us, shaking hands and slapping backs as he went. Mayor Packer was always in election mode.

"Hey, if it isn't the lazy mermaids." Keats Packer chuckled, his blue eyes crinkling. He was a cheerful supporter of local businesses, especially restaurants. Though we'd been open only a couple of months, he'd become a regular at the Lazy Mermaid.

"Morning, Allie. You visiting from Boston, Lorelei?"

Lorel reddened. She hated her given name, preferring to go by the more professional-sounding Lorel. I grinned as she gritted her teeth in a smile. "Here to help, Mr. Packer."

"I haven't eaten since yesterday." Packer patted his stomach. "Had to make room for all the goodies I'm going to try today. Let me tell you, I'm delighted two of the four finalists for best lobster roll are from right here in Mystic Bay and beat out dozens of other lobster shacks to do it."

A guy in a navy blue blazer pushed past us. "Mayor, can we get a few words about the festival? By the monument on the green?"

"Happy to, Leo. Meet you in five. Say, have you met the Larkin sisters? Girls, this is Leo Rodriguez, my favorite reporter." Packer beamed as we greeted Leo. "May the best lobster roll win." He winked, then moved into the crowded hall.

I'd recognized Leo Rodriguez from the television that was always on in Aunt Gully's kitchen. Leo was tall, dark, and handsome—and knew it. He flashed a grin. "Mermaids. Cute clams. Here for the competition?"

I stiffened at his condescending tone. Lorel put a hand on my shoulder.

"Absolutely! I'm Lorel. We're with the Lazy Mermaid Lobster Shack." She handed him a business card. "Please stop by. My aunt would love to meet you."

"The new place on Pearl? Right at the piers?" Leo tucked the card in his pocket.

"Fresh lobster delivered all day long." I jumped in with Aunt Gully's sales pitch.

"Hey, would you two be willing to do an interview later?"

"With Aunt Gully, of course." Lorel smiled.

"Of course." Leo grinned.

I didn't think they were talking about lobster rolls anymore.

Leo turned to me. "Wait a sec. You're Allegra the dancer, right? Got injured, now works in the lobster shack?"

"That's me, but you can call me Allie." I waved at my walking boot. "Almost healed, but I have to be careful, do my PT."

"I'd love to do a story on you, too," Leo said.

The local papers had already written up my Tale of Woe. The headlines read "Spunky Ballerina Doesn't Let Injury Stop Her" and "Pirouettes to Pier."

I caught Lorel's look. "Maybe."

He handed his business card to Lorel. "See you later."

"Later," Lorel said.

Leo's gaze lingered on Lorel a moment longer, then he jogged after the mayor.

"Lorel, how can you flirt with that guy? He's so smarmy."

"Allie, publicity's all a game. Just play the game and stop being such a serious *artiste* all the time."

"Serious?" I waved at my T-shirt. "I'm a woman wearing a clamshell bikini T-shirt. How is that serious?"

Lorel sighed. "I'm going to talk to Aunt Gully about these T-shirts."

Chapter 2

Having security at the festival made sense for the celebrities, but I couldn't believe the long line waiting to flash their badges to enter the kitchen wing of the church.

I had no intention of waiting in line.

Since I'd been a bridesmaid at Elodie Daggett's wedding here last summer, I knew there was a back stairwell that led down to the kitchen. Lorel and I tiptoed through the hushed church nave. Well, she tiptoed, and I clomped as quietly as I could in my walking boot. Sunlight streamed through tall windows onto a half-dozen people seated in the 150-year-old gated wooden pews. We crept through a door behind the pulpit and down a tightly turning iron staircase to the lower level of the building.

We emerged into a hallway full of cables and wires that was evidently a celebrity-free zone. Several kids nearly collided with us as they pushed past a volunteer wearing a Red Sox cap, their shouts ringing as they banged through the door to the playground. No one checked badges there. Perhaps the organizers hadn't known about this entry.

I pulled open the door to the church kitchen, but the

sound inside made me slam the door shut. "Good grief. She's singing."

Over the general kitchen hubbub of running water and clanging pot lids, through the closed door, a voice screeched. Not just any voice. Aunt Gully's.

If you heard Aunt Gully sing, you wouldn't wonder where she got her nickname. Aunt Gully has a voice like a seagull, sharp and squawking, capable of setting off a shiver like nails on a chalkboard. And she likes to sing while she cooks.

"God help us," Lorel whispered.

We pulled open the door a crack. The sound blasted into the hallway. Two little boys covered their ears and ran out the playground door.

Lorel and I winced as Aunt Gully hit, well, missed a high note. She was singing "her" song, "You Are My Lucky Star" from *Singin' in the Rain.* Despite Aunt Gully's treatment, it's a charming melody. I couldn't help but hum and sway along until my ankle reminded me that it had been broken in two places and those two places hadn't completely healed yet.

Inside the kitchen, cameramen prowled as the four chefs prepared their lobster rolls, but as Aunt Gully sang, all eyes and cameras swung to her. Ernie Moss, in his gaudy Kahuna's Hawaiian shirt, had frozen in the act of tasting a scoop of his famous lobster salad. Volunteers laughed and raised their cell phones to record Aunt Gully serenading her lobsters as she put them into a large pot.

"That's their favorite song," she explained to a cameraman.

"Let's get out of here." Lorel inched away from the door.

"I thought you wanted to help her," I said.

"She needs more help than we can give."

Lorel hadn't spent as much time with Aunt Gully as

I had since Uncle Rocco died. Aunt Gully knew exactly what she was doing. Aunt Gully was a ham. She knew her off-key singing would make for good television. A tiny flicker of hope glowed inside me. I hummed "Lucky Star" as I shouldered my way through the laughing crowd near the door, feeling more excited than I had since Aunt Gully announced she'd won an entry into the contest. Maybe the best New England lobster roll would win after all.

A large section of the green had been roped off around the stage for the Best Lobster Roll judging. Lorel and I flashed our badges again and took seats three rows back from the front row, which was reserved for the contestants. My seat was on the aisle near the church building.

The faultless blue sky promised good weather. A YUM-TV banner rippled across the stage behind a table with four seats. Huge screens flanked the stage. Red-white-and-blue bunting hung, well, everywhere. Cameras on a platform at the back of the crowd stood ready to catch the action.

Patriotic music wafted in the air as a group from Mystic Bay High School played Sousa marches from the bandstand.

"Gorgeous day," Lorel said, tilting her chin and closing her eyes.

I dug in my bag for sunscreen and applied it to my nose.

"Fingers crossed for Aunt Gully." Lorel raised her crossed fingers.

"Fingers crossed." I looped my pinkie finger around hers, just as we did when we were little girls. "Let's hope she doesn't sing during the judging."

A guy from the YUM Network warmed up the crowd, but I tuned him out. All I could think of was Aunt Gully's lobster roll. It was absolutely delicious, but honestly, so plain. Lorel said that it was the essence of lobster roll, that we should market it as classic, pure food, but my stomach churned again. Maybe it wasn't special enough.

Excitement rippled through the crowd. After a squawk of feedback, an announcer's voice boomed from the PA system. "And now, the star of YUM-TV's *Leftovers,* Cameron Kim!"

A guy in skinny jeans, a plaid shirt, and black Converse sneakers bounded up the steps to the stage. The crowd erupted in applause. Cell phone cameras were raised. He brushed his floppy black hair out of his eyes, grinned, and waved.

"Hello, Mystic Bay!" Cameron Kim bounced as he talked about how happy he was to be in such a beautiful and historic New England town, but my attention turned to the side door of the church. Volunteers held it open while the chefs exited.

I'd researched Aunt Gully's competition. At the front of the line, Paul Pond ambled with his hands thrust in the pockets of his denim overalls. He owned Pond's, an old-time shack on a tiny island in Maine. With his snowy white hair and beard, he looked like the quintessential Maine sea captain.

Paul Pond was followed by a stocky man in a yellow polo shirt with a navy sweater knotted over his shoulders—preppy Chick Costa of Chick's World Famous Lobsters in Chatham, Massachusetts. Deeply tanned with sun-bleached hair, Chick Costa looked like he'd just stepped off a yacht.

Behind Chick walked Ernie and Megan Moss of Kahuna's, just a half-mile down Pearl Street from the Lazy Mermaid. Ernie and Megan sported loud orange Hawaiian shirts, chinos, and deck shoes. Ernie beamed, his ruddy face shining, but Megan huddled close to his side, her chin tipped down, her dishwater-blond hair hanging in her face. Everyone else wore their Mystic Bay Food Festival badge on a lanyard, but Ernie and Megan hung theirs from plastic leis.

"Hardly New England," Lorel sniffed.

The church door banged shut. No sign of Aunt Gully. "Where's Aunt Gully?" I shot to my feet as the other contestants walked toward the stage. "I'll go check on her."

By the time Lorel rose to her feet, I'd run to the side door of the church, doing my best to ignore the twinge in my ankle. I slid through the mob of volunteers who held their cameras high to film Cameron Kim and stepped inside the building.

"Aunt Gully?" The door banged shut behind me. The hallway was dim and the silence sudden after the excitement at the festival stage. "Aunt Gully?"

For a moment all I heard was my own panting breath.

"Here I am!" At the far end of the hall, Aunt Gully turned the corner, her sneakers squeaking along the linoleum floor. "Oh, Allie, I forgot my apron again!" She hurried toward me, looping the fluorescent-pink apron, also with strategically placed clamshells, over her head. "I hope they don't start the party without me!"

"You nut." I should have stayed with her. "Turn around."

I tied the strings of her apron and Aunt Gully sang an old nursery rhyme as we went out. " 'Rings on her fingers and bells on her toes, she shall have music wherever she goes!' "

"No time for singing, Aunt Gully!"

The door banged shut behind us. Aunt Gully scurried to join the line of contestants, laughing and waving. My hands were sweating as I sank back into my seat by Lorel.

"It's time to meet our contestants," Cameron announced from the stage. "Paul Pond! Of Pond's in the great state of Maine!"

When he heard his name, Paul Pond jogged up the stairs, ran to center stage and did a little Rocky dance, flexing and raising his sinewy arms over his head. Laughter bubbled through the audience. Cameron chuckled and shook Paul's hand.

"Next, Chick Costa of Chick's World Famous Lobsters in Chatham, Massachusetts!"

As he joined Paul and Cameron, Chick Costa whooped and pointed at his supporters, a row of people also clad in yellow polo shirts.

"Megan and Ernie Moss from Kahuna's, right here in Mystic Bay!"

"Godlobster! Godlobster!" A Godlobster chant started behind us. I turned and saw two rows of people in Hawaiian shirts and leis. I forced myself to smile and wave.

Ernie and Megan Moss joined the group onstage. Chick Costa shook hands with Paul Pond and Ernie Moss. Chick and Megan did an awkward back and forth as he went for a hug and she put out her hand for a shake. Everyone laughed. Megan, her face bright pink, huddled close to Ernie's side.

"And the new kid on the block, also from right here in Mystic Bay, Gully Fontana of the Lazy Mermaid Lobster Shack!"

My pent-up energy shot me to my feet. I twirled my scarf over my head. "Whoo-hoo!"

Lorel pulled me back to my seat. The applause for Aunt Gully was loud and long. Locals who had eaten her food were showing their support. My heart warmed.

Once onstage, Aunt Gully waved and blew kisses to the crowd. Her hot-pink sneakers matched her fluorescent Lazy Mermaid apron and pink jeans. Lorel had tried to get Aunt Gully to try a new hairstyle, but Aunt Gully had waved her off and kept her silver hair in the same bob she's had forever.

The contestants trooped back down the stairs and took their seats in the front row. Ernie and Megan Moss sat closest to the aisle. I couldn't see Aunt Gully over all the people sitting in front of us.

"And now our panel of judges!" Cameron said. "Long-time mayor of Mystic Bay! The Mayor of Good Eats, Keats Packer!"

Keats Packer ambled across the stage, shook Cameron's hand, and waved to the crowd. Mayor Packer took the smattering of boos in stride as he sat at the far end of the judges' table.

"Next, beloved actress on Broadway and in Hollywood, just off a guest starring role on *CSI,* starring here at Broadway by the Bay in *Mame.* Let's welcome singer, dancer, and actress triple-threat Contessa Wells!"

A petite woman with bright red lips and glossy black hair cut in Cleopatra bangs climbed the steps on the arm of a teen escort. She thanked him with a squeeze of the hand and waved to the crowd, her silky jade-green dress fluttering in the light breeze.

Lorel leaned to me. "Remember ringing the doorbell at Contessa's house when we were kids?"

"How could I forget?" Lorel had dared me and my friends to trick-or-treat at the Wells House. It was an old sea captain's house up on Spyglass Hill in Rabb's Point that had sat empty for years. Folks said it was haunted by a sea captain's wife who still waited for her husband's return, two hundred years too late. No ghost had answered the door but Lorel and her friends had water-ballooned me and my terrified friends.

"She looks great for her age," Lorel said. "She's what, in her seventies?"

"She played a dead body on *CSI* last week," I whispered.

Contessa strode across the stage oozing energy the way Broadway performers do, broadly gesturing to the crowd and greeting Cameron with exaggerated pleasure. A flowery scarf flowed behind her trim figure. Unlike virtually everyone else at the food fest, Contessa didn't wear a security badge. A good choice, I thought. It would've ruined the look of her outfit.

"I never met a Contessa before." Cameron laughed. Contessa gave him her hand with a flourish and a jokey curtsy. Cameron kissed her hand. The crowd burst into applause. Contessa took her seat at the table as Keats Packer gallantly held her chair.

"She's appeared at Broadway by the Bay at the Jake several times," I whispered. "The Jake" was what locals called Mystic Bay's Jacob's Ladder theater complex, which hosted Broadway by the Bay. "Terrible reputation. Total diva."

Cameron waved the last judges up the steps. "Last but not least, my YUM Network buddies, stars of *Foodies on the Fly,* Rio and Rick Lopez!"

The audience didn't need the producer's GET LOUD signs. Applause rang out across the green. A slender man and even more slender woman in ripped skinny jeans sauntered onstage and wrapped Cameron in bear hugs.

Rio and Rick waved to the crowd, their silver concha belts gleaming in the sun, his black hair spiked and gelled, hers flowing in the wind. Rio wore an intricately embroidered denim jacket and gleaming red cowboy boots. Rick wore a tight black T-shirt that showed off a sleeve of tattoos.

Their show was one of the top ranked on the YUM network. They cruised the country in a vintage Airstream motor home, stopping at local restaurants to showcase regional cuisines. I hoped they'd appreciate Aunt Gully's traditional approach.

"Are you ready for a Lobster Roll Rumble?" Cameron shouted. "Get loud, Mystic Bay!"

I looked around at the crowd, filled with many locals who were typical New Englanders. There were a few wolf whistles from Chick Costa's group, and the rowdy Godlobster people hooted, but most of these people were not getting loud. They applauded politely, shaded their eyes with their programs, and waited for the contest to begin.

"All right!" The tepid applause didn't affect Cameron's boyish energy. "We're doing blind taste testings. Applause is okay. Show the love for your favorites, but remember. This contest will be decided by taste alone."

The Godlobster crew grumbled.

Cameron beamed at the camera. "Are you ready, judges?"

The judges applauded with vigor. Keats Packer tucked his napkin into his collar.

"First up, we have a lobster roll with a mayonnaise-based lobster salad. The lobster is mixed with a combination of over twenty vegetables, herbs, and secret ingredients!"

The audience *oohed* when Cameron said "secret ingredients."

"Doesn't that look fantastic?" Cameron pointed to large screens on either side of the stage.

The Godlobster flashed onscreen. The audience *oohed* again. Someone in the crowd blared the theme from *The Godfather* from a megaphone.

My stomach twisted. Lorel shot me a worried look.

Like everyone else in Mystic Bay, I'd enjoyed one of Ernie and Megan Moss's giant lobster rolls. Well, more than one. The chopped vegetables and herbs added color that Aunt Gully's lobster roll lacked. Instead of a traditional hot dog roll, the Godlobster was served on an oversized brioche bun.

I love brioche.

I squirmed in my seat.

Lorel twisted her hands.

Six volunteers marched up the stairs to the stage. One carried a large tray covered with a gleaming silver cloche. With a flourish, one volunteer lifted the cloche. Four helpers each took a plate and set the plates before the judges in unison.

"Oh, yeah!" Cameron shouted. "Thank you, volunteers from Mystic Bay High School!"

The teen volunteers shuffled offstage.

"Oooh, looks good!" Rio exclaimed. "Beautiful dish."

"Great color," Rick agreed. "You can see the flavor."

The judges bit into the overflowing Godlobster. Tiny Contessa Wells laughed as lobster salad fell from the bun onto her plate. She scooped it up with a fork and said "Divine!" before popping it into her mouth.

Several people sitting near me leaned forward, their folding chairs creaking in the expectant silence while the judges chewed.

Was it my imagination? Did I see a tiny frown flicker across Contessa Wells's face?

Rio and Rick glanced at each other then took another bite, as if they weren't sure about the dish and were giving it another chance. Keats Packer wolfed down several bites and wiped his mouth with his napkin. He burped, setting off a wave of laughter.

The camera captured a close-up of Contessa Wells. She'd taken a large bite and now struggled to chew it. She swallowed hard and reached for her water glass.

"Judges?" Cameron prompted. "You first, Rio."

"An interesting preparation." She took a sip of water. "A bit, er, tangy?"

"Ha!" Rick folded his arms. The audience held its breath. Rick was known for his blunt culinary assessments.

"The tangy went off the rails into bitterness. Actually, quite a lot of bitterness." He shook his head and reached for his judging sheet. "The chef took some chances on this one. Didn't pull it off. Hey, that's what happens in the kitchen sometimes, right? Go big or go home. Sorry, this one's going home."

The audience groaned.

Mayor Packer leaned into his microphone. "I liked it," he said.

"You'll eat anything," someone shouted from the back of the crowd. Laughter rolled toward the stage.

Contessa leaned toward her microphone. "The brioche was out of this world." The audience applauded.

Lorel and I shared a look. Contessa hadn't said anything about the lobster salad.

I couldn't see Ernie's face, but the back of his neck reddened. Megan shook her head and he wrapped his arm around her. They must be devastated.

Volunteers cleared the dishes while the judges filled in their judging sheets.

"And the Mystic Bay High School band will provide a musical interlude while the judges fill in their scorecards and we get the next delicious lobster roll to the stage!" Cameron said.

Music filled the air as Rio and Rick conferred, their heads close together. Contessa wrote on her scorecard, then rubbed the side of her face. Mayor Packer loosened his tie and leaned away from the table as the band brought to a close "The Washington Post March."

"And next up, we have a lobster roll done in a very traditional preparation, what I believe is called the Connecticut style," Cameron said.

Aunt Gully's lobster roll flashed onscreen, the meat piled high, a little cup of her secret-recipe lobster sauce perched next to the golden-brown toasted hot dog roll. "Now I understand that the judges are to pour some of that secret-recipe lobster sauce onto the lobster meat, right?" Cameron read from the teleprompter. The audience cheered and hooted.

"That's some lobster overload!" Cameron shouted.

Contessa Wells reached for her water glass.

Rio whispered in Rick's ear.

The volunteers carried a covered tray onto the stage. Once again they flourished the silver cloche, set Aunt Gully's lobster rolls before the judges and exited stage left.

Keats Packer cupped his hand over his mouth and staggered off the stage toward a row of Porta Pottis.

"Um, Mayor?" Cameron said.

Rick's microphone captured a groan and a muttered expletive.

Then Contessa Wells stood, clutched her stomach, and doubled over on top of Aunt Gully's lobster roll.

Chapter 3

The audience gasped, an intake of breath followed by a few seconds of silence that seemed to suspend time.

Rick pushed away from the table and darted to Contessa's side. He caught her limp form just as she slid from the table to the floor.

Rio struggled to stand, then fell to her knees, panting. Cameron rushed to her side and put his arm around her. "Help! Help up here, help up here!" Cameron looked about wildly. "What's going on?"

YUM Network staff rushed toward the stage. I, too, rushed forward. I had to see if Aunt Gully was okay.

"Oh, my goodness," she cried. "Those poor things! Keats Packer's ill, too. Someone had better go check on him."

Lorel squeezed through the crowd that now milled helplessly, waiting for someone to Do Something. A siren wailed in the distance. Discordant notes floated over the crowd as the musicians in the bandstand tried to see what was happening on the festival stage.

A loud thud set off shrieks from the audience. Rick Lopez had fallen, writhing and groaning, next to Rio. Cameron Kim, still cradling Rio, reached out to him.

Contessa Wells lay on her back in a little heap of green fabric, alone behind the judging table.

"I've got to help." I started toward the stage, but Aunt Gully grabbed my hand.

"Look, Hayden's on his way. He's an EMT," she said.

Hayden Yardley, who'd been my classmate at Mystic Bay High School, vaulted onto the stage and ran to Rio's side.

The crowd pushed toward the exits. Spectators blocked the stairs, so two volunteers boosted May Strange, Mystic Bay's pediatrician, onto the stage. Dr. Strange struggled to her feet, then hurried to help Rick.

But before I knew what I was doing, I'd run forward and pulled myself up onto the stage. I rushed to Contessa, unwinding my scarf as I went.

High school first-aid class flashed into my mind. It's dangerous for an unconscious person to be on their back in case they vomited and choked. I knelt beside Contessa. Using my scarf to cushion her head, I raised her shoulder and rolled her to her side. Her makeup stood out on her pale skin, garish and clownlike. Her eyelids fluttered.

"Miss Wells?" She didn't answer. I brushed aside her dark hair and scarf so I could see her face. Whitish foam from the side of her slack mouth dripped onto the stage floor. A jolt of horror made me catch my breath.

"Let me." Hayden Yardley materialized at my side. Gently, he took Contessa's shoulder and pressed his fingers to her neck. "She's got a pulse."

He glanced at me, concern in his deep brown eyes. "You okay, Allie? You're pretty pale."

"I'm okay." I sat back on my knees and took a deep breath to steady myself. "I'm always pale, Hayden."

Two volunteers joined us. My ankle throbbed as I walked to the edge of the stage and lowered myself back to the ground. I rejoined Aunt Gully and Lorel, but couldn't stop watching Hayden and the volunteers tend to Contessa.

Loud sobs drew my attention from the stage. Ernie Moss wrapped Megan in a bear hug, holding her close as she wept.

"It was our lobster roll, Ernie!" She pulled back and looked wildly into his eyes. Her tears had splotched the front of his Hawaiian shirt. "It was the only one they ate. The only one."

"Babe, shh." Ernie rocked her in his beefy arms.

Aunt Gully reached out to Megan. "Oh, Megan. It couldn't have been your lobster roll. This is just"—she groped for words—"a terrible accident."

A few feet away, a teenage guy stepped onto a folding chair. His black Mystic Bay Landscapers T-shirt and baggy khaki shorts hung on his angular frame. He held his cell phone high to record the scene on the stage.

Ernie's face reddened.

"Stop!" Ernie let go of Megan and charged at the teen. He yanked the kid off the chair with such force that they both fell to their knees. Ernie wrapped his hands around the teen's cell phone.

"Hey, old man, what's your problem?" the teen shouted.

Ernie and the teen grappled for a few seconds, then Ernie wrested the phone away.

With a snarl, Ernie staggered to his feet and hurled the phone into the crowd. The teen jumped to his feet and swung at Ernie's head but connected with his shoulder. Somebody screamed. Ernie's shining, already red face purpled. With both hands, Ernie bulldozed the teen into a row of folding chairs. Two other guys helped the teen up from the tangle of chairs, then they all rushed Ernie, whose stocky body crashed into and toppled several chairs.

"Let's get out of here." I wrapped an arm around Aunt Gully and tugged Megan's hand, pulling her out of the way just before one of the teen's friends backed into her. Megan's face was blank, her arms hung limp. Lorel gently slipped an arm around her.

We all backed toward the stage, passing two ladies in black volunteer T-shirts. They spoke into walkie-talkies but didn't move toward the fight. I didn't blame them. Curses filled the air as bodies ricocheted from one side of the aisle to another, knocking into chairs and bystanders. Some of Ernie's Hawaiian-shirt-clad supporters pushed through the crowd.

"Ooh, boy, now it's gonna get real," one of the volunteers said.

"Just a minute!" Aunt Gully roared. The two volunteers jumped. Aunt Gully strode toward the fight and tapped one teen on the shoulder just as he raised his arm to land a punch on Ernie. He spun.

"Whoa!" He raised his hands. "Mrs. Fontana!"

Aunt Gully put her hands on her hips, pulling herself up to her full five-foot-two-inch height.

"I thought that was you, Brendan Hart. Now that man"—she pointed to Ernie, Hawaiian shirt torn, panting and sweating on the ground—"had a mighty bad shock. I want to see you apologize to him and then head on home."

The teenage boy, panting, blushed. He looked at the ground, then mumbled something that sounded like "Sorry."

One of his friends held a phone in the air. "Got your phone."

Brendan and his friends straightened their clothes and looked around at the disapproving crowd.

"Let's roll." He jerked his head toward the exit, then looked back at Aunt Gully. "Um, bye, Mrs. Fontana."

Aunt Gully crossed her arms and watched them slip away through the crowd.

Lorel smoothed her hair. "You know those juvenile delinquents?"

"They went to Mystic Bay Elementary School." Aunt Gully sighed as some men in Hawaiian shirts helped Ernie to his feet. "They were trouble then, too."

The crowd streamed out of the exits. EMTs in the tan uniform of Mystic Bay's emergency squad fought against the tide of moving bodies. We stood with the other contestants, watching in silence as EMTs worked on the sickened judges. They carefully but quickly put the judges on stretchers. Mystic Bay police officers cleared the aisles as ambulances arrived.

As the EMTs carried her off the stage, Contessa Wells's arm swung limply from the side of her stretcher. Megan Moss moaned.

"How could this happen?" Megan swayed and crumpled into a chair, shaking her head, her eyes half closed. Ernie sat next to her and wrapped her in his arms.

Paul Pond walked past us, talking on his cell. He threw a glance toward the Mosses, and turned away. I caught the words "food poisoning."

Food poisoning. I thought of all the people who'd done just what Aunt Gully's juvenile delinquents had done—recorded the ghastly scene of the judges falling ill and being taken to the hospital on stretchers. I glanced at the Mosses. The weight of what had happened was clear to them. They were crushed. I felt for them but all I could think was, *What about Aunt Gully? What if some cell phone video named the wrong lobster shack? What would the fallout be for her?*

And would all those poor judges be all right? A wave of fear passed through me. How still Contessa Wells's fragile body had been! She was in her seventies for sure. Could she recover from this?

Chick Costa and his yellow-polo-shirted friends joined us by the stage. "Man, this is messed up," he said. He caught sight of Megan Moss and frowned. "Is she okay? What do we do? Can we leave?"

What did we do now?

"I don't see why we have to stay," Lorel whispered. "Let's go, Aunt Gully."

Aunt Gully sat next to Megan, patting her hand. Megan's blank face frightened me.

A tall man in a stylish tan suit and a woman in black jeans and a short leather jacket hurried over to us. He opened his arms and looked from one contestant to the other.

"I'm Stan Wilder from the YUM Network. This is my assistant, Ashley Singh." The young woman nodded. "I'd like all the contestants to accompany us into the church building for a few moments."

Chick Costa pointed at Wilder. "Listen, man, my lobster roll got nowhere near those judges—"

"Let's go someplace private so we can talk." The way Stan lowered his voice when he said "private" made everyone look around. Suddenly it seemed like a very good idea to go someplace private.

Chick Costa waved off his followers. "Be back in a few." The Hawaiian-shirt-clad crew from Kahuna's patted Ernie on the back and melted toward the exits. Several of Aunt Gully's friends gave her quick hugs but her focus remained on Megan.

We shuffled into line and followed Stan and Ashley into the building. I caught sight of Leo Rodriguez shouldering through the crowd from the other side of the green. I was glad when the heavy church door closed behind us.

Ashley Singh wore all black, but her high-style jacket

and pricey boots told me she was no volunteer or under-paid assistant. Stan Wilder exuded a similar air of expensive executive responsibility. Lorel and I exchanged glances as we trooped into a classroom in the church's education wing.

Stan and Ashley asked us to wait and moved into the hall, phones to their ears.

We milled around the room, lined with wooden students' desks that were older than I am. One desk had hearts and initials carved onto the top. I ran my fingers along the scarred wood and wondered what had happened to *M.W.* and *J.S.*

Paul Pond and Chick Costa sat in the back of the room, Paul hunched over his phone, Chick throwing worried glances at Aunt Gully and Megan Moss.

The classroom clock ticked away the seconds. Two volunteers brought us cups of tepid coffee and then hurried back in with Aunt Gully's requested tea. She added a heaping spoonful of sugar to the cup and pressed it into Megan's hands.

My phone buzzed with texts from my friend Verity, but I stopped answering them. There was nothing new to say. I stretched to relieve the tension in my back and legs. Paul Pond moved to a seat by the window and stared out at the green. Everyone avoided each other's eyes. A very slow hour passed.

Lorel raised her eyebrows and showed me her phone. The screen displayed posts on the Mystic Bay Food Festival Facebook page.

Don't go to the Mystic Bay Food Festival! Seriously. You'll get food poisoning. STAY HOME.

Just watched the Godlobster take out four judges at the festival. Never going to Kahuna's again.

How did YUM and the board of selectmen allow this to happen? They can't even get a simple lobster sandwich right? Kick 'em all out of office. Inept and corrupt!

Due to circumstances beyond our control, this year's Mystic Bay Food Festival has been canceled. No refunds will be given for passes.

I'm suing. I want my money back!

Then I realized what this meeting was. This was damage control.

Then Stan and Ashley returned with two police officers, and I realized it was something even worse.

Chapter 4

"Everyone, please take a seat." The two officers stopped just inside the door, their thumbs hooked on belts heavy with equipment, guns, and handcuffs.

Lorel and I exchanged glances as we sank into our undersized wooden chairs. My ankle throbbed, payback for that jump onto the stage. I propped my foot on a chair.

Aunt Gully remained next to Megan, patting her arm, urging her to sip her tea.

I recognized both of the officers, Murdoch and Petrie. The Lazy Mermaid was just down Pearl Street from the volunteer fire station and public safety complex. Locals called it the Plex. Aunt Gully always gave the firefighters and police officers free coffee.

"Ah, yeah." Murdoch took a deep breath and blew it out. "The judges were transported to Mystic Bay Hospital. All went into intensive care."

Paul Pond stood. "But they're going to be okay, right? It's just food poisoning, isn't it?"

Ernie Moss stiffened.

"Unfortunately." Murdoch shuffled his feet and cleared his throat. "One of the judges died at the hospital."

I froze.

Stan and Ashley looked at the floor.

"No," Megan whispered.

Aunt Gully pressed her hand to her chest.

"Who was it?" Chick Costa demanded.

"Contessa Wells." Murdoch cleared his throat again. "And the others aren't out of the woods yet."

Chapter 5

Dead. I recalled Contessa's bloodless face, her slack jaw, the awful white foam seeping from her glossy red lips.

Paul Pond sank into his seat.

"You can't tell me my food had anything to do with it." Chick leaped from his small student desk, the chair ricocheting with a loud bang against the wall. He held up a hand. "I'm sorry about Miss Wells, and the judges, but my food wasn't even onstage."

"Mine, either," Paul Pond added. "Maybe there was something in the lobster roll she ate"—Megan Moss moaned—"but not mine. It was still in the church building."

Megan slumped against Ernie. The two police officers rushed to her and eased her limp body to the floor. Murdoch spoke into his shoulder mic.

Ernie cradled Megan's head while Aunt Gully knelt next to her, murmuring soothing words. Lorel and I moved behind Aunt Gully. Ernie's ruddy face paled and I wondered if he would faint next.

While everyone hovered around Megan, Ashley Singh ended a call on her phone and whispered with Stan.

Heavy footfalls and chatter grew louder in the hall. Stan opened the door to two EMTs with a stretcher, then leaned into the hall to speak with a thin man wearing a gray suit.

Lawyer. Figures. The YUM Network would protect themselves. Lorel, Paul, Chick, and I pushed back chairs and desks as the EMTs maneuvered next to Megan. As Ernie hovered, the EMTs helped Megan onto a stretcher and wheeled it from the classroom.

I wrapped my arm around Aunt Gully. If you were to catch Aunt Gully on a good day, which is pretty much every day for her, you'd see a cheerful woman with a quick smile and an often naughty wit. Sparkling, that was Aunt Gully. Now she looked washed out, her bright clothes and pink apron contrasting with her colorless face, her inner light extinguished by worry.

"I'm taking my aunt home," I said. Lorel and I flanked Aunt Gully and we started toward the door.

"Of course." Stan ran his hand over his close-cropped hair. "Please, before you go, the police have asked for everyone to leave their contact information."

"Why?" Chick countered. "There's no crime here, right? What's going to happen with the contest, Stan? Huh?"

"We're on it," Ashley said.

Lorel and I exchanged glances at Ashley's nonanswer.

Officer Murdoch returned to the room. "Folks, Stan's right. Let us know where you're staying, please."

"I'm heading back to Maine," Paul Pond said.

"Plan to stay at least until tomorrow." Murdoch's expression said he wasn't taking no for an answer. "You're at the Harbor Inn, right?"

Stan Wilder stepped forward. "We're sure that everything will be okay. Perhaps just a case of food poisoning. Unfortunately, Miss Wells was of advanced age and perhaps not in the best of health. Perhaps she had an undiagnosed heart problem."

Funny, she'd looked absolutely vibrant as she'd taken the stage. But he was right, maybe she did have some undiagnosed problem. Plenty of older people did.

Then it dawned on me. Stan was giving us the network's spin: older lady, advanced age, weak heart. You know how these things go.

Lorel handed Officer Murdoch one of Aunt Gully's Lazy Mermaid business cards, but he waved it off. "I know where to find your aunt. You girls take good care of her now."

We hurried down the church steps.

"Let's get home," Lorel said.

"My mermaidabilia, I can't leave it," Aunt Gully said.

As we swept her mermaidabilia from the booth, friends and neighbors swamped Aunt Gully, giving her hugs and, of course, angling for news.

Finella Faraday sidled up. "I was at my shop and missed what happened." Her eyes glittered. "Was it your lobster roll that made everyone sick? Did Contessa die right onstage?"

Aunt Gully's face paled. "No."

"Honestly, Finella," one of Aunt Gully's friends cut in. I'd never liked Mrs. Farraday, ever since I heard her call Aunt Gully's restaurant "that cafeteria food shack." Her insensitive snooping pushed me over the edge.

"Gotta go, bye." I slung a tote bag over my shoulder, not caring that it almost hit her. Lorel and I hefted boxes and herded Aunt Gully toward the parking lot.

A news truck with a satellite dish pulled in front of the church. Stan and Ashley hurried from the door, Leo Rodriguez right behind them. Stan waved Leo off and he and Ashley got into the back of a black SUV. Leo's head swiveled. His gaze settled on us.

"Oh, no, not the right time for an interview," Lorel said.

"Let's move," I said. "Before Leo corners us."

We pushed through the crowd. I felt a hand on my arm.

"No comment!"

"Hey, it's me!" My friend Verity Brooks gave me a quick hug, then reached out to hug Aunt Gully.

I set down the box of mermaidabilia and quickly adjusted the tote bag on my shoulder. "Thank goodness it's you. We've got a reporter on our tail."

Verity spun around to see, her colorful patchwork skirt swirling, then ran with us. "Ooh, that hunk Leo Rodriguez? No worries, I've got your backs. But what happened?" She held my arm and we dropped back. "People came into my shop and said four people died eating the lobster rolls," she whispered. Verity owned Verity's Vintage, a vintage clothing shop right across the town green from the church.

"No, four people became ill." I hefted the box. "Just poor Contessa Wells died."

"Oh, no! I loved her in *Gypsy's Daughter*!" We hurried to catch up with Lorel and Aunt Gully, the mermaid tchotchkes clinking in the box as I ran. Verity's eyes went wide. "It wasn't—"

"No, it wasn't Aunt Gully's lobster roll."

"Thank God," Lorel muttered.

"Whose was it?" Verity panted.

"The Godlob—"

"Mrs. Fontana!" Leo Rodriguez jogged down the path behind us. "Mrs. Fontana!"

Behind him a heavyset man with a shoulder-mounted camera fast-walked, his face red and sweating.

"Oh, it's that nice Leo Rodriguez from the television." Aunt Gully turned and waved.

"Aunt Gully, we don't need a reporter now," Lorel said.

"No time! Maybe later, Aunt Gully," I said, shifting the box to one arm and taking Aunt Gully's arm with the other.

"I got this," Verity said. "Get Aunt Gully home and call me."

Verity ducked behind the large weathered wooden MYSTIC BAY CONGREGATIONAL CHURCH sign as we ran toward the van.

I hurled my box of mermaidabilia into the passenger side and we all jumped into the van. As Aunt Gully slid the van door closed, I looked back. Just as Leo Rodriguez passed the sign, Verity shot out from behind it. She pretended to stumble, then executed an expert martial arts leg sweep. Leo's legs scissored out from under him and he thudded to the ground. His cameraman cried out as he tumbled over Leo and dropped the camera. Verity did a SWAT roll and flashed me a thumbs-up.

"Your friends are so weird," Lorel muttered as she floored it out of the parking lot.

Chapter 6

"Lorel, you drove past the turn for the Mermaid," Aunt Gully said.

"We're going home. Trust me, Aunt Gully, you don't want to be easy to find." Lorel's eyes flicked to the rear view mirror.

"But people will think I'm hiding. I have nothing to hide, young lady." Aunt Gully's voice resumed its feisty tone.

"You don't want to be associated with this mess. If people see you on television now, they'll think you're involved," Lorel said. "We'll let it blow over."

Lorel's death grip on the wheel told me she didn't really believe this would blow over. I'd checked my phone. The Mystic Bay Food Festival site was filled with ridiculous rumors. Food poisoning. YUM Network tricks to boost ratings. A plot to murder the mayor. Lorel was right. Best to go home.

"Tell you what, Aunt Gully, just go home and have a lie-down. I'll head over to the shop and help Hector and Hilda," I said. "It's my usual shift anyway."

Aunt Gully exhaled. "Well, I'm not going to sit around. I'll go check on Megan and bring Ernie some chowder."

"Great idea, Aunt Gully." I didn't believe some chowder was going to make anything better. We'd just watched the Mosses' lives implode in front of hundreds of people, but Aunt Gully had an almost pathological need to take care of others.

Lorel pulled into the driveway of Aunt Gully's house, parking next to her brand-new BMW sedan. Living in Boston, I hadn't needed a car. Now that I was living at Aunt Gully's, I often borrowed the same van in which I'd learned to drive. I tried not to think about how pathetic that was.

Aunt Gully's cottage was the same 1920s style as its neighbors, with a broad front porch, tidy gray cedar shingles, and lace curtains at the windows. Unlike the neighboring cottages, Aunt Gully's door was painted bright blue, garden gnomes ran rampant, and rainbow-hued whirligigs spun among the bushes flanking the porch. A sign above the door, carved by Uncle Rocco, read GULL'S NEST.

Lorel and I unloaded the van while Aunt Gully put on the teakettle. The ancient black wall-mounted phone rang, jangling my nerves. I lifted the receiver and a loud voice brayed "Gully!" Aunt Gully's chum Aggie Weatherburn. The news had spread. I gave Aunt Gully the phone, and she settled in Uncle Rocco's lumpy Barcalounger, the phone cord stretched from the kitchen wall around the corner into the living room.

I turned to Lorel. "Now what?"

Lorel smoothed her already smooth hair. "It blows over. I hope."

"Except someone's dead." Contessa's pale face flashed before me. I cringed, trying to shake the horrible image. "I didn't think food poisoning could act that fast. It doesn't make sense. Kahuna's has been in business for years.

There's no way he would've used anything but the freshest ingredients in that lobster roll."

"Just thank God it wasn't Aunt Gully's roll." Lorel yanked shut the lace curtains on Aunt Gully's broad living room windows.

"I'm heading down to the Mermaid to let Hector and Hilda know what happened," I said. Hector and Hilda Viera were the shack's only other full-time employees.

"Just remember, Allie," Lorel whispered, throwing a glance at Aunt Gully. "No comment, okay? You can say that Aunt Gully's deeply saddened by what happened"— her cool blue eyes held mine—"but that's it."

Normally, I would've rolled my eyes at Lorel's bossing, but I was too stressed. I waved at Aunt Gully, grabbed the keys to the van, and drove back along the water to Pearl Street.

Aunt Gully's Lazy Mermaid lobster shack was in one of the oldest parts of Mystic Bay, an area once known as Fishtown, but now referred to by real estate agents as Mystic Bay Village. Tiny streets lined with painstakingly restored Greek Revival homes and trim fisherman's cottages flowed into two distinct areas: Spyglass Hill, an area of large, historic whaling captains' mansions overtaken by expensive, sprawling vacation homes, and Pearl Street, a twisting lane that led to specialty shops, small homes, and a bustling marina.

My tires crunched into the gravel parking lot of the Lazy Mermaid. It was empty. I'd never seen it empty.

The Lazy Mermaid was three cedar-shingled buildings. The main building was bright with fluttering blue pennants and an American flag. This is where customers lined up for Aunt Gully's lobster rolls and took them to picnic tables scattered on the grass and pier. Inside was space for only four tables and counter space with ten seats. For years the building had housed a bar/restaurant called Petey's. When Petey had had to sell the property, Aunt Gully had jumped at the chance to make her dream of owning a lobster shack a reality.

Behind the main building stood a small shed that held seawater tanks of live lobsters. Behind that was another freestanding shack, where Aunt Gully planned to expand. A broad pier led to the Micasset River, which flowed behind it all into Long Island Sound.

Who could have imagined that underneath years of Petey's grime and spilled beer was a sparkling gem of a restaurant waiting to be born? One weekend the entire corps de ballet had come from Boston to join with Aunt Gully's friends to clean, paint, strip the sticky wood plank floor, toss three Dumpsters' worth of trash, and then throw a celebratory party that people in Mystic Bay still talked about.

Artist friends of Aunt Gully's painted a mural of fishbowl castles and sea creatures, using a special finish to give the walls the opalescent sheen of a shell. The ceiling was similarly painted in a fish-scale pattern. Aunt Gully's antique-dealer friend Aggie had found a figurehead of a mermaid, which had regal pride of place by the door. Well, after Aunt Gully put a bikini top on the figurehead's naked torso. "It's a family restaurant," she said.

Dozens of knickknacks from Aunt Gully's mermaid collection crowded a shelf by the ceiling. Plastic lobsters and octopuses, nets, and an old wooden lobster pot brightened the walls. Plastic red and white checked table-cloths added cheer to the already eclectic décor.

But the shack was empty as I walked in.

"Allie, what happened!" Hector rushed forward. "It's all over the news! Is your aunt okay? I couldn't get through to on her phone."

Hilda, like Aunt Gully, believed that tea cured all. She brought me some, the cup shaking in her hand.

Hector's and Hilda's eyes widened as I told them what happened.

Leo Rodriguez's face filled the television screen high on the wall.

"Breaking news from Mystic Bay and the food festival, now closed by tragic events. As we reported earlier, Broadway star Contessa Wells has died at Mystic Bay Hospital after falling ill with the other judges at the Mystic Bay Food Festival. Joining me now is one of the contestants in the Best Lobster Roll contest, Chick Costa, owner of Chick's World Famous Lobsters in Chatham. Very sad events, Chick."

Chick Costa had changed out of his yellow polo shirt and into a yellow T-shirt that said CHICK'S WORLD FAMOUS LOBSTERS, CHATHAM. He pulled back his shoulders so the T-shirt was taut across his bulging bodybuilder pecs.

"Yeah, very sad, Leo."

"Tell us what happened, Chick."

"Well, it's of course tragic."

Leo Rodriguez glanced at the camera and then back at Chick. "Tell us what you saw."

"Well, before my lobster roll even got served, they all got sick. All the judges. Right after they served the God-lobster roll from Kahuna's."

Hector whistled. "Kahuna's!"

"Then they fell ill," Leo Rodriguez prompted.

"Yes. Everyone got sick and then the EMTs came and took everyone away to the hospital. It's a tragedy," Chick said. "I'm just glad my lobster roll had no part in it. Wasn't even on the stage at that point."

"We know there was a meeting with the YUM Network, the organizers of the event. Can you tell us what they said?" Leo asked.

"Well, they said it's tragic of course, but you know, Miss Wells was an older lady, and she might have had some undisclosed health problems. Maybe a heart problem."

"There you have it, right from one of the contestants." Leo Rodriguez put a finger to his ear. "And now we're going to Mystic Bay Hospital for a follow-up on the judges. Thank you, Chick Costa of Chick's World Famous Lobsters in Chatham. This is Leo Rodriguez reporting live from the canceled, I repeat canceled, Mystic Bay Food Festival. Over to Terri LeDuc."

The news switched to a woman in a chic navy blue suit standing in front of Mystic Bay Hospital. She glanced at her notes and then looked up suddenly, composing her face to read sadness and gravity.

"Leo, I've just talked with a Mystic Bay Hospital spokesman. As you know, we've reported on the tragic death of Broadway and Hollywood star Contessa Wells. Despite treatment en route and here at the hospital, Miss Wells died shortly after arriving at the ICU at noon. The other judges, Mayor Keats Packer and YUM Network stars Rio and Rick Lopez, of *Foodies on the Fly,* have received treatment, and doctors are cautiously optimistic that all will recover. Doctors here, however, have told me that this is one of the most unusual cases they've seen, and they've asked for toxicology tests from the state crime lab. We'll let you know just as soon as we have those reports.

"And I have this exclusive information." The camera zoomed in as Terri looked into the camera with wide hazel eyes. "One of the medical personnel who attended Miss Wells spoke to me anonymously. He was deeply, deeply moved. He was a fan of Miss Wells." She took a deep breath, composing herself. "He was with the celebrated actress as she drew her last breath."

Terri LeDuc read from her notes. "He said, 'Miss Wells struggled to take a breath. I held her hand in mine. I could tell she wanted to say something important so I leaned close. She looked right into my eyes and spoke her last word.'"

Hector, Hilda, and I leaned toward the television screen.

Terri LeDuc stared into the camera. "Her last word was 'Contessa.'" She paused a beat. "Reporting live from Mystic Bay Hospital, I'm Terri LeDuc."

"That's weird." Hector leaned back. "Her last word was her own name?"

"She was in terrible shape." I told them how Hayden Yardley and I had tried to help her.

Hector clapped one of his big, callused hands over mine as Hilda hugged me. "You poor thing! And your poor aunt! Poor Contessa, of course." Hilda's eyes welled.

"I wonder what'll happen to the Wells House. It's worth a fortune," Hector said.

"And her sister," Hilda said.

"Her sister?" I said. "Oh, I'd forgotten. I thought she died years ago?"

"Yeah, the crazy one who lives in their house on Spyglass Hill," Hector said.

Hilda gave him a disapproving look, grabbed a dishrag, and wiped down the counter. "Neither of the Wells sisters has lived here in like forty years. Few years back they renovated it and rented it out. But Contessa came back what, two or three months ago?"

Hector nodded.

Hilda continued. "While you were dancing in Boston, Allie, so you wouldn't have known. Well, everyone says what an angel Contessa is because her sister is—"

"Off her rocker," Hector said.

Hilda frowned. "Contessa brings, well, brought in

private nurses to care for her. They say she's harmless, but you can imagine what it's like to live with someone like that. Most folks think Contessa is a saint." She frowned again. "Was a saint."

"So sad," I whispered. "So what happens to the sister now?"

Hilda shrugged. "Probably an institution. I don't think there's any other family."

"What's the sister's name?" I asked.

Hilda looked at Hector. He shrugged. "Not sure, everyone just called her Contessa's sister, or the Crazy Lady." He snapped his fingers. "Juliet! Like Romeo and Juliet."

"How's your aunt?" Hilda asked.

"Okay, but she's taking it hard. Megan Moss had to be hospitalized, she's so upset."

Hilda clucked and straightened already straight salt and pepper shakers.

Hector looked out the window toward the end of Pearl Street, where it wound along the river to Kahuna's. Kahuna's was located on a pier by the marina.

"I thought something was wrong," Hector said.

"What do you mean?"

"There's hardly any traffic. At this time of year, with the food fest, Pearl Street's a solid line of cars looking for a place to park, like the mall at Christmas."

We all looked out the window that faced the street. Pearl Street was as quiet as I'd ever seen it. The usually terrible traffic had driven a wedge between the residents of Pearl Street and Kahuna's, and now, I realized with a jolt, residents would have the same concern with the Lazy Mermaid.

Pearl Street traffic activists had won a fifteen-mile-per-hour speed limit on the street. The Lazy Mermaid was certainly adding to the congestion. Aunt Gully was born and raised in Mystic Bay, had worked at the elementary school, and was part of Mystic Bay life. But still. Could traffic issues be the reason someone sent those threatening letters to Aunt Gully?

"What's that?" A piece of cheap white poster board was pinned to a light pole just outside the Lazy Mermaid's door. Our little doorbell jangled as I stepped out of the shack.

STOP OR WE'LL STOP YOU! was written in marker over a pot with two red claws sticking out. A stop slash on top. It was signed "Lobster Liberators." My hands shook as I took a photo with my phone and then pulled down the sign.

"Look at this." I showed the paper to Hector and Hilda.

"First those crazy letters, now this!" Hilda breathed.

"There was a sign like this at Kahuna's. I saw it when I went jogging this morning," Hector said. "Somebody threw red paint on the sign, too."

First the letters, now signs, and the disaster at the food festival. How I wished Aunt Gully hadn't dismissed those letters so easily. "I'm taking this sign to the police."

Hilda's brow furrowed. "Do you think there's a connection to those crazy letters?"

"I'm going to find out. Did we get another letter today?"

Hector and Hilda shook their heads. For the past three days, the threatening letters had been slipped under the door. Had the letter writer stopped because they'd been busy at the food festival?

A news van sped past our window.

"We're closing today out of respect for Contessa Wells." I turned the sign on the door to CLOSED. "If any newspeople call just refer them to Lorel."

Chapter 7

As I hurried up Pearl Street to the Plex, I turned the lobster libbers sign over in my hands. No contact information. No Web site. Just a crude drawing and a few words. "Stop or we'll stop you."

A threat. Just like the anonymous letters.

What would be a good way to stop people from eating lobster or going to lobster shacks? I thought of the post I'd seen on the Mystic Bay Food Festival site: "Maybe it was the lobster libbers."

Just an hour earlier, the idea of lobster libbers seemed ridiculous, a bad joke. Come on, lobster libbers? But this paper in my hand put the food poisoning at the food festival in another light. Could it be the work of an organized group? Could they have caused the death of poor Contessa Wells, and almost killed three other people, for their cause?

It was insane, just insane.

As I pulled open the Public Safety Office door, the receptionist looked up from her computer screen.

"Well, if it isn't Legs Larkin."

My old middle school nickname. I smiled. "Hi, Bron. How are you?"

"Been better." My friend Bronwyn Denby worked as a receptionist at the Public Safety Office while studying for her criminal-justice degree. She held up her wrist, encased in a blue cast.

"What happened?" I asked.

"Bike race. Two miles from the finish, my tire hit some loose gravel."

"Ouch, sorry."

"How about your ankle? Didn't slow you down too much on television."

My confusion must've shown. Bronwyn pointed to the television mounted near the ceiling. "They played some video from the food fest. Saw you vault up onto the stage. Pretty impressive with your foot in a boot."

"Didn't do my ankle any good, that's for sure. Hope my physical therapist didn't see that."

I put the sign onto the counter and told her about Aunt Gully's anonymous letters. Bronwyn whistled and ran her fingers through her dark, pixie-cut hair.

"Did you save the letters?"

"No, Aunt Gully threw them away. She thought someone was playing a joke."

"Too bad." Bronwyn shook her head. "I can't imagine anyone doing this to Aunt Gully. Everyone loves her."

"Not Finella Farraday," I said.

"I can't see Finella making this crazy sign. She might chip a nail," Bronwyn said. "Listen, everyone's up at the food fest now." She put on a plastic glove and put the sign on a broad shelf behind her desk.

"Fingerprints!" I said. "I forgot about fingerprints."

Bronwyn laughed. "I thought you watched *CSI*? Where did you find the sign?"

"Tacked to the light pole right outside the front door. And get this, Hector saw another sign by Kahuna's."

Bronwyn jotted notes.

"Just be careful, okay, Legs?" The serious expression in Bronwyn's gray eyes confirmed my feeling that the disaster at the food fest wasn't over yet.

Chapter 8

I barely saw the shops I passed on the way back to the Lazy Mermaid—the Tick Tock Coffee Shop, Sirius Pet Grooming, Mystical Arts and Crafts, Millie's Psychic Vibes. The same words turned in my mind: *Food poisoning. The lobster libbers.*

Poisoning.

After helping Hector and Hilda close, I pulled the van out of the Lazy Mermaid's gravel parking lot. As I came to the fork in Pearl Street where I usually turned right toward home, a sudden thought made me turn left toward Kahuna's.

Yellow police tape crossed the front door of the sprawling restaurant. A shock went through me. The police had closed Kahuna's?

A woman stroked white paint over the large Kahuna's sign by the road, covering red streaks that slashed an *X* over the image of the swaggering Godlobster. I stopped and shot a photo.

Had lobster libbers also sent threatening letters to Kahuna's? Who were they? Why had Kahuna's sign been smeared with red paint and not the Lazy Mermaid's?

Chapter 9

Several vehicles lined the curb by Gull's Nest, but I was
relieved to see that no news trucks were among them. I
parked and hurried into the house.

My phone buzzed with a text from Verity.

DOING BANG UP BUSINESS. ALL THESE PEOPLE
WITH NO PLACE TO GO.

THANKS FOR TAKING CARE OF LEO, I texted
back.

MY PLEASURE. HE'S GOING TO DO A SEGMENT
ON MY VINTAGE SHOP! SCORE! HA! HOW'S
AUNT GULLY? ARE YOU OK? she texted.

FINE. TOO MUCH TO TEXT. TALK TO YOU LATER.

I put away my phone.

Friends and neighbors crowded the kitchen. The scent
of coffee brewing blended with the creamy and briny
scent of Aunt Gully's clam chowder.

The kitchen clock said 4 P.M. How had that happened?
My stomach rumbled and I gratefully accepted a cup of
chowder. Aunt Gully sprinkled some oyster crackers on
top, just the way I liked it.

Lorel sat in Uncle Rocco's recliner, her feet up, her
phone to her ear. She waved at me. "Yes, Aunt Gully will

talk with you tomorrow. She's exhausted and I can't wake her now."

I looked back at Aunt Gully bustling about the kitchen, her face pink, her equilibrium restored by taking care of others, then turned back to Lorel. "Leo Rodriguez," she mouthed at me.

Lorel was trying to get some distance between the food festival disaster and Aunt Gully's television appearance. Sometimes I thought cold salt water ran in Lorel's veins instead of blood. I flopped onto the couch and set my soft boot on top of a pile of *National Geographic* and *People* magazines stacked on the coffee table. Then I lost myself in the creamy goodness of Aunt Gully's chowder.

Over the clink of spoons in mugs and the whistling teapot, I listened to the crowd in the kitchen rehash the morning's events.

"Terrible, but it looks like food poisoning."

"Tsk-tsk."

"Worst food poisoning I've ever seen."

"The mayor was okay, gabbing like usual from his hospital bed."

"Pack It In Packer. Did you hear about that time at the VFW picnic he ate five lobster rolls in five minutes?"

Laughter rolled from the kitchen.

"I love Rick and Rio. The doctors say poor Rio's in trouble."

"You know my friend Judy, the one in real estate? She said Rio and Rick were looking for a spot to build a spa. That's how they found you, Gully, when they were looking at real estate."

"They came in the second day the Mermaid was open," Aunt Gully said, "but I didn't know it. You know how they disguise themselves."

"You know Chick Costa used to date Megan Moss, when they were teens? His people summered on Fox

Point. He never came back after she turned him down for Ernie."

"That Leo Rodriguez is so handsome. Did you see the way he looked at Lorel?"

I smirked at Lorel.

"No, you should've seen the way he was looking at Allie."

Lorel stuck her tongue out at me. I threw a pillow at her, then went in to the kitchen.

"Did you hear the police closed Kahuna's?" I rinsed my mug in the sink. "There was a lobster libber sign posted there, with red paint splashed on it."

The room went quiet. Aunt Gully's friends turned to me, faces expectant, eyes alert.

They all started talking and asking questions at once.

"Lobster graffiti?"

"Red paint, in a big *X*," I said.

"Was the red *X* supposed to look like blood?"

"What color is lobster blood?"

"Juvenile delinquents. This town's going to hell in a handbasket."

I showed them the photo I'd taken of the lobster libber sign. "And this sign was in front of the Lazy Mermaid."

Aggie Weatherburn's black seagull eyes glittered as she held my phone at arm's length. "Stop or we'll stop you." She passed the phone to Aunt Gully.

Aunt Gully peered at the photo under her glasses. She looked up, concern in her big brown eyes.

"That sign was posted in front of the Mermaid," I said. "I brought it to the Plex. Bronwyn Denby said she'd show it to the officers when they got back from the food festival."

Aunt Gully's forehead creased. "Was red paint splashed on the Lazy Mermaid sign, too?"

"No."

"Maybe they ran out?" Aunt Gully suggested.

Aggie scoffed. "These dumbasses have a red lobster in the pot. A red lobster's a cooked lobster. A dead lobster. Everyone knows that."

After more speculation and expressions of support, Aunt Gully's friends gathered their things.

Aggie wrapped the remains of the coffee cake and took her plate to the door. "I'll come sit with your aunt if needs be," she whispered.

"Thanks, Mrs. Weatherburn."

Lorel joined Aunt Gully and me at the door as we waved everyone off.

"Aunt Gully, I wish we'd saved those anonymous letters."

"Do you really think they're from the same people that made the signs at the Mermaid and Kahuna's?"

I shrugged. "I'm wondering if they're connected somehow."

Aunt Gully rubbed my arm. "The police will figure it out."

I followed her to the kitchen, deep in thought

Aunt Gully reached for a dishrag. Lorel pulled it from her hands and tugged her to Uncle Rocco's chair.

"Aunt Gully, sit. We have to talk."

"I can talk and work at the same time," but Aunt Gully sagged into the recliner. I popped the handle so her feet were raised and sat on the arm of the chair.

"Okay, Miss Executive." Aunt Gully folded her arms.

Lorel rolled her eyes. "Look, Aunt Gully, we've got to manage the situation. You're going to have to get in front of this and make a statement."

"Lorel," I said. "Did you see Chick Costa on the news? That appearance reeked of bad taste."

"He didn't have me running things," Lorel said. "I never would've let him wear that god-awful T-shirt or be interviewed so soon after what happened."

"How were things at the Mermaid, Allie? I should be there." Aunt Gully started to get up.

"Fine. Actually." I glanced at Lorel. "I told Hector and Hilda to close for the day."

"I suppose that's best." Aunt Gully sank back into the recliner. Lorel looked at me. I could tell exactly what she was thinking. I'd made a decision without consulting her. But it was a decision she agreed with, so I'd get no flack. Lorel bent over her phone.

"Who're you calling?" Aunt Gully said. "That handsome reporter?"

Lorel didn't look up. "Updating our social media. I'll make a statement about how saddened we are by the events at the food festival, best to be vague about that—"

"And that we'll be open tomorrow." Aunt Gully rocked forward and the recliner creaked upright. "No matter what you say, Miss Executive, I'm going to clean that kitchen and bring chowder over to the Mosses' house and if Megan's still in the hospital I'll go to the hospital to check on her and those poor judges."

There was no stopping Aunt Gully when she made up her mind. We all trooped into the kitchen and helped tidy the already spotless table and countertops while Aunt Gully took down a woven basket from a shelf full of them. She collected baskets—among other things too numerous to mention—but since she was always giving them away stuffed with food to new mothers, bereaved families, or friends needing cheer, the collection constantly changed.

I nibbled some of Aggie's coffee cake.

"Food of the gods." I wrapped a large piece of cake and added it to the covered bowl of chowder that Aunt Gully'd already placed in the basket. Aggie Weatherburn was hell on wheels, but she baked a darn good coffee cake.

"We'll go the Mosses' house," Aunt Gully said. "If Megan's still at the hospital Ernie'll stay by her side. Megan's a quiet one, but as sweet as can be. And a hard worker." That was the highest praise Aunt Gully gave— that someone was a hard worker. "If they aren't home we'll leave the basket with Lucia." Lucia Barreto was the Mosses' housekeeper. I'd often seen her sunning on one of the multiple balconies in front of Kahuna's Kove, the Mosses' massive beachfront home. Aunt Gully didn't say anything about Lucia being a hard worker.

We drove across the stone causeway to Fox Point. Kahuna's Kove was one of the largest homes on the Circle, a private enclave of massive homes. The windows were dark, the drapes drawn. We pulled into the drive.

"We'll go around to the kitchen door. Lucia's here. I texted her," Aunt Gully said.

Lorel and I followed Aunt Gully to the rear of the house, across a flagstone patio with a lap pool and hot tub. A border row of tall grasses swayed, providing a buffer and privacy to the backyard without obstructing the glorious ocean view.

A woman with a glamorously long waterfall of honey-colored hair and bright red lips opened the door. Lucia always looked like she'd wandered in from a *telenovela*.

"Come in," Lucia stage-whispered. She poked her head out and then stepped back into the darkened kitchen. We followed her, stepping carefully. A single candle burned on a granite countertop.

"Can we turn on some lights?" I said.

Lucia took the basket of food. "Thank you, Gully. You're so kind."

"Why are all the drapes closed and the lights off, Lucia?" Aunt Gully asked.

"So many television people," Lucia said, but she flipped a switch, illuminating a huge open-plan kitchen that flowed into a dining area and sunken living room with a towering stone fireplace. "I drew the drapes and stopped answering the door. Mr. Ernie hasn't called. I don't know how Mrs. Megan is. I'm so worried!"

Aunt Gully settled Lucia in a chair in the breakfast nook and bustled to the stove. She filled a kettle with water. Lorel and I exchanged glances. Not more tea.

Lucia opened a low cabinet door. "It's okay, Gully, I had enough tea today. I think I need this." She set a bottle of Scotch on the table and brought out four shot glasses.

I stifled a laugh when Lucia offered me a drink, as did Lorel, but Aunt Gully nodded. Lorel shook her head, but I accepted a glass. I took a sip and sighed as the amber liquid warmed me.

Lucia knocked hers back and poured herself another shot. Aunt Gully's eyebrows rose. "You've had quite a time, I think, Lucia."

"Gully, you wouldn't believe it. The phone rings all the time." As if on cue, the phone rang. Lucia glanced at the caller ID and ignored it. "People banging on the door. Trampling flowers. Trying to peek in the windows. They even called my house, my sister said. They wanted a statement. I told her, no statement! Not until I talk to Mr. Ernie. But he's at the hospital and I don't want to bother him." She cupped her face in her hands, gold rings gleaming. She had kept rings from all her past husbands. "I don't know what to do."

I went through the sunken living room and pulled aside the edge of the curtain. A dark sedan slinked down the street and slid to a stop in front of the house.

"Do you see someone?" Lucia called.

"A car. I think someone's staking out the house. Probably going to wait until Ernie comes back home." I smoothed the curtain into place and returned to the table.

Aunt Gully set a slice of coffee cake in front of Lucia.

"Oh, Aggie's cake!" For the first time since we entered the house, Lucia's tense expression softened into a smile. We waited while she took a few bites. "Do you want some coffee?" she asked.

"No, thanks," Aunt Gully said. "We're heading to the hospital."

Lorel rolled her eyes.

"Let me know how things are, okay? Tell Mrs. Megan I'm thinking of her. Oh, what she's been through these past days." Lucia shook her head.

"These past days?" I asked. Megan had certainly had a bad day today. "You mean with all the preparation for the lobster roll competition?"

Lucia mashed up the last coffee-cake crumbs with her fork. "No, that was easy. They just took the lobster salad they make all the time. The flavors must meld for at least twenty-four hours, so the salad was made as usual, at Kahuna's."

"So that's why they closed Kahuna's," I said.

Lucia sniffled. "They thought it was a bad batch and the police took it for testing," she wailed.

Aunt Gully sipped her Scotch and patted Lucia's hand. "There's no way on God's green earth there was anything wrong with that lobster salad."

Her words echoed in the cavernous kitchen.

Our drawn faces reflected in a glass breakfront across from the breakfast nook. I felt like an exhibit under glass in a museum, a still life called *Four Women Hiding Out with Scotch*.

Lucia knocked back the rest of her drink. "That's not the only thing. For the past few months, Mrs. Megan sometimes got phone calls that upset her. And letters."

Aunt Gully, Lorel, and I exchanged glances. "What kind of letters?"

Lucia shrugged. "All I know is, she'd open the letters out on the deck. She'd read them. And cry."

"Poor thing," Aunt Gully said.

"Not from lobster libbers?" I said.

Lucia shrugged. "She never said anything about lobster libbers. But it's strange. As far as I know, she never told Mr. Ernie about them. I saw her stuff one in her pocket when he came home."

I leaned forward. "Return address?"

"None," Lucia said.

"Postmark?" I asked.

The sound of a car door slamming made us jump.

"Smudged, but it was from Massachusetts," Lucia said.

I knew Lucia would've checked.

"Then Mrs. Megan had a visitor. He upset her," Lucia said.

"A visitor? Who was it?" I asked.

"You know that guy in the yellow shirt from Chatham? On the news?"

Lorel and I exchanged looks. "Chick Costa."

Chatham is in Massachusetts, I thought.

Lorel got up and looked out the front window. "Two cars," she whispered.

"He came early this morning, in that fancy red sports car. Wanted to see Mrs. Megan. He was so bossy. He knocked right after Mr. Ernie went to Kahuna's. Like he was watching the house and came when Mr. Ernie left."

I leaned forward. I'd heard something about Chick and Megan in the conversation at Aunt Gully's.

"They dated years ago, when they were in high school? When he was summer people?"

Aunt Gully's eyes took on a faraway expression. "She

was waitressing at her family's ice-cream shop. Well, they had ice cream, hot dogs, clams. In the same building that Kahuna's is in now. It used to be called Scoops by the Sea."

"Well, I had no idea who he was. He had a big bouquet. Red roses, a whole armful. When she came downstairs and saw him"—Lucia hesitated—"she was angry."

All this drama with Megan Moss. I tried to square this with the quiet middle-aged woman who wiped tables and served lobster rolls at Kahuna's. She usually had a smile on her chapped lips, her long light brown hair pulled into a messy braid. Her soft voice made me think of a sixties folk singer, wispy and sweet, strewing daisies, barefoot in a field. Funny that she ended up with a man with such a bullish personality.

"She was angry?" I asked.

Lucia shifted in her chair. "Well, she was getting ready for the competition. Mr. Ernie had to go down to the restaurant early. He got a phone call about something bad that had happened and he left. Swearing. He said something like, 'I don't need this this morning.'"

The paint-splashed sign. Ernie was probably going over to handle the lobster libber crisis before they left for the lobster roll competition.

Lucia continued. "When Chick came I said, Mrs. Megan, do you want to see this guy? She said yes. They went into the study off the foyer and shut the door. I heard her voice. At first she sounded mad. But then." Lucia paused. "Like she was begging. Please. I heard her say 'please.'"

I pictured Lucia dusting the table across from the study door, over and over, waiting to hear some juicy tidbit.

The rumble of the garage door made us jump. Car doors slammed, muffled voices rose. The phone started ringing again. Pounding rattled the front door. I felt a guilty jab of sympathy for Lucia. The door to the garage opened and Ernie and Megan Moss entered, Megan leaning heavily on Ernie's arm.

Lucia swept the bottle of Scotch off the table into the cabinet. Aunt Gully hurried to the Mosses.

"I'm so glad you're home, Megan," Aunt Gully said.

I gathered the shot glasses and put them in the sink.

"So sorry to intrude; we were just going," Lorel said.

Megan embraced Aunt Gully. "Oh, you couldn't possibly intrude, Gully. I'm just so tired. Thank you for taking care of me today. The doctors say I've had a shock and need to rest."

Megan blinked as if she couldn't stay awake. Probably sedated.

"Let's get you to bed, Mrs. Megan," Lucia said.

As Lucia helped Megan upstairs, Ernie turned to Aunt Gully. "Damned reporters are harassing me, plain and simple. I called the cops."

Fox Point had its own tiny police force. Its usual duties included enforcing noise ordinances on parties, checking on empty houses in the winter, and taking down speeders. They were a cross between a police force and a private security company.

Moments later blue lights flashed around the front curtains, car doors slammed, and engines fired up. We peeked around the curtains. The reporters were in retreat. They probably figured they wouldn't get anything out of Ernie now. I wondered if they would chase down the other contestants—like Aunt Gully.

Fatigue hit me. All I wanted was to get Aunt Gully home safely, where she could rest. As she and Ernie spoke, I studied their faces. Ernie, beefy and red faced, seemed older than he had that morning. What was he, in his fifties? Megan was maybe in her late thirties, early forties, but it was hard to tell. Though the effects of the terrible events of the morning had taken their toll, Ernie was probably at least ten years older than his wife.

I circled to the sink and washed out the shot glasses. I looked for a towel to dry them as Lorel swiped on her ever-present phone.

The Mosses' kitchen had beautiful mahogany cabinetry. When I slid open what I thought might be a drawer of towels, I pulled open a concealed trash bin. It was stuffed full of red roses. The red roses that Chick had given Megan. Had she angrily stuffed them into the bin this morning? Did she want to hide them from Ernie? She'd probably had little time to get rid of them before she left for the competition. I remember how busy we'd been this morning, which suddenly seemed a hundred years ago. I slammed the bin shut but the scent of the roses lingered.

We took our leave, wishing Ernie good night, though I knew that was futile. The man had just had his whole life blown up in front of him. How could he sleep? Perhaps the doctors had also given him a sedative. Ernie was going to need it.

We nodded to the police officer outside Kahuna's Kove and got in the van. I just hoped the reporters didn't have Gull's Nest staked out. We didn't have a private police force to run interference for us.

Chapter 10

No news trucks staked out Aunt Gully's cottage, but two unfamiliar vehicles were parked in front of the house. One was a white pickup truck with Maine license plates. The other, a little red sports car, gleamed expensively under the streetlight. Paul Pond and Chick Costa stood by their vehicles, deep in conversation.

We pulled into the driveway next to Lorel's BMW.

"Aunt Gully, you just go in. I'll get rid of them for you," I said.

"Allie, don't be silly." Aunt Gully turned to look at the men. "They've had a bad shock, just like me. I'll invite them in for some chowder."

I caught Lorel's eye. I couldn't imagine why these guys were here. Didn't Paul Pond say he wanted to leave? Maybe they'd heard if you showed up at Aunt Gully's you got free food. This was true.

I looked through the van window at the two men: rangy Paul Pond, overalls over his Pond's T-shirt, working that Maine seafarer look. Chick Costa leaned on his car, which probably cost as much as Aunt Gully's cottage, his sweater still knotted around his neck, sun-bleached hair slicked back, a chunky watch gleaming on his wrist.

He'd changed out of his Chick's World Famous Lobsters T-shirt into his signature yellow polo shirt and navy blue sweater.

"How did they find her?' I said.

"She's still listed in the phone book," Lorel said.

"Nobody's listed in the phone book anymore," I said.

"You girls behave." Aunt Gully gathered her things. "Let's see what they're up to."

The two men approached the van, Paul Pond tall and stooped, hanging back behind Chick's broad-shouldered frame.

Aunt Gully opened her door. "Good evening, gentlemen."

"Gully, how are you?" Chick said.

Aunt Gully lifted her chin. "It's been a difficult day."

"True, that," Chick said.

Paul Pond offered Aunt Gully a hand as she stepped from the van.

"We should discuss the network's position," Chick said.

"Network's position?" Aunt Gully's brow furrowed.

"They called about an hour ago. They want a meeting tomorrow afternoon," Paul Pond said.

"Aunt Gully, have you checked your cell phone?" Lorel's exasperation showed.

Aunt Gully shrugged. "I always forget my cell phone. Let's go inside and have a bite to eat and you gentlemen can tell me about it."

"Very kind of you," Paul Pond said.

Aunt Gully settled the men at the dining room table and served them each a steaming bowl of chowder in her vintage Fiestaware, the red, yellow, and orange (Aunt Gully did not believe in matching) bright pops of color on her vintage tablecloth, this one a map of Hawaii, with hula girls and surfers. The unnaturally cheerful colors contrasted with the strained expressions of those sitting around the table.

We ate quietly. Paul Pond's and Chick Costa's sober faces brightened after their first spoonfuls of chowder.

"Mighty fine chowder, Mrs. Fontana." Paul lifted his spoon in appreciation.

"Thank you. Please call me Gully."

"Paul." Paul nodded and returned to his soup.

"We've got to talk damage control," Chick said.

Aunt Gully waved him off. "When did you get into town, Chick?"

"Drove down this morning, bright and early. Now, the network—"

Aunt Gully turned to Paul Pond. "Tell me about your shack, Paul. I understand it's been in your family for quite a long time."

"My many times great-grandfather started lobstering back in the 1800s. Shack's been in my family for so many generations I've lost count. I've worked there since Moses wore knee pants," Paul said. Everyone but Chick laughed; his eyes were on the phone on his lap.

Paul continued. "It's right on Kitt's Harbor, prettiest place you'll ever see."

"How about you, Chick?" Aunt Gully passed a tray of her homemade dill bread.

"Oh, I've always been a lobster lover." He looked up, took the tray and several slices of bread. "My family owns a chain of sandwich shops called Seaside Sandy's all up and down the coast. Then about ten years ago, I saw a place called Grand Clam was going under. Family run, poorly managed. Typical. Some of these family-run outfits have no idea how to turn a profit."

Paul Pond lowered his eyes.

"But the location on the water was primo. Got it for pennies and turned it around. Did a fair amount of testing and surveys to get just the right lobster roll. Rick and Rio tried it and liked it. And here I am." He spread his hands. "Just like you guys. But you got here a little faster than most, Gully." Chick's smile was cold despite his perfect white teeth and square jaw.

I didn't like the way he said that, but Aunt Gully smiled right back at him.

"Rick and Rio came on the second day I was open. Barely knew what I was doing." Aunt Gully chuckled. "They were in disguise, as they do on their TV show. But they liked my lobster roll and next thing I know, I get an invitation to the contest."

"Overnight success." Chick folded his arms and leaned back in his chair.

"Aunt Gully's been making her lobster rolls for years." I leaned forward, my face hot.

Chick cleared his throat. "Well, the network's talking about canceling the Best Lobster Roll contest for this year. I don't want that. I want a redo. That's my position for the meeting tomorrow." He looked around the table. "Thought it might be best to present a united front."

Paul Pond took a piece of bread and sopped up the last of his chowder, avoiding looking at Chick. Aunt Gully blinked. Lorel's face was composed, thoughtful. Oh, God, she's actually considering this, I thought.

"Absolutely not," I said. "I held Contessa Wells in my arms. It's absolutely gruesome."

"So some old lady died, yeah, that's sad." Chick tried to look sad. "You heard the network, she had undisclosed health problems."

"That's what the network says." I tried to keep my voice level. "The news said the lobster roll's being tested."

"And it wasn't our lobster rolls. We shouldn't pay because of what Ernie Moss did. Not. Our. Fault." Chick's finger poked the air with each word. "You know as well as I do that winning this contest is golden as far as marketing's concerned. Two news cycles from now and nobody's gonna remember some dead old lady."

I shot to my feet. "That's a terrible thing to say."

Chick stood, flipping his key chain so we couldn't help but see the Ferrari emblem. "Maybe the other Larkin sister'll talk sense into you guys." Chick winked at Lorel. Lorel met his eye, no change in her expression. Ice princess.

"Gotta jet. See you guys tomorrow." None of us offered to see Chick out.

When she heard the door close, Aunt Gully turned to Paul. "What an awful man."

Paul Pond stood and ran his hands along the straps of his overalls. "I shouldn't take up any more of your time. You do whatever you think's best for your business," he said. "But I'm inclined to agree with your daughter." He nodded at me. Aunt Gully didn't correct him.

Aunt Gully drew a shaky breath. "Is that what people say about me? That I shouldn't have been in the contest?"

"Gully, you didn't know it, but I stopped by your place yesterday. Checking out the competition." Paul smiled. "Speaking as a man who's eaten a lot of lobster rolls over the years, you deserved to be in the contest." He jutted his chin at his empty bowl. "And your chowder's just as good as my grandmother's, and that's saying something."

Aunt Gully took his hand in hers. "Thank you."

"Getting late. Best be getting back to the inn. Then back to Maine." He winked at Aunt Gully. "Got a family business to run."

Aunt Gully saw Paul Pond out then gathered the empty bowls and went into the kitchen.

I leaned toward Lorel. "You aren't seriously considering what that jerk said."

"He's a jerk. Agreed." Lorel adjusted the sleeves of the

camel-colored cashmere sweater she'd put on over her Lazy Mermaid T-shirt. "But we've got to do what's best for Aunt Gully and that's helping her business succeed," she whispered. "It's all she's got now that Uncle Rocco's gone."

"She's got us," I whispered. "Aunt Gully's a decent person and no decent person wants any part of a contest where one person died and three people almost died. Anyway, we should ask what she wants to do."

Over the sound of the little television in the kitchen, I could hear Aunt Gully running water in the sink, pots and pans clinking, getting her fix of soap bubbles and the evening news.

"Chick Costa's a jerk but he makes sense, Allie," Lorel stood. "We've got to watch what's happening and react the right way. We'll watch social media, the news, and see how public opinion goes. That's how you manage a crisis."

A crash came from the kitchen.

We ran into the kitchen, narrowly avoiding the bright orange shards scattered on the black-and-white checkerboard linoleum. Aunt Gully pointed at the tiny television on the shelf of her vintage Hoosier cabinet.

"Poison!" Aunt Gully clutched her chest with a soapy hand. "They found poison in Kahuna's lobster rolls!"

Chapter 11

We stayed up late to watch the news, but there was little beyond the report that a "toxic substance"—which Aunt Gully translated into poison; were they even the same thing?—had been found in the Kahuna's lobster rolls served to the judges. Test results would come soon from the state police lab.

After I called Verity to fill her in, we'd all stumbled to bed, Lorel and I to the bedroom we'd shared at Aunt Gully's since we were little girls. Bedsprings creaked as Lorel tossed all night. My sleep was fitful as images—the lobster libber sign, the threatening letters, Contessa's scarf, Rio's red boots, Aunt Gully's pink apron—swam in and out of my dreams.

When my phone rang the next morning, I struggled to form the word "hello."

"Allie!"

I rolled over, smiling. "Dad! How are you?"

"Question is, how are you two doing? The food fest's all over the news." Dad's rich tenor voice touched something in me and tears sprang to my eyes. I cleared my throat.

"We're fine, Dad, really. Hard on Aunt Gully, that's for sure."

Aunt Gully had been exhausted when she finally went to bed. We talked her into a cup of tea with a large shot of her book-club brandy and tucked her in.

"You girls staying with her?"

"Yes." Lorel and I still had bedrooms at my dad's house just around the corner from Aunt Gully's, but growing up we'd spent so much time at Aunt Gully's she had a bedroom with two matching twin beds for us, cozily tucked under the slanting roof, my bed with the same purple crocheted afghan she'd made me when I was eight and everything had to be purple.

Lorel's side of the room held little but the bed and a photo on the bedside table of my dad and mother holding Lorel. The wall on Lorel's side of the room had a single seascape. Posters of bands, dancers, and figure skaters still covered the wall on my side of the room.

I curled up on Lorel's bed and set the phone on speaker.

"Hi, Dad." Lorel sat up and yawned.

"Lorelei, honey, how are you?" My dad and Aunt Gully were the only ones who could call Lorel by her given name without getting a death glare.

"Okay, Dad," Lorel said. "But it's been crazy."

"I expect it's going to get crazier," he said.

We filled him in on our upcoming meeting with the YUM Network, the "toxic substance" found in Kahuna's rolls, the judges, the Mosses, the mayor, the lobster libbers, and Contessa Wells.

"Just the other day Esmeralda was saying what a blessing it is that you two girls help Gully with the shack."

Lorel and I shared a look. What Esmeralda meant: Aunt Gully has you two so she won't need her brother to help.

Dad had been dating Esmeralda Lima for nine months. She'd sailed into Mystic Bay on her yacht, the *Sea Queen*, had taken one of Dad's whale-watching cruises, and decided to stay on. All the men of a certain age in Mystic Bay had been captivated by the flamenco-dancing widow, but she'd had the good taste to pick Dad. I wished she'd had worse taste in men. She'd taken her trip to get over a previous relationship. She was a quick healer. She asked Dad to sail with her on her yacht to the British Virgin Islands. Dad left his whale-watching business in his partner Sprague McCoy's hands while on this trip with Esmeralda.

Neither Lorel nor I were happy about Dad's infatuation with the woman we called the Firecracker. From what we knew of Esmeralda, she changed her men as often as she changed the color of her nail polish. Ever since Mom died when I was born, Dad had always put us first. He'd dated a few Mystic Bay ladies over the years, but nothing serious. I didn't mind Dad having a companion, I just didn't want to see him get hurt.

"Now, your aunt says everything's under control. Is that true?"

"Absolutely." Lorel looked at me.

"Yes, Dad, don't worry," I said.

"All right then. Remember, I'll be back in a jiffy if you need me. Things'll look up. They always do." Dad's sympathetic voice was soothing.

"Right, Dad." I meant it.

"Stick together," he said, as always. "Love my girls."

"Love you, too, Dad," we chorused.

When we got downstairs, Aunt Gully was just hanging up the phone. She looked so dejected, I rushed to her. "What is it?"

Aunt Gully sat heavily in a kitchen chair. "That was the

director of health and sanitation for Mystic Bay. Robbie Vasquez. He's ordering the closure of the Lazy Mermaid until the state police have a handle on the substance that was in the lobster rolls."

All my calm from the conversation with Dad evaporated. "What! It wasn't your rolls that made everyone sick!"

"That's ridiculous," Lorel said.

Aunt Gully blew out a breath. "Well, he has the authority. He said until the state police definitely knew what caused the illness, he had to protect the people of Mystic Bay." To my surprise, she chuckled. "Robbie Vasquez always was the most cautious soul you'd ever see. Won't dip a toe into the water unless he's wearing water wings. Well, I guess it's better safe than sorry. But I told him I've got people depending on me. I've got to call our lobstermen."

Several lobstermen and women delivered their catches right to our dock. The Lazy Mermaid had seawater tanks for the lobsters, so none would die, but Aunt Gully believed that keeping the lobsters too long stressed them and affected their flavor.

"I'll get in touch with our other suppliers." I mentally started a list with the bakery that supplied our rolls.

"Robbie said he'd do an inspection later today," Aunt Gully said. "Personally."

"Well, he'll be impressed," I said.

"I'll call Hector and Hilda," Lorel said. "When can we reopen?"

"Robbie said if all goes well, tomorrow. He'll let me know."

Aunt Gully's phone shrilled. She was now back in stride, humming the song "Tomorrow" from *Annie* as she answered.

"I have to pick up some things at Dad's." I'd moved most of my stuff back after my injury and it was split fairly evenly between Aunt Gully's and Dad's house.

"Don't forget you girls promised to go to church with me this morning," Aunt Gully said.

"We did?" Lorel and I exchanged looks. I couldn't think of an excuse. "Be back soon."

I walked around the corner to Dad's house, a tidy cottage with MERMAID MOTEL carved over the door. My sister and I had gone through an extended mermaid phase, pretty much expected for two imaginative little girls who lived on the beach. The Lazy Mermaid was Dad's nickname for me and I loved that Aunt Gully'd used the name for her shack. Lorel, to her credit, didn't seem too jealous.

The Mermaid Motel's cedar shingles were dark brown and none of Aunt Gully's whirligigs spun by the door. Dad's idea of decorating was to hang old lobster buoys on the shed in the backyard. Since Lorel and I'd left for school and Boston several years earlier, the house had taken on a bit of a man cave feel, though Dad kept everything shipshape.

Like Aunt Gully's cottage, the top floor had two bedrooms with a bathroom in between. Lorel, ever practical and organized, had moved most of her stuff to her Boston condo. But Lorel's white four-poster was still in her room, along with a vanity that had been our mother's.

My dad had allowed me to paint my room a sea green when I was in my mermaid phase. Little fluorescent stars I'd glued to the ceiling still gave off a dim glow. My bookshelves were stuffed with Trixie Belden and Nancy Drew mysteries that had been my mother's, Harry Potter, and biographies of famous dancers. Rows of dance trophies lined a shelf and battered old toe shoes hung from my ballet barre in front of the window.

Tucked in one corner was an oversized rocking chair. My mother had rocked Lorel in it. She never had a chance to rock me in it; my dad and Aunt Gully had done that. Still, when I curled up in this chair, often with a favorite book, I felt embraced by the mother I never knew.

I tossed a few clothes in a bag, removed my walking boot, put on some music, and ran through the exercises of my floor barre.

Every morning since my injury, I did floor barre, an adaptation of the dancer's regular exercises that are usually done standing, plus Pilates, since it allowed me to isolate my left ankle and foot. Along with my regular physical therapy sessions, I was doing everything I could to stay in top shape to speed up my recovery and my return to the ballet company. How I missed dancing.

For an hour, I wasn't a woman worried about her aunt's livelihood, stale rolls, or deliveries of lobsters. As I moved, my mind emptied of everything but the music and the strength in my body. I stretched into a split, resting my upper body and face against my leg. When the music stopped, the relaxing sound of the ocean waves curling into shore filled the room.

Timing, I thought. Everything that had happened— from the first threatening letter to the death of Contessa Wells—flashed through my mind. Aunt Gully thought the letters were a joke, but why had they arrived the week of the food festival? Why did the sign appear the morning of the food festival? Were they all connected?

Chapter 12

In the early years of the twentieth century, St. Peter's Church had been built in a rocky field not far from Mystic Bay. In a moment of spiritual whimsy, the church planners had incorporated a carved statue of Saint Peter in a wooden hull that jutted over the front door of the church. Almost one hundred years later, the fields were gone and the building and Saint Peter were marooned by strip malls and busy Route One. Everyone called the church St. Peter in the Boat.

Saint Peter's somewhat surprised expression welcomed Lorel and me as we accompanied Aunt Gully into church. During the service, the sound of St. Peter's well-regarded choir helped relieve the suffering inflicted by the hard wooden seats.

My phone vibrated with a text from Verity.

I GOT THE JOB OF THE CENTURY. COME WITH? THREE OR FOUR HOURS?

Lorel frowned as I texted back. YES. PICK ME UP AT ST PETES. I couldn't wait to tell Verity my thoughts about Aunt Gully's threatening letters. She'd help me sort it out.

At coffee hour, I explained that I was going with Verity for a few hours. Lorel rolled her eyes. I was ditching her and at a church coffee to boot. Friends mobbed Aunt Gully, most offering hugs and sincere support, some just angling for news. Finella Farraday cut through the crowd toward Aunt Gully like a shark intent on a kill, eager to say something mean. Strange how such a beautiful woman would always say such ugly things.

"I've got her." Lorel headed off Mrs. Farraday.

I stepped outside, throwing an apologetic glance at Saint Peter.

Verity's car skidded to a stop in a tow zone. I walked quickly to the car, a gray seventeen-foot-long 1962 DeSoto complete with fins. Even Verity's car was vintage. We called it the Tank.

I've been friends with Verity every since she, Bronwyn, and I were the Three Little Kittens in the St. Peter's Preschool Snowflake Revue. Verity had insisted that her kitten should wear not only mittens and a matching hat, but also a feather boa. Even as a child, she'd been a fashionista.

"Allie, you're not going to believe this," Verity said.

"Tell me!" I slid into the vast front seat of the Tank. "What's this job of the century?"

Verity grabbed my shoulders. "You can't tell a soul. Promise."

"Cross my heart! Tell me!"

"This morning I got a call to buy clothes and"—she sat up straight and pursed her lips—"accoutrements."

"Accoutrements? Someone actually said 'accoutrements'?" I laughed. "Who was it?"

Verity tightened her grip on my shoulders. "Juliet Wells."

"Juliet Wells?" I remembered my conversation with Hector and Hilda. "Contessa Wells's sister? The crazy lady?"

"One and the same. She wants to sell her sister's stuff."

I stared at Verity. "Contessa just died yesterday."

"I know. She told me she's having the funeral on Tuesday, if the police allow it. She wants to know if I can pay cash." Verity's eyes glittered. "Still want to come?"

Of course I wanted to come. Verity and I discussed the reservations a normal person would have about buying the clothing of a recently deceased movie/Broadway star not even twenty-four hours after she died. But then excitement took hold.

"We're awful people," I said.

Cars and churchgoers streamed from St. Peter's parking lot.

"Just wretched. Think of it this way. What kind of income does a crazy lady have?" Verity asked. "She probably needs the cash. I'm helping her. That's good karma, right?"

"Hey, speaking of good karma, thanks for taking care of that pesky reporter yesterday," I said.

"We live to serve." Verity grinned, but squeezed my shoulder. "The whole thing must've been awful. You okay?" Verity's almond-shaped brown eyes were huge behind her cat's-eye glasses.

"Pretty okay. My dad called to check on us, wondering if he should come home. We told him to wait. Lorel said everything'll blow over."

"Lorel's right, right?"

"Maybe?" I shrugged.

Finella Farraday exited the church. Verity and I slid down in our seats as she power walked past the Tank and Aunt Gully's van to her car.

"She looks steamed," I said. "Though she always looks steamed."

"Yesterday her corgis got away from her and tore through my store, mangled some really sweet old handkerchiefs and she blamed me!" Verity said. "But then one of my customers said something about the mess at the food festival. Finella ran over there like a shot."

I remembered Finella's insensitive questions as we'd packed Aunt Gully's mermaidabilia.

"We're supposed to meet with the TV people later today. Chick Costa wants them to reschedule the competition," I knotted my hair into a bun.

Verity's perfectly arched eyebrows shot up. "After what happened to Contessa?"

"Exactly. Aunt Gully doesn't want to do it, but Lorel thinks everyone'll forget about Contessa soon enough. If Aunt Gully did the competition somewhere else and won, having the YUM Network star of approval would be great for the shack."

"Your sister's cold."

Lorel exited the church, texting on her ever-present phone. She exuded a Grace Kelly cool in white linen pants and a soft blue sweater. She drew admiring glances from men and women, but she was oblivious. Business above all else—that was Lorel.

"When do you have to be at the Wells House?" I said.

"Miss Wells said twelve-thirty."

"We'd better get going." As Verity steered toward Rabb's Point, I told her about the letters and the lobster libber sign. "I think it's all connected somehow. Why would we start getting those letters just days before the competition?"

"Make Aunt Gully so upset she'd mess up her lobster rolls?" Verity said.

I shrugged. "Maybe? Still, I'm going make sure the police know about them."

"Call my uncle." Verity's uncle was Emerson Brooks, Mystic Bay's chief of police.

"Didn't you tell me he's always too busy to take your calls?"

"Yeah, but call him anyway. Use my phone, his number's programmed in."

The call went to voice mail. "Hi, Chief Brooks, it's Allie Larkin. I know you're probably really busy, but could you please call me back? I want to talk to you about some threatening letters my aunt received. It's important." I left my number and hung up. "It's too bad Aunt Gully didn't save the letters."

Verity threw me a look. "You still look worried."

"I am worried, Verity. Nobody came to the Mermaid yesterday, and today the health and sanitation director has us closed until he can do an inspection. What if people think Aunt Gully had something to do with the poisonings?"

Chapter 13

Verity steered the Tank into Rabb's Point, up historic Spyglass Hill past several old whaling captains' houses, and through ivy-covered walls into a property that looked like a movie set.

The Wells House had looked down on Mystic Bay from the top of Spyglass Hill for over two hundred years. The towering white mansion was crowned with an ornate cast-iron widow's walk. I imagined the view from high above, the anxious ancestor of the famous Contessa Wells watching the harbor, praying for the return of her husband's ship.

Abutting the property was the Mystic Bay Ancient Burial Ground. Halloween night most kids in Mystic Bay made their way through the cemetery to the Wells House, which had sat empty for many years.

The house had been completely transformed from the Halloween-night haunted house of my memory. Ivy that had choked the walls had been cleared away, the brick repainted, the fountain in the circular driveway cleared of debris and repainted. But still a hushed feeling remained, a feeling of stepping out of time, of a house in the grip of a fairy curse, destined to be reclaimed by twisting vines and thorny branches.

"Wow. I don't remember this." Verity parked the Tank next to a small rusted Toyota.

"I remember toilet paper hanging from all the tree branches. This is gorgeous," I said.

Verity took a deep breath. "Let's go. But, Allie—"

"Yes?"

"The less we say inside, the better. I just want to buy and go, okay?"

"This is legal, right, Verity?"

Verity gathered cardboard boxes filled with large trash bags. "This could be the buy of a lifetime, Allie. Contessa and Juliet were fashion icons, especially Contessa. She ran with the A-list in the seventies and eighties. Studio 54, all that. It's my big chance."

Excitement coursed through me as we carried the boxes to the door. Every kid in Mystic Bay had wanted to get into the old Wells place. Now was our chance. The circumstances were beyond sketchy. Would the police show up at any moment? Were Contessa's clothes somehow evidence? I didn't care. I couldn't wait to get inside.

Verity rang the bell. I imagined the door being opened by Contessa's sister, dressed perhaps in a Chanel suit or movie star lounging pajamas.

Instead, a middle-aged woman holding a broom and dustpan opened the door. She wore baggy jeans and an oversized gray Heart's Ease Homecare sweatshirt. Everything about her was gray: her thinning hair, pulled back into a sloppy ponytail, her dull skin, her pale lips.

"Yeah?" she said.

Verity and I looked at each other.

"Miss Wells asked me to come over. My name is Verity Brooks and this is my associate, Allie Larkin."

The woman's eyes flicked over me. I had the sense she

was trying to place me. Perhaps she'd seen the TV footage of me with Contessa. I tilted my chin and let my hair fall forward to obscure my profile.

But the woman simply stepped aside to let us in and shut the door, snuffing out birdsong and sunlight. We stepped through a marble foyer, past a grand carved wood staircase that led to a gallery above. Several flamboyant floral arrangements and potted plants lined a long side table.

One arrangement lay smashed against the base of the stairs, lilies, roses, and broken glass littering the floor.

The woman said, "Leave the boxes by the stairs. This way."

We obeyed, silently stepping around the mess.

"She's in the morning room."

Verity and I looked at each other. It took me a moment to realize that the woman meant "morning." "Mourning" had come to mind, and I think Verity had heard the word the same way.

The woman opened a door at the end of the hallway. "In here." She left without a backward glance.

After the dark hallway, the room was a burst of sunlight. Wide French doors opened onto a walled garden where pink azaleas had burst into bloom. The garden made a feminine backdrop for a petite dark-haired woman seated on a powder-blue upholstered couch. She was dressed in an oversized white button-down shirt and black leggings. From her short black bob and high, round cheekbones to her wide red lips, she looked exactly like the woman I'd held in my arms the day before. Déjà vu. I willed myself to take a deep breath.

Rings sparkled on every finger of the woman's gnarled hands, heavy cuff bracelets circled her wrists. She held an ornate silver vial that hung around her neck on a black velvet cord.

"You're the clothes girl." Her voice rasped and made me think of rusty hinges.

"Yes, Miss Wells. Thank you for calling me. This is my, um, associate, Allie Larkin. Um, my sympathies about your sister."

"Do you know what this is?" She held out the small vial.

Verity nodded. "A lachrymatory. A tear bottle. Used in Victorian times."

"For holding tears." Miss Wells covered her face. Her shoulders shook.

Verity and I shared a look. Was she weeping?

When Miss Wells looked up, her shiny red-painted lips curved in a smile. "I have so many tears I'd need a million of these." She stood abruptly. "Well, come on. Pack up her stuff. I don't need it. I don't want it. I need the cash. Okay?"

Juliet didn't seem particularly broken up about her sister's death. Well, I'd heard she was a crazy lady and this was a crazy reaction. I tried to keep my breathing steady and make no sudden movements.

"Look." Juliet pointed to two framed silhouettes on the wall beside the door. "There we are. Two sisters, just two years apart." Verity and I stepped closer to see the profiles of two little girls with large hair bows and identical upturned noses. Brown braided material ringed each. I stiffened as I realized what the braid was.

"Oh, I love hair art," Verity cooed.

"We had an old-fashioned governess." Juliet strode from the room.

We scurried after her, dodging the broken glass and scattered petals, scooping up the boxes, and following her up the grand staircase. She moved quickly for a woman who must be in her seventies.

"We rented the house out for years but my sister kept

many old family things in these rooms, which"—Juliet stepped into a room—"were locked to keep the renters out." She pulled the door closed as I caught sight of a portrait over a fireplace. A woman in a crimson gypsy dress, a black mantilla over her wild black curls. The walls matched the color of the woman's dress, intensifying her look of triumph. It was a portrait of Contessa Wells in her most famous role in *The Gypsy's Daughter*. Verity caught my eye. She'd seen the portrait, too.

Juliet unlocked a door across the hall. Unlike the cleaner lines and more modern style of the room downstairs, this room's décor had old-fashioned sophistication and glamour. Velvet swags topped large windows through which Mystic Bay glittered in the distance.

We followed Juliet through another door. Verity swayed. "Oh, my stars."

"We made this room into a walk-in closet," Juliet said.

The term "walk-in closet" didn't do the vast, clothing-lined room justice. It was twice the size of the large bedroom we'd walked through. Floor-to-ceiling shelves were jammed with wigs, shoes, and hatboxes. A shelf running the length of the room held dozens and dozens of handbags. A chandelier hung in the center of the room over a gold-upholstered pouf. It was California Closets by way of Versailles.

Juliet opened a drawer in a tall chest and said, "Jewelry."

Verity walked to the drawer like a woman sleepwalking through the best dream of her life. "Miss Wells, I'll have to come back, this is far beyond what I expected—"

"You brought the cash, right?"

Verity handed Juliet an envelope. "Yes," she whispered. Verity looked stunned. I was stunned, too. We were surrounded by gorgeous clothes, accessories, and jewelry of every description. Just one of the Birkin bags on a shelf would sell for more money than Verity had paid Juliet.

Juliet took the envelope without looking inside.

"I'll have to pay you more, for the jewelry," Verity stammered. "I'll come back on Tuesday after the bank opens."

"You girls can come to the funeral. Tuesday at three at our family mausoleum in the burying ground. Come back Wednesday morning. You can take all this stuff then."

This was a gold mine for Verity but still I shuddered at the way Juliet called her dead sister's things "stuff."

"The police came, you know. To tell me about my sister." She turned to face me. "I saw you. You're the dancer."

I nodded, not sure what to say. She must have seen me on the news.

"I saw you when we visited once, years ago, when Broadway by the Bay did *Brigadoon*. You were in the chorus. I knew you'd be a ballerina." Her voice softened. "We dancers can tell. You have a gift, my dear."

I remembered that Juliet had also been a dancer and actress. "Thank you. You're a dancer, too." Her carriage was unmistakable. Her posture was perfect, her neck long, her back straight.

"I still do a barre every day. Well, what I call a barre." She spun slowly to my right, her movements surprisingly graceful. She stopped and ran her fingers along the sleeve of a velvet jacket. "I love dancing."

"Me, too."

She jutted her chin at my walking boot. "I hope you're healed soon."

"Thank you."

"Is that your sister?" Juliet pointed at Verity.

Hadn't Verity just introduced us? "We're friends."

"Friend." Juliet said the word as if tasting a strange new fruit. "Friends keep sending flowers. Theater friends." Her voice rose. "I'm tired, I need to lie down."

The gray woman stepped into the room. "Is everything all right, Miss Wells?"

"Where are my manners? Susan, will you get our guests some tea?" Juliet said. "And open the windows for some air."

Susan slid open a window as Juliet continued. "Susan, they're taking the old clothes. They'll come back for more the day after the funeral."

"Yes, Miss Wells."

"No more visitors today. Even the police. They can go pound sand." Juliet left the room.

Susan took a rag from her back pocket and passed it over a desk. Verity and I exchanged glances as we stepped back into the closet.

"No tea for us," I whispered.

"I guess she's here so we don't slip the stuff into our pockets," Verity whispered.

I rolled my eyes. "Juliet just offered to give you thousands of dollars' worth of jewelry. I think Susan's just biding her time until we're gone."

I raised my voice. "Are you Juliet's, um, nurse?"

Susan looked up. "Yeah, plus chief cook and bottle washer. It's just me taking care of her and the house until summer renters come in July."

"Big house for two people." Verity opened a drawer of lingerie.

Susan shrugged. "It's just Juliet. Contessa lives in her house in Beverly Hills. Lived. She put"—Susan hesitated—"she let Juliet live here for the past couple of months. She only came out herself because of the job at Broadway by the Bay."

"Oh. So Juliet moved here from California?"

"No, they didn't live together. Juliet was in a"—again Susan stopped—"in a place in Chicago."

Verity turned to me and mouthed "Loony bin."

Through the open window came the sound of car tires crunching over the gravel drive. A door banged somewhere down the hallway.

Juliet shrieked, "Susan! If it's newspeople, get rid of them!"

Susan threw down her rag and hurried from the room.

Verity and I ran to the window. A black sedan parked by the Tank.

"Oh, crap. If they see me taking boxes out I'll look like a vulture," Verity muttered.

From above, we saw a dark-haired guy get out of the car, smooth his hair, and jog to the door. Verity and I jumped back from the window.

"That's Leo Rodriguez!"

We eased down the hall where we could see down into the foyer. An old-fashioned buzzer echoed, magnified by the marble floor. We heard Susan's sneakers squeak.

A door along the gallery banged open. Verity and I hurried back into the doorway of the bedroom, peering around the doorjamb.

"Susan!" Juliet leaned over the gallery rail, dangerously far, I thought. I moved forward, but Verity pulled me back.

"Tell them I'm distraught," Juliet screamed. Verity and I froze.

Juliet stomped away and seconds later we heard a door bang shut.

The door below opened.

"Hello. May I speak to Miss Wells? I'm—"

"Just go already. She doesn't want to talk to anyone," Susan said.

"Leo Rod—"

The door slammed. Susan muttered a stream of obscenities as her sneakers squeaked across the floor.

We rushed back to the window. Leo Rodriguez got back into his car and drove down the driveway.

"We'd better move. He'll be back," I said.

For two hours we packed trash bags and boxes. At first, I worried that Juliet would come back and make a scene, but the clothes were so beautiful I forgot her. As Verity pulled silky gowns, wrap dresses, and tweed suits from their hangers, she checked labels and sobbed out the name of a designer.

"Halston!"

"Chanel."

"Givenchy."

She staggered to the door of the walk-in closet, a magnificent red velvet ball gown held out in front of her. "Dior!" I took the dress from her and held it in front of me, bemoaning my height. Contessa's petite frame meant all the clothes were too short for me.

Verity gazed out the window. "My life finally has meaning." She gasped. "Oh, no!"

I hurried to the window. A television news truck parked at the end of the driveway.

Verity's eyes went wide behind her glasses. "We're trapped!"

I laid the crimson dress on the bed and took Verity's arm.

"Verity, look at me. They can't block the driveway. Let's see if we can sneak out a back way. The driveway probably goes around to the kitchen door. From what I heard before, Susan can handle them."

Susan's sullen expression didn't change when we asked her about a back exit. Perhaps caring for Juliet Wells made her feel like she'd seen it all. We followed as she plodded to a gleaming, updated kitchen. She unlocked a dead bolt with a key on a chain around her neck. We hustled packed bags and boxes down to the kitchen and set them outside the door.

"I'll get the car." Verity panted. "We'll be back Wednesday."

"Thank . . ." Without a word, Susan closed the door, I heard the bolt shoot home.

". . . you, Susan." I rolled my eyes.

As I'd thought, the kitchen opened onto the gravel drive as it curved behind the house. Verity hurried past a brick wall to the side of the house away from the driveway. I peered around the corner of the house. The news truck hadn't exactly blocked the exit, but the Tank would have to squeeze past.

I clambered onto an iron garden bench and looked over the top of the brick wall. The wall was part of a courtyard that encircled the garden just outside the morning room where we'd met Juliet. The enclosed flower beds were lush and well tended. On the other side of the wall, just below where I stood, was a moss-covered garden bench.

I lowered my injured leg carefully to the ground and walked around the garden wall, trailing my fingers along its rough surface. Though the house had been renovated, the garden wall was in poor shape. Ivy covered the crumbling mortar and brick; its lovely but destructive tendrils had worked their way into the masonry, weakening and undermining the wall. A heavy iron gate set into the back wall was flecked with rust, but a shiny metal chain and padlock were threaded through the bars.

The padlock on the inside of the kitchen door had also been shiny and new. Was the gate padlocked to keep people out or was it padlocked to keep Juliet in?

The Tank's engine rumbled up the drive. I hurried to load the car.

"Oh, God, the reporters saw me drive back here," Verity said.

We heaved bags into the backseat and vast trunk of the Tank. I cringed thinking of the glamorous silk and satin fabric crushed within the cardboard boxes and plastic trash bags.

"Don't look at them." I slammed the trunk and we got in the car. "Just drive right past. No eye contact."

"Here, I took some wigs." Verity handed me blond Marie Antoinette curls. She slid a curly brown bob over her dreads.

"Sunglasses on." Verity slid on her cat's-eye glasses.

I put on my own aviator sunglasses. "Just don't stop."

Like that's going to help, I thought. We were driving a rust-spotted 1962 DeSoto. There was only one in Mystic Bay. Heck, there was probably only one in all of New England.

"What if they stop us? We need a story," Verity babbled. "Why am I here? Hello, Leo. Why I am buying a dead lady's stuff?"

"Verity." I took her shoulders. "You always buy dead ladies' clothes."

"Oh, yeah, that's right." She frowned. "But why does this feel different? It feels different. What if her clothes are important? Huh? What if they're evidence?"

It did feel different. But would the police care? I had to calm Verity down. I parked my glasses on top of my towering wig. "Honestly, Verity, what on earth could her clothes have to do with anything? You heard Juliet, they've been locked up for decades. Listen. We did buy clothes. But we also paid our respects, right?"

Verity nodded.

"Okay, if anyone asks, we paid our respects. We're big fans of Contessa's, right?"

Verity nodded. "Big fans."

"And if anyone asks, that's all we say." I slid my sunglasses back into place. "Just don't hit anyone on the way out."

Verity floored it. The car roared, spitting gravel from the rear tires. As we rocketed down the drive, Leo Rodriguez poked his head around the corner of the house and held up his hand.

Verity screamed but didn't stop. I covered my eyes. As we skidded through the gates, just missing the news truck, I looked back. Leo jogged down the drive after us.

"Did I hit him?" Verity said.

"No."

We high-fived.

"We need to stop for ice cream." I pulled off the wig and fanned myself with it.

"You've got it." Verity headed for Route One.

As air streamed in the open window, I lifted my hair and let it cool the back of my neck. "You know something funny, Verity? Juliet never said her sister's name. Not once."

Chapter 14

After ice-cream cones at Sea Swirl and several unanswered calls to Verity's police chief uncle, we drove to the Plex.

I expected to see Bronwyn Denby, but instead there was a woman I didn't recognize at the reception desk. Suddenly, my mouth went dry, but I squared my shoulders.

"Yes?" She looked up from her computer screen.

"I need to talk to someone. About some letters, threatening letters, that my aunt received," I said.

"Do you have the letters?" the woman said.

"Um, no. My aunt threw them out."

The woman looked at me for several long seconds. "She threw them out."

"She thought they were from kids playing a trick," Verity said.

"But you think they're important." The woman's eyes drilled into mine.

"Yes. Well, they might be important." A blush crept up my neck. "Related to the, er, what happened at the food festival."

The woman tilted her chin and looked at me over her reading glasses.

"All I've had today is people with theories about what happened at the food festival. Is there a crime in progress?"

"Well, no, but—"

"Just fill out this form." She handed me a clipboard. "I'll make sure it gets to the right people." Her look said, When hell freezes over.

I filled out the form and handed it back. We got back into the Tank.

"That went well," Verity said.

If the police weren't looking into the letters, I would. "Verity, turn down by the Mermaid and park by the stone wall."

The Tank slid to the curb in front of a multicolored Victorian across the street from our shack. A skinny boy with floppy black hair sat on the front porch holding a skateboard.

In the Mermaid parking lot, a group of guys got out of their Jeep and posed for a photo by Aunt Gully's life-sized wooden mermaid. They cupped their hands to peer in the windows, then shrugged and headed down the street.

"Well, you'd have customers if you were open. Why are we here?" Verity asked.

"I want to talk to Bit Markey." I waved to the boy on the steps.

The boy on the porch stood. His T-shirt read IF HISTORY REPEATS ITSELF, I'M GETTING A DINOSAUR.

"Hey, Bit!" I called.

"Hi, Allie." Bit ran up to the car and leaned in, his dark hair flopping into his eyes. "Hi, Verity."

"Hey, Bit."

Two angry scratches crossed his forearm under several colorful sailors' knot bracelets. "What happened?"

"One of Mrs. Farraday's corgis got away from her. Muffy. I helped Mrs. Farraday catch her."

"God, those dogs." Verity rolled her eyes.

"Why're we closed today?" Bit helped with odd jobs every day at the Mermaid. Aunt Gully had noticed him hanging around the Mermaid, and ever since she'd asked him to "taste-test" a lobster roll, Bit had taken responsibility for the shack. Even when we weren't open, Bit picked up trash and kept an eye on things.

I wondered if he'd seen anyone leaving the letters. "This past week, did you notice anybody hanging around or putting anything under the front door of the Mermaid? Before we opened? Or at night?"

Bit's eyes went wide. "I don't think so. Did someone leave something bad?"

"No, no. Someone left letters. And put up a sign about lobster liberation." I forced a laugh. "Silly, right?"

Bit's green eyes were steady. "Lobster liberation? Does that mean they want to let all the lobsters go?"

"Free the lobsters," Verity said.

Bit shook his head. "They have a place in the food chain like other animals."

"If you remember seeing anything strange, or out of the ordinary, let me know, okay?" I said.

"You mean like the guy in the health inspector's car that was here a little while ago?"

"You saw him?" Bit didn't miss a thing.

"Yep." Bit scratched a scab on his knee. "He looked happy."

"Good. That means we'll be open tomorrow." Relief flooded me.

Bit smiled. "I'll be there."

"Thanks, Bit." Verity and I waved.

"Peace," Bit said.

Verity pulled out.

"How did such crummy parents get such a nice kid?" My eyes flicked to the rearview mirror. Bit propped his skateboard against the low stone wall across from the Mermaid and sat cross-legged on top. Keeping watch.

Chapter 15

After I promised to come over later to help her sort clothes, Verity dropped me back at Gull's Nest.

In the kitchen, Aunt Gully was exuberant. "Robbie says we can reopen tomorrow!"

Lorel frowned as she flipped grilled cheese sandwiches.

"You don't look happy." I pulled plates from the cabinet.

"Reopening's great. But you won't believe this," Lorel said. "Aunt Gully's van got another flat tire."

"Again? She just had one!" I set the table.

"The mechanic said her tire was punctured several times," Lorel said. "Deliberately."

"Where was this?" My pulse raced.

"At church," Lorel said.

Aunt Gully rooted in her tote bag. "The mechanic found this." She laid a narrow silver lobster pick on the kitchen table.

"A lobster pick?" I said.

"Kids! The things they get up to." Aunt Gully shook her head.

A decorative red enamel lobster topped one end. The

other end curved in a nasty sharp point. "Our tire slasher has nice taste. Looks like the kind of thing you'd find at a fancy gift shop." Hadn't I just seen boutique owner Finella Farraday in the parking lot at church? Good grief, would Finella puncture Aunt Gully's tire?

I tested the sharp point with my fingertip. Finella hated Aunt Gully, thought the lobster shack building should've been hers. Why wouldn't Finella puncture Aunt Gully's tire?

Lorel's voice surfaced. "Since you'd already put on the spare Saturday I didn't have one."

My heart pounded. Flat tire Saturday. Flat tire today. Threatening letters.

"Two flat tires and threatening letters!" I said. "Aunt Gully, this isn't kids. Lorel, you know who was parked next to Aunt Gully at church? Finella Farraday."

"Do you think Finella saw who slashed my tire?" Aunt Gully said.

Finella'd slashed the tire. I was sure of it.

"I know that look." Aunt Gully opened a bag of potato chips. "I cannot believe that a lady like Finella Farraday goes around slashing tires."

"Well, what kind of weirdo goes around using a fancy lobster pick to poke holes in tires?" I grabbed a handful of chips.

"Ridiculous!" Lorel snapped. "Finella Farraday's a respected businesswoman on the town council! I hardly think she goes around slashing tires."

Aunt Gully patted my hand. "See? Maybe the flat on the day of the food fest was just a flat. My tires're pretty old."

Lorel slid sandwiches onto our plates. "No matter what happens, you need to think about getting a new van, Aunt Gully."

I dropped the pick into my bag. "But the letters said

'lobster libbers.' This is a lobster pick. That ties them in—"

"You've been so very concerned about those letters," Aunt Gully said.

Her phone shrilled.

"Hello?" Aunt Gully listened intently, then started wrapping the cord around and around her wrist. I'd only seen her do that a few other times—when on the phone with Uncle Rocco's doctors and when her friend Anna called to talk about her no-good son.

Lorel and I exchanged glances.

"Call me when you know more." Aunt Gully hung up.

"What happened?"

"That was Lucia." Aunt Gully took a deep breath. "The police are searching the Mosses' house. They've taken Ernie and Megan in for questioning."

Chapter 16

Stan Wilder had arranged a meeting at the Harbor Inn at 5 P.M. Lorel tossed her overnight bag into the trunk and then we drove over in her car. She'd drop us home after the meeting and return to Boston to prepare for a big presentation Monday morning. I knew it was killing her to leave.

"You work too hard, Lorel," Aunt Gully tsked. "Tomorrow's Memorial Day. A holiday."

"Life in the big city." Lorel shrugged. Even when she wasn't in the office or traveling for work she was glued to her work phone. "But I'll come right back after my presentation," she said. "I can telecommute."

Aunt Gully patted Lorel's shoulder. "Honey, just knowing you're a phone call away is a help. But don't you worry. We'll be fine, right, Allie?"

"Right, Aunt Gully." I forced a smile, but my mind reeled. Ernie with his crazy Hawaiian shirts and sweet wispy Megan were being questioned by the police. How could the police think Ernie would poison people with his very own lobster roll?

"Lorel, drive past Kahuna's, okay?" I said.

Lorel threw me a glance in the rearview mirror but

did as I asked. A few minutes later we pulled into Kahuna's parking lot. Police tape still fluttered at the front door. The painter had covered the red *X* on the Kahuna's sign, but now the sign was simply a shiny white blank. Just like Kahuna's future. A minivan pulled into the lot and, seeing the tape, pulled out again. "Ernie and Megan are losing business," Lorel said as she spun the wheel.

"He's lost more than just business," I said.

We met Paul Pond and Chick Costa in the wood-paneled lobby of the Harbor Inn. Paul stood and greeted us. Chick nodded as he strode outside to take a call.

"How are you, Paul?" Aunt Gully asked.

"Been better," Paul said.

We stepped into a quiet parlor off the main lobby.

"I thought you were heading back to Maine?" I said.

"You heard about Ernie and Megan?" Aunt Gully said in a low voice.

"Ayah, to both questions." Paul waited until we'd taken seats, then sat in a Windsor chair by the fireplace. He rubbed his bright blue eyes. "I'd like to be on my way, to tell you the truth, but the police wanted to ask me some questions. And my lawyer called. Said that somewhere in that pile o' papers we signed was a clause about YUM having the right to tell us when"—he looked upward—"'our participation was no longer required.' Figured I'd best see what Stan had to say."

Aunt Gully turned to Lorel and me. "Should I call John Dombrowski?"

John Dombrowski was Aunt Gully's lawyer. I considered. Mr. Dombrowski had helped Aunt Gully with the purchase of the Lazy Mermaid property. He'd helped with Uncle Rocco's insurance. He was a nice guy I'd last seen dressed in a green lobster suit for the St. Patrick's Day Fun Run. I shrugged. Mystic Bay wasn't exactly full of lawyers experienced with television contracts and the poisoning deaths of famous actresses.

Chick returned, his face red, his lips set in a thin line.

Stan Wilder stepped into the parlor. "Glad you're here. Please join me in the meeting room." We followed Stan and took seats at a conference table.

"Where's Ashley?" Aunt Gully asked.

"Ashley has a shoot in L.A." A smile lit Stan's face. "Thank you for asking."

Paul Pond cleared his throat. "Stan, what've the police told you?"

"Very little. They asked to see footage of the judging. Of course we cooperated. Answered a lot of questions, same as many of you. Wish I had more to share, but that's it."

Chick leaned forward. "Listen, Stan, I'm not a quitter. Yeah, we've had a huge setback, but I'm still in."

Setback? Could Chick get any more insensitive?

Stan tented his fingers, the gesture revealing hands of surprising strength. I remembered he'd played for the Patriots before going into television. "The purpose of this meeting," he said, "is to communicate the network's decision as far as continuing with New England's Best Lobster Roll Contest." He looked at each of us as he let the quiet stretch. Good dramatic timing.

"Yeah?" Chick raised his chin and folded his arms.

"The YUM Network does want to host a best lobster roll contest this year," Stan said.

Chick sat back, a satisfied smile curling his lips. Paul Pond frowned.

"However." Stan cleared his throat. "However, we feel that association with the tragic events of yesterday are not in congruence with the upbeat personality of the YUM Network. We plan to discard the existing footage. We'll continue with the lobster roll contest in a different venue."

"Come on up and do it in Chatham. Perfect setting," Chick crowed.

Stan shot Chick a look that said the contest would be held anywhere in the world but Chatham. "The network will decide and extend the invitations."

"To the same lobster shacks, right?" Chick pressed.

Chick was a jerk, but he asked the question we all wanted answered. This was the bottom line. Would we be in the running again for the title?

Stan shifted in his seat.

My breath caught in my throat. Aunt Gully bit her lip.

"Pond's and, ah," Stan said, "Chick's will be invited to participate again." Chick whooped and punched the air. Across the table, Lorel struggled to keep her face composed.

"Unfortunately, we don't want to, ah, bring up the memory of what happened Saturday." Stan turned toward Aunt Gully. His voice softened. "I'm sorry, Gully, but we won't be inviting anyone from Mystic Bay."

Heat surged into my face, but before I could say anything Aunt Gully put a hand on my thigh and squeezed a warning. Lorel beat me to it.

"But what if the Lazy Mermaid has the best lobster roll?" Lorel prided herself on her professional behavior but her voice was shrill and the cords in her throat stood out.

"I truly am sorry," Stan said. "But the network's decision is final."

After promising to stay in touch, Stan shook hands around the table and left the room, trailed by Chick Costa. "Stan, Chatham's a great setting . . ."

We shuffled toward the door. "Don't worry, Aunt Gully," Lorel said, tapping on her phone. "I'm going to check our contract with YUM—"

Aunt Gully stopped short. Lorel bumped into her.

"Lorel." Aunt Gully slipped an arm around Lorel. "Do you remember the time you got caught in the rip off Seal Rock?"

"When I was ten?" Lorel said. "Yes, I'll never forget it."

"The rip carried you right out into the sound. But you remembered what to do. You didn't fight it. You rode it till it let you go, and then you could swim back. This is one tide I can't fight. I'm not going to try. I'll ride it out and then"—she squared her shoulders—"I'll just get back to the Lazy Mermaid. That's what I'll do."

"Aunt Gully, it's not fair." Tears pricked my eyes.

"Allie's right," Lorel said. "It's not fair. You have the best—"

Aunt Gully raised her hands. "It's what I want to do. Stan's a smart man. And . . ." She took a deep breath. "I think he's right."

I couldn't fathom where Aunt Gully was getting her Zen today. I slipped an arm around her as we headed through the lobby, leaned my head against hers. No matter how hard I tried, I couldn't swallow my disappointment. Why should Aunt Gully suffer when she hadn't done a thing wrong?

Paul Pond followed, silently hanging back. I turned to him.

"Are you going to do the lobster roll contest again?" I asked.

Paul Pond shook his head. "No. If they won't let me out of the contract, I'll fight it. Every morning when I open, there's a two-hour line of people waiting to get in. I don't need any more customers. Pond's was fine before the contest. We'll be fine after." He took Aunt Gully's hand.

"Gully, I think you'll be fine, too."

"I will," Aunt Gully said. "At our age, we know the storms come and the storms pass."

"I hope someday you'll come to Maine and visit," he said.

Aunt Gully smiled. "I'd be delighted. And anytime you're in Mystic Bay, I hope you'll stop by."

"Thank you. Pleasure to meet you. All of you."

We stepped onto the inn's broad porch. The wind had risen and it whipped the flag around the flagpole in front of the hotel as Paul got into his truck.

The twist of Lorel's lips told me she wasn't done, but Aunt Gully looked serene. We got into Lorel's car and headed home.

I leaned back and closed my eyes while Lorel and Aunt Gully talked, Lorel arguing that they should fight the network's decision. I knew Aunt Gully well enough to know that her decision was final.

Lorel's leather seats were so comfortable. My mind drifted. Scenes from the past few days flitted through my mind. The roses in Megan's trash. Juliet Wells's red lips. Rick and Rio waving to the crowd. Ernie Moss in that gaudy orange Hawaiian shirt. Ernie Moss with a spoon to his lips while Aunt Gully sang in the church kitchen.

I sat bolt upright. "Turn around, Lorel! Go back to the inn."

"Did you forget something?" Aunt Gully said.

"Remember Stan said the police asked for video of the judging? Did the police know there's behind-the-scenes footage? Because that footage proves that Ernie didn't poison the lobster rolls."

Chapter 17

We asked for Stan at the reception desk and met in the same meeting room. After I explained what I was looking for, Stan opened his laptop and clicked on a file.

"I have the behind-the-scenes stuff here," he said. "I assumed the police just didn't want it. Maybe they didn't realize we'd shot it."

We huddled around the laptop. Had the food festival been only yesterday? It seemed like a decade had passed since then.

Stan fast-forwarded through scenes of Mystic Bay, happy faces at the festival, the quaint beauty of our small town on a sparkling May day. All the cheerful activity as the chefs bantered with the producers, volunteers hurrying to and fro. I watched the screen intently.

Aunt Gully's hair-raising singing rang into the room. We winced.

"Great TV." Stan chuckled.

"There!" I said.

On the screen, Ernie dipped a small tasting spoon into a tub of his lobster salad. Ernie tasted the salad as Megan plated their lobster rolls.

"See, if he tasted the same lobster salad that went to

the judges, and he was fine, then the poison couldn't have been in the lobster salad," I said.

We watched as the four plated lobster rolls were placed on a tray and a silver cloche was lowered over them. Volunteers set the covered plates on a long counter on the side of the kitchen near the door. Ernie and Megan took seats across the room from the covered lobster rolls and chatted with a woman in a blue YUM Network polo.

"Who's that?" Lorel asked.

"One of the producers," Stan said.

"I remember," Aunt Gully said. "Ernie and Megan finished faster than everyone else because their preparation's cold. All they had to do was assemble their lobster rolls."

"And that's why their rolls were judged first. They were done first," I said. "Their rolls were closest to the door."

We watched for a few more minutes. From what we could see in the footage no one approached Kahuna's covered lobster rolls.

The camera swung often to Aunt Gully, who bantered with the producers and other chefs. Her sunny personality filled the screen. Stan sighed. He pressed a button on the laptop and Aunt Gully's image froze. Stan straightened. "Well, I'd better make sure this gets to the police."

Aunt Gully squeezed my hand as we walked back to the parking lot. "That'll help Ernie's cause. The police will figure it out, this whole nightmare will be over, and we'll all get back to normal."

Chapter 18

"So Ernie and Megan couldn't have poisoned the rolls," Lorel said. "Ernie and Megan owe you one, Allie."

"Someone must've added the poison after Ernie plated the rolls," I said slowly. But why? Why poison Kahuna's rolls? "YUM didn't film every single moment in the prep kitchen. And maybe Ernie still could've poisoned the rolls after he plated them."

"There were so many people," Aunt Gully said. "Wouldn't someone notice?"

"Maybe yes, maybe no. If the poisoner looked like he or she belonged there? I remember how distracted we all were when you were, er, singing, Aunt Gully. All eyes were on you for quite a while."

So many volunteers and television people were crammed into the kitchen. Kids running in and out. It was hard to tell who belonged and who didn't.

Lorel pulled into the driveway. "Well, it's still good for Ernie and Megan. That's your good deed of the day, Allie. I'll come back tomorrow, after my meeting," she said. "We'll talk about how to go forward."

"Of course, dear. We'll get a good night's sleep tonight, right, Allie?"

"Right after I go to Verity's." I'd promised to help with Juliet Wells's clothes.

"And right after I go to the hospital and check on the judges," Aunt Gully said as she unbuckled her seat belt.

"What!" I said.

"Weren't all the judges in ICU? They won't let you see them, Aunt Gully," Lorel said in her trying-to-be-reasonable voice.

"Aren't you tired, Aunt Gully?" I was exhausted.

"I want to see how Rick and Rio and the mayor are doing," she said.

"They might not let you in," I repeated.

Aunt Gully got out of the car. "I'm getting a sweater. Don't worry, Lorel, Allie can drop me on her way to Verity's."

I sighed. There was no stopping Aunt Gully when she made up her mind. She was a smiling, rainbow-colored steamroller. I opened the door.

Lorel checked her watch. She drummed on the steering wheel. "I'll take you over."

"Don't you have to get back to Boston?" I said.

"It can wait. I want to keep an eye on Aunt Gully." That was Lorel. If there was a chance that Aunt Gully would be on TV or social media, Lorel wanted to be there.

"I can keep an eye on her," I said.

"This won't take long," Lorel replied.

Translation: she didn't trust me to do it.

I slammed the door and folded my arms.

Aunt Gully emerged from the house, pulling on a yellow crocheted sweater.

"I'll drive," Lorel called.

"Thank you, Lorel." Aunt Gully settled back into her seat, perching her glasses on her head as she bent over the glowing oblong of her smartphone, intent as she texted.

Dusk was falling. Wind-whipped waves crashed onto the seawall as we drove past on the way to the hospital.

"Lorel," I said softly, "aren't you worried about the newspeople?"

I couldn't see Lorel's face clearly but I could hear her certainty. "Aunt Gully going to see the poor folks who were sickened by someone else's poisoned lobster roll? Nope. That's nothing but positive, Allie."

Two news trucks hulked by the brightly lit main entrance of the hospital as we turned into the parking lot.

"In the back, Lorelei." Aunt Gully directed Lorel to the staff parking lot. A woman wearing faded purple scrubs stood in the golden rectangle of light spilling from an open door. She waved us inside.

"It's Mrs. Yardley," Lorel whispered to me as we hurried inside.

"Hello, Darcie," Aunt Gully said.

"Gully, how are you?"

Mrs. Yardley greeted us both, but her eyes lingered on Lorel. Lorel had dated her son Patrick in high school. It hadn't ended well. Patrick's crowd of partying lacrosse players had been too fast for Lorel, the lifelong Girl Scout. Still, I knew Lorel's feelings for Patrick ran deep.

"Gully, what a time you've had." Darcie Yardley embraced Gully.

"Seen better, that's for sure, but those poor judges, Darcie! How're they doing?"

"Well, the reporters created such a scene. We had to have the police help our security team. Reporters and others trying to sneak in." She grinned at Aunt Gully. "They don't have your connections."

"Now you know I'm not going to go barging in or break any rules," Aunt Gully said. "I just want to know how they're doing."

Mrs. Yardley led us past a bank of elevators and

through a waiting area. She gave Aunt Gully a conspiratorial look.

"When you texted me, I asked the mayor if he'd like to see you. He said yes. He's sitting up, doing pretty well, considering. Let's just say he got whatever it was out of his system pretty fast."

"Ugh," I muttered to Lorel. She was wringing her hands. She cannot stand hospitals. Or bending rules.

"What's wrong?" I asked.

"Aside from everything?" Lorel said.

"What was the toxic substance?" Aunt Gully stagewhispered to Mrs. Yardley.

Mrs. Yardley raised her sparse gray eyebrows. Her eyes were the same dark brown as her son Hayden's. "No one's saying exactly what it was. Believe me, they never get results this fast from the police lab, but because it involved celebrities, it all happened like lightning. They said something organic. Plant based."

A poisonous plant? Lorel and I shared a look.

"And you heard about Ernie and Megan Moss being questioned?" Mrs. Yardley asked.

Aunt Gully waved it away. "Ridiculous."

Mrs. Yardley shrugged. "I've seen Ernie Moss in here a few times. When he was younger. Bar fights."

"Poisoning and bar fights are two different things," Aunt Gully said in a low voice. "And we know Ernie couldn't have done it." She whispered to Mrs. Yardley. Mrs. Yardley's mouth formed a surprised O. No doubt what we'd seen on the YUM video would soon be reported across Mystic Bay via the gossip hotline.

"Here we are." The ICU was a glare of white paint and glass. Curtains screened individual cubicles. Thank goodness. Hospitals made me nervous. Amid the beeps of equipment and low voices of conferring medical staff ran an undercurrent of excitement.

A clutch of people hovered at the door of a room down the hall.

"Rick and Rio down there." Mrs. Yardley nodded to nurses at the main desk and asked us to sign a visitor's log. Then she greeted a security guard who sat by a door. We followed her in.

Mayor Packer was propped up in bed, a table across his legs. His normally ruddy face was as white as his pillows.

When he saw Aunt Gully, he grinned. "I think it was something I ate, Gully."

Lorel and I hovered by the door. Seeing the mayor pale and weak, a hospital gown slipping from one shoulder, made me feel awkward, but Aunt Gully went to the bedside and squeezed his hand.

"Serves you right, gulping your food like that," she said.

"How nice of you to come. You, too, girls." Bliss Packer sat on the other side of the bed. The mayor's wife was a tanned tennis blonde, as angular as her husband was round. Her coral lipstick coordinated with her coral cardigan, skirt, and flats.

"Doctor said he's going to be all right. Said it was a toxic substance, can you believe it?" Mrs. Packer twisted the double strand of pearls at her throat. "What kind of toxic substance ends up in a lobster roll is what I want to know."

Mayor Packer drew a shaky breath. "Takes more than a lobster roll to stop me."

"Why would someone poison my husband, I ask you? And the other judges, of course," she added. "And why on a television show? The mayor thought this would bring so much great attention to Mystic Bay. Now, all people're talking about is the poisoning!"

"And poor Contessa Wells," I said.

"Of course, Contessa Wells." Mrs. Packer rolled her eyes and sighed, as if the whole disaster had been Contessa Wells's fault.

Mayor Packer's eyes fluttered. "Not good for the town."

"No, it's not." Mrs. Packer folded her arms.

"We'll let you rest," Aunt Gully said.

Mayor Packer whispered, "Gully, nobody's blaming you."

"Of course not," Mrs. Packer snapped. "We know who's responsible."

"Who's responsible?" I said. "Seriously, do you know who did this?"

Mrs. Packer drew herself up.

"Obviously," she said. "It's that awful Ernie Moss. He's been out to get the mayor ever since he put the kibosh on that idiotic street-widening project Ernie proposed." Mrs. Packer's eyes flashed. "I'm going to make him pay."

Aunt Gully shot us a warning look. There was no need to engage with Bliss Packer.

We edged out of the room. Four security guards stood by Rick's and Rio's cubicles. Two hospital staffers in white lab coats conferred by the door. A sense of urgency surrounded the room that wasn't apparent in the mayor's.

"Touch and go with Rio," Mrs. Yardley whispered. "She's so slight, like a bird. You can't believe she eats all that food on TV. They had to use a child's gown on her."

Aunt Gully nodded at a gray-haired woman who pushed a walker slowly out of the elevators.

"Is that Cindy Opalski?" she whispered to Mrs. Yardley.

"Yes, I believe it is." Mrs. Yardley nodded.

I caught Lorel's eye. Was there anyone in Mystic Bay that Aunt Gully didn't know?

A shout rang out. Two of the security guards hurried down the far corridor by Rick's and Rio's rooms.

Mrs. Yardley threw up her hands. "Reporters. People trying to get photos to sell to Web sites. Can't remember this many reporters trying to get into the hospital since that rock and roller ran his motorcycle off the pier at Gold's Marina ten years ago."

We followed Mrs. Yardley back through the corridors of the hospital, our footfalls—Mrs. Yardley's rubber-soled nurses' shoes, Aunt Gully's pink tennis shoes, my sandal and walking boot, Lorel's ballet flats—echoing loudly in the ghastly fluorescent-lit hallways.

Was Bliss right? Was it possible that Ernie, or someone else, wanted to kill the mayor? Could someone hate so much that they would poison three other perfectly innocent people in order to get to him? It wasn't just crazy, it was depraved. Evil.

We said good night to Mrs. Yardley. She waved, smiling wistfully at Lorel. The one who got away.

"Nice to have connections to sneak you into the hospital, Aunt Gully," I said as we got back into the car.

"Lorel, are you . . . bummed out that we didn't get on the TV news?" Aunt Gully's peppery tone made me smile. She always enunciated carefully when using what she called "young people's lingo."

Lorel shrugged.

Aunt Gully settled back. "I don't do things for the cameras, Lorel. I'd still like to thank Rick and Rio. They did me a huge favor by nominating me for the competition. I owe them a lot."

"Maybe Mrs. Yardley can smuggle you in tomorrow, Aunt Gully." I clicked my seat belt. As the dome lights went out when Lorel started the car, the lines of Aunt Gully's face settled into an uncharacteristic frown. "What is it, Aunt Gully?"

"It's terrible," she said. "Why would someone hurt all those innocent people? What did poor Rick and Rio, Mayor Packer, and Contessa Wells ever do to hurt someone?"

I leaned forward. "What street-widening project was Bliss Packer talking about?"

Aunt Gully sighed. "Ernie's been trying to get the town council to widen Pearl Street and raise the speed limit to make it easier for cars to get to Kahuna's."

"There's no place to widen it to," Lorel said.

"A speedway to Kahuna's?" I scoffed.

"Ernie didn't win many friends with that idea," Aunt Gully said.

"Mrs. Packer actually thinks that Ernie Moss would poison the mayor using his own lobster roll? In front of all those people? What else would that accomplish but ruin his own business?" Lorel said.

"Agreed," I said. "Ernie Moss doesn't strike me that way at all." I remembered the way he cradled Megan. "Maybe if the mayor had hurt Megan. Ernie's definitely the protective type."

"It must've been an accident," Aunt Gully said. "A terrible accident."

Lorel parked in the driveway of Gull's Nest. "I'll be back late tomorrow after my meeting."

Aunt Gully patted Lorel's shoulder. "We'll be fine, right, Allie? The Mermaid'll be open tomorrow and back to normal."

Aunt Gully got out of the car and headed toward the house. As she opened the door, I saw a flurry of paper fall from the doorjamb in the porch light. Aunt Gully picked them up. "Oh, look! Business cards," she said. "Four different TV stations!"

"Aunt Gully has a funny definition of normal," I said.

Chapter 19

Verity lived on the first floor of a tumbledown 1850s house a block off the main drag of Mystic Bay. Pre-renovation, her landlord called it. Since her shop was jam-packed, she used two of the bedrooms of her three-bedroom apartment to store stock.

Verity sat on the wide plank floor, surrounded by a wall of boxes and green plastic trash bags stuffed with the clothes from the Wells House.

"I thought you'd be done by now." I tossed my purse on the couch.

"I did, too. I'm in awe. Look at this." Verity stroked the boning of a green silk ball gown. "Those tiny stitches were all done by hand. Nobody does that anymore. I'm in vintage heaven."

"I don't know how long I'll last. I've got to work at the Mermaid tomorrow."

"I'm glad Aunt Gully can reopen."

I pulled a stuffed garbage bag toward me and set my booted foot on a low stool. My ankle throbbed, payback for that vault onto the stage. I'd have to be more careful or my ankle would never heal properly.

I reached in the trash bag and pulled out several evening bags, popped them open, searched the insides, then set them on a shelf. Once, I'd found some diamond earrings and a clip of money inside a yard sale purse.

"Look at this." I pulled out a little golden spoon.

"Ha. I find those sometimes in eighties stuff. Cocaine spoons."

I set it aside. Deep inside a gold sequined clutch I spotted a small twist of tissue paper. I unwrapped it. Multicolored pills and capsules tumbled into my palm.

"Whoa," I said. "Looks like she took a bit of everything."

I rewrapped the pills and set them on Verity's fireplace mantel.

"How did Contessa even function with all that stuff?" I asked. "Though maybe I'm assuming that stuff was Contessa's. Could be Juliet's."

Verity nodded. "I researched Juliet online. She had a huge drug problem. Fried her brain."

I shuddered thinking of Juliet, locked inside the big house on Rabb's Point.

"What happened at the meeting?" Verity's question brought me back.

I filled her in on the latest, including my realization about Ernie Moss in the YUM footage.

She grinned. "So you saved an innocent man from the gallows. Not bad work, Allie!"

I hung a vintage Diane von Furstenberg wrap dress on a hanger. "Maybe not. Lorel says that Ernie still could've put poison in the rolls. I just can't imagine how or why he'd do that. At least the judges are getting better. We saw Mayor Packer. And his wife."

Verity scoffed. "Bliss Packer's a loon. She's always in the shop, trying to squeeze herself into dresses that are two sizes too small." She glanced at her watch. "Rick and Rio's show's on now." She flicked on the TV.

Jangling guitar and banjo music filled the room with Rick and Rio's bluegrass theme song. Their trademark silver Airstream motor home flashed onscreen.

"I love that little motor home," Verity said.

"Eating from coast to coast," I said. "That's my kind of trip."

We helped ourselves to bowls of chocolate-chocolate-chip ice cream topped with cherries, crumbled potato chips, and whipped cream, and settled in to watch. It was an episode where Rio and Rick visit a Maine restaurant famous for its—what else?—lobsters.

Rio, Rick, and the restaurant owner raced to see who could pick a lobster fastest. As Rick knocked lobsters to the floor, Rio speedily and neatly separated the lobster meat from the shell. She finished before the restaurant owner.

"Queen of the lobstahs!" Rio raised her arms in victory.

"She's fast!" I licked my spoon.

"Did you hear that Rio wants to build a spa in Mystic Bay?" Verity set aside her bowl.

Where had I heard that? "One of Aunt Gully's friends mentioned it."

"Rio and Rick want to turn that old farm near the Jake into a spa."

"Gruber's Farm, right? That would be perfect. People could walk over to Broadway by the Bay shows from the spa. All that's there now are a couple of falling-down barns."

"Rick and Rio and some other celebrities from the YUM Network are in on it. It's going to be one of those healthy-eating spas." Verity wrinkled her nose. "Yoga, kale."

"For a treat you get a glass of iceberg water." I laughed. "Still, that's good for Mystic Bay."

Rick and Rio gave their signature send-off: "Here's to the best food in America."

"Should've been Aunt Gully winning that contest," Verity groused.

I didn't want to talk about the contest. "Let's finish up."

Soon we had every dress hung and each box stacked. Verity's storage room was a rainbow of sumptuous fabric.

"Good haul." I yawned and stretched. "I'd better get home. I'll be picking a lot of lobster tomorrow. I could use Rio's help."

Chapter 20

The sun rose entirely too early on Monday morning. Along with the scent of coffee brewing, the sound of Aunt Gully's mixer rose from the kitchen. She was singing "Oh, What a Beautiful Morning" from *Oklahoma*. Even with a pillow covering my ears, the sound still seeped in. I reached for my headphones and slid from the bed to the floor to stretch.

After floor barre and a shower, I went downstairs to the kitchen as Aunt Gully set golden-brown muffins on the table. The *Mystic Bay Mirror* was folded next to my plate. My early-bird aunt had already finished the crossword puzzle.

The scent of lemony blueberry-raspberry muffins made my mouth water. I reached for one and managed an appreciative "mmm" as Aunt Gully whisked eggs.

I scanned the newspaper's headline. "Network Target of Food Fest Attack?" A photo of the empty stage, chairs upended, ran above the fold.

Attack? Attack made me think of a military attack, or aliens. Something organized. Below the fold ran a picture of Ernie Moss, hand raised in an attempt to shield his face from the photographer. "Kahuna's owner questioned." The photo had been taken at the Mosses' house. No wonder Lucia wanted the drapes closed.

"And now for more on the Mystic Bay Food Festival fatality." The news anchor's voice made me turn toward Aunt Gully's television. "We have Leo Rodriguez at the state police lab. Leo, what have you learned?"

Aunt Gully stopped whisking eggs.

Leo's handsome face filled the screen. "Let's start with some good news. Doctors are confident all three of the hospitalized judges of New England's Best Lobster Roll Contest—Rick Lopez, Rio Lopez, and Mayor Keats Packer of Mystic Bay—will go home soon."

"That's good news," Aunt Gully resumed whisking.

"An autopsy performed on the fourth judge, Broadway and screen star Contessa Wells, showed no abnormalities, but because of her advanced age, doctors think the toxic substance affected her more strongly and led to her death.

"The big news is that the lab isolated the substance that investigators think caused the dramatic illness and death." Aunt Gully's vigorous whisking stopped again. I held my breath.

The report cut to a shot of a purple flower with long, almost bell-shaped petals. "Monkshood," Leo said, "also known as aconite or wolfsbane."

"Wolfsbane?" Aunt Gully and I shared a look.

"This plant grows wild and is highly toxic. Every part, from the root to the leaves, is dangerous," Leo Rodriguez continued. "The question remains: how did such a toxic substance get into the lobster rolls served to the judges at the Mystic Bay Food Festival? Reporting live from the state police lab, I'm Leo Rodriguez."

Aunt Gully poured the eggs into the frying pan. "Monkshood! Sounds like something out of P. D. James."

"Where on earth do you find monkshood? Have you ever seen it in a garden?" I asked.

Aunt Gully shook her head. "Looks like a weed to me."

Through the gingham curtains on the window, I could see Aunt Gully's own garden, an impressionist painting of vegetables and plants. Roses would soon cover several trellises. Pots of succulents she called hens and chickens lined her flagstone patio. Herbs flourished in raised beds. Every inch of her small garden worked in the service of good food and beauty.

I flipped through the newspaper. The *Mystic Bay Mirror* had nothing new on the poisonings, except one line that said police were investigating "lobster liberation" and "other" groups that might have reason to ruin the competition.

"It says here the police are investigating lobster liberation groups." I wished Chief Brooks would return my calls, but evidently he didn't think Aunt Gully's letters were a big deal.

Aunt Gully set a bowl of fruit salad in front of me, along with a plate of scrambled eggs. "Do you think those letters . . . Allie, I can't believe there's a whole group of people who'd do something so terrible."

"If you get another letter, save it so I can bring it to the police."

"Yes, yes." Aunt Gully started on the dishes.

I turned back to the paper. The article about Ernie Moss was damning, simply by stating the facts—it was his lobster roll, after all—but also by reporting Ernie's belligerent behavior. When taken to the Plex for questioning, he'd pushed several officers and they'd had to call in backup.

"Ernie didn't help himself." I cleared my dishes.

"Some people are their own worst enemies." Aunt Gully shooed me from the sink.

I hurried upstairs to dress. It didn't take long to slip into my Lazy Mermaid T-shirt and jeans. When I went back downstairs, Aunt Gully was packing extra Lazy Mermaid aprons in her tote bag. "I think we'll be busy today," she said.

I thought of the news coverage. Ernie on the front page should quash any rumors about Aunt Gully's lobster rolls.

"I hope so, Aunt Gully."

As we got into the van, Aunt Gully resumed her singing. A spanking wind came up from the water, setting her whirligigs spinning. The sky was a blue so bright and clear it almost hurt to look at it. My spirits lifted.

We parked in the farthest spot of the Lazy Mermaid parking lot and crunched across the gravel. Hector and Hilda waved as we entered the kitchen. "Let's get back to work," Aunt Gully said.

"But, how many people do you think'll come?" Hilda fretted. "It's Memorial Day, but . . ."

"You mean, do people think they'll get poisoned if they eat here?" Aunt Gully harrumphed. "No. Mystic Bay's made of sterner stuff than that. Let's get ready for a big crowd. A really big crowd."

I looped my Lazy Mermaid apron around my neck as I passed the weather-beaten shed housing our lobster tanks. A collection of old buoys, their colors sun faded, covered the rough gray cedar shakes. Aunt Gully and I went down to the pier to supervise lobster delivery. Our lobstermen knew she'd accept no culls or sleepers. "Happy lobsters are delicious lobsters," Aunt Gully said.

Back at the shack, Hector readied our steamers while Hilda and I mixed a massive stainless steel bowl of coleslaw. Aunt Gully raised the American flag by the front door. She blew it a kiss, her salute to Uncle Rocco, who'd been a Marine.

Aunt Gully believed we'd get a crowd. Lorel had confided to me she thought our numbers would suffer due to the tragedy at the lobster roll contest. She probably had some kind of spreadsheet with sales statistics, but Aunt Gully went on feel.

Aunt Gully's feel beat Lorel's spreadsheets.

Cars pulled into the parking lot at ten. Even though it was an hour before our official opening time, Aunt Gully opened the doors. The thought of someone "going hungry"—though none of the foodies at our door looked in danger of starvation—jolted her into action.

I pulled my hair back into a braid and put on a hairnet Aunt Gully'd bedazzled with sequins. "Gorgeous, dahlink," Hilda said. I laughed.

I needed a laugh. Picking lobster was hot, messy work. Using my hands and tools similar to nutcrackers, I twisted and cracked to separate the hot, cooked shells from the delectable meat. Aunt Gully spread the torn meat on the golden buttered-and-toasted rolls. Hilda took orders and rang people up. Several of Aunt Gully's friends were on hand to help. Hilda and I switched places every hour or so, since picking lobster isn't the most fun thing in the world. I set my boot on an inverted milk crate, tried not to channel Cinderella, and sank into the messy monotony of cracking claws.

"I hope we sell as much lobster as Aunt Gully thinks we will," I said.

Hector crossed his fingers. The top of the pinkie finger of his left hand was missing, an offering to the sea gods when he got a little casual with a lobster. "Never get casual with lobsters," he said.

Hector and I fell into the easy rhythm of people who work well together. As the lobsters cooked and their mottled brown shells turned bright red, Hector moved them from steamer to worktable where I picked the meat into a tray. As we worked, I filled him in on our visit to the hospital.

"I've missed all the drama about Ernie Moss's parking plan," I said.

"You know how bad the traffic gets in summer. With Ernie's plan, it'd be even worse for the people who live here." Hector rubbed sweat from his bald head. With his hoop earring he looked like the man on the bottle of cleaner. "I don't want to take my life in my hands every time I walk down to the marina. Get run over by some out-of-towners who can't wait to get a lobster roll. Present lobster rolls excepted."

"What did Ernie propose?" One of Aunt Gully's friends moved the tray of picked lobster meat to the other end of the kitchen, where she and Aunt Gully assembled lobster rolls.

"Taking people's front lawns to widen the street. I was at the town meeting last week when Ernie floated his plan." Hector shook his head. "Ernie and the mayor really got into it. Mrs. Mayor let loose. Man, she's got a potty mouth for such a classy-looking dame. Even the Crazy Lady got into it."

That was a surprise. "Juliet Wells was there?"

Hector nodded but kept an eye on the cooking lobsters. "She was there with her, well, what would you say? Nurse? I heard she gets a new nurse every couple of weeks. Maybe they won't stay. Well, Juliet came in wearing sunglasses and this was at night, right? With a big walking stick. She pounded that stick on the floor and pointed at Ernie. She said, 'You'll be the death of this town!' Then she swooped out. Believe me, people got out of her way fast."

Hector piled the cooked lobsters on my worktable, steam and heat rising. He flicked on a fan by the stove.

"Death!" I said. "And look what happened."

Hector met my eyes. "Creepy, right?"

"Hey." Bit banged in through the screen door, tying a bandana into a sweatband. "The cavalry is here."

"How are you doing, Bit?"

"Fantastic, Allie. Ready to rumble. It's crazy out there!"

I'd been so busy that the hum of conversation and rhythmic clang of the register drawer had been background noise to my own work. I peeked out the pass-through window. A line stretched through the front door into the parking lot, but the air was festive and the customers looked happy.

The beautiful day certainly contributed to a holiday mood, but first-time customers always smiled when they entered the Lazy Mermaid. Our artist friends had transformed Petey's dingy walls, the color of decades of cigarette smoke and despair, into a shimmering blue-green mural of fanciful underwater creatures and Gothic fishbowl castles.

A little boy pointed at the ceiling, painted in a swirl of curved scales, as if a giant sea creature swam overhead. People in line took selfies with Aunt Gully's walls and mermaidabilia.

"Change partners!" Hilda said.

We quickly washed our hands and changed into fresh aprons, then switched places. Aunt Gully had called in reinforcements. One of her friends hustled between the kitchen and the order counter while another bussed tables. Out the front windows, I watched Aggie hand out free samples of her magical coffee cake.

"Great idea with the coffee cake, Aunt Gully!" I said.

The picnic tables and pastel-hued Adirondack chairs filled. Some diners snugged two to a chair. People sitting on the dock watched boats go by.

Customers seemed unconcerned about the events of the food fest and yesterday's closure. There was no evidence of Robbie Vasquez's visit from the previous day, so my heart leaped into my throat when Mr. Vasquez came through the door with five others wearing the white polo shirts of the Health and Sanitation Department.

"It's Robbie Vasquez," I whispered. Hector and Hilda hurried to the pass-through window. We shared a worried look.

After a few minutes, Robbie Vasquez and his group reached the order counter. Aunt Gully greeted him. My heart pounded.

"Good morning, Gully. We're going to the parade and thought we'd get lunch first." Robbie Vasquez had a walrus mustache that added to the droop of his dour expression. But his eyes were bright behind his oversized glasses. "I've seen a lot of restaurants, but never one as pristine as yours."

"Clean bill of health?" Aunt Gully beamed.

"Absolutely, positively," he said. "I wish every restaurant in town had your high standards. We'll take ten rolls."

Hector and I shared a fist bump.

"Good grief," Hilda said. "If everyone orders like that, we'll be here all day."

"That's a good thing!" Hector grinned, showing a gold tooth that gleamed like the little hoop in his ear.

The rest of the day passed in a festive whirl of activity. I called in a couple more of our part-time helpers to pick lobster and take deliveries from the lobstermen and women who came in to the dock. Even though it was a holiday, they knew it was a busy day for tourist dining. Some restaurants used frozen lobster, but Aunt Gully insisted on fresh preparation, which meant live lobsters.

From the kitchen I watched Aunt Gully take a selfie with a man wearing a red watch cap with two foam lobster claws. "She's a rock," I said. "I mean, sure she feels for all the judges and feels awful about Contessa. But she keeps going."

"She's a truly centered individual." Bit leaned on a broom. "Her karma's good."

As the day wore on, my shoulders knotted. I started suspecting I was getting carpal tunnel syndrome when another of Aunt Gully's friends showed up to help. As I watched her nimble fingers pick lobster, I remembered Rio Lopez.

"Did you see last night's episode of *Foodies on the Fly*?" I asked.

"Yes, Rio's speed was impressive." Aunt Gully's friend wiped a bit of shell from her cheek with the back of her hand. "She used to pick lobster down at Red Bridge Lobster Co-op."

"Wait a minute," I said. "Isn't she from New Mexico?"

"No, she was born right here in Mystic Bay. Rita Opalski."

"Rita Opalski?" Where had I heard that name before?

"Ri. O. She made a new name from her old."

I wanted to ask more, but Hilda hurried back. "I have an order for a group of twenty tourists on one of those culinary bus tours. Best of New England Eats."

Rio Lopez was from Mystic Bay? Why had I never heard this before?

The Mermaid usually closed at 9 P.M., but we cleaned and closed the door by 8:30 P.M. because we'd run out of everything.

"Now I know why your sister wants me to have a cooler with chowder for sale. I could buy one if I have another couple of days like this," Aunt Gully said.

I raised my aching body into the driver's seat of the van. Visions of the ballet company masseuse gave me a deep pang of regret. Best not to think of it. A hot bath in Aunt Gully's claw-foot tub would have to do the trick.

"Aunt Gully, why didn't you ever mention anything about Rio Lopez being from Mystic Bay? We've watched her show together a dozen times."

Aunt Gully busied herself with her tote bag. "It was years ago, twenty years ago? More? You were a little tyke when she lived here."

She sighed. "Everyone, especially kids, take a wrong path sometimes." Aunt Gully was struggling. She liked a good gossip session as much as anyone, but she hated to say anything negative about anyone, either. She turned the thick wedding band she still wore and looked away. "She had a very unhappy childhood. I don't speculate. Nobody ever said, especially back then. But her mother left her father when Rio was about ten. They moved into a poor little trailer out by Route One. Her mom cleaned motel rooms."

The motels by Route One were rundown. The trailer park was even shabbier.

My stomach clenched with what Aunt Gully wasn't saying.

"Rio's father left, went up to Maine, drank himself to death." Aunt Gully sighed. "Well, Rio acted out, people say now."

I concentrated on driving, not wanting to do anything that would stem Aunt Gully's flow of memory.

"Many times, she'd stay after school and wait for the late bus, you know, just hang around me in the cafeteria kitchen. Usually, she'd sit and read, or I'd let her help with little things, you know, like wiping down counters. She was even happy to mop the floor. Even if I'd already done it, I let her do it again. It made her feel good to help. To feel needed. Truth is, she didn't want to go home." Aunt Gully fished a tissue from her pocket and wiped her eyes.

"Kids made fun of her. She got in with a bad crowd and then, when she was sixteen, she left town. Disappeared. Never heard a word from her, except she sent me a Christmas card every year."

"What!" I said. "You never told me you got Christmas cards from Rio Lopez!"

Aunt Gully patted my arm. "I didn't get cards from Rio Lopez. I get Christmas cards from Rita Opalski. Still do. When I saw that television show the first time, I thought she looked familiar, but I wasn't sure.

"Well, I didn't recognize her when she visited the Lazy Mermaid, either, though you know how they disguise themselves. I'd love to give that girl a hug—thought I'd get my chance at the food fest—but then everything went crazy. The good thing is I saw her mother when we were at the hospital. I know for a fact she hasn't seen Rita these past twenty years. So at least there's that."

"Why wouldn't she get in touch with her mother?"

"I imagine it's complicated." Aunt Gully's cell rang.

"Lorel!" Aunt Gully listened as Lorel's voice squawked. Lorel was miffed about something. Aunt Gully threw me a look, her eyes wide behind her glasses.

"Sorry your meeting went so late," Aunt Gully said. "We didn't have a minute to pick up the phone." That was true. I'd felt my phone vibrate several times but hadn't had a spare moment to answer.

My mind drifted as Aunt Gully talked. Her tone took on some pepper. "No, your sister wasn't able to get a picture when Robbie Vasquez came in."

I rolled my eyes. Lorel was complaining about my failure to take pictures while I was up to my elbows in lobster meat. "Seriously?" I muttered.

"The culinary bus tour stopped by today!" As soon as the words were out of her mouth, Aunt Gully threw me a wild look. Lorel's voice shrilled. I hadn't gotten photos of the tour group and neither had Aunt Gully.

Aunt Gully let Lorel go on while I considered. Maybe Paul Pond was right. He already had enough business. If today was any indication, with lines out the door and hundreds of happy customers, maybe the Lazy Mermaid didn't need any more publicity. Didn't need YUM Network to give us a gold star.

"Well, see you soon, dear. Glad you're coming home tonight. Drive carefully." Aunt Gully's voice was warm. She didn't get mad or stay mad long.

I could just make out Lorel's voice squawk, "But we've got to talk strategy—"

Aunt Gully cut her off. "Tonight I'm putting some of my book-club brandy in my tea and then I'm going to bed with a Maeve Binchy. Give me a kiss when you get in, dear. But we're pooped and are getting a well-deserved rest. Bye-bye."

A well-deserved rest was just what I needed. First, a good stretch to untie all the knots in my back and then that bath, or maybe a swim. Aunt Gully hung up and started singing again.

As I pulled into the driveway, a car roared in behind us.

"What on earth?" Aunt Gully turned.

I turned but was blinded by the headlights behind us. "What a maniac!"

A hulking, broad-shouldered man got out of the driver's seat and slammed the door. He left his engine running. I reached for my cell.

"Why, it's Ernie Moss!" Aunt Gully said.

Ernie rapped on my window so hard I thought it would shatter. I made a "just a minute" gesture while Aunt Gully got out of the van. I scrolled to 911. I wanted to be able to summon help in a moment if I needed it. Ernie's fists were clenched and he turned from side to side. His coiled energy and the crazy way he'd boxed us in amped my adrenaline.

"Ernie!" Aunt Gully walked around the van, unconcerned by the wild look on Ernie's face or his disheveled clothing. I turned off the engine and jumped out of the van as they met in the glare of Ernie's headlights. I scanned Aunt Gully's garden ornaments, looking for something heavy in case I had to hit Ernie.

"How are you, Ernie? I've been thinking of you." Aunt Gully's voice was full of genuine concern.

"Oh, yeah. Thinking about me when you were open all day." Ernie laughed, a derisive bark. His Hawaiian shirt was wrinkled, his hair mussed.

"Yes, Robbie Vasquez gave us the go-ahead," Aunt Gully said.

"I'm still closed. Police tape on my door. But I heard you had big crowds down at the Mermaid. My loss was your gain."

Aunt Gully reached for Ernie's arm, but he flung his arm back, triggering the motion-activated spotlight on her front porch. "Now, Ernie—"

Ernie's voice rose and I caught a whiff of alcohol. "My staff called all day. How long will we be closed? Will they still have jobs?" He swore and picked up one of Aunt Gully's garden gnomes. "Hell if I know," he bellowed as he hurled it across the lawn.

"Now, Ernie." Aunt Gully raised her hands.

"Cool it, Ernie!" I stepped in front of Aunt Gully.

Shoulders heaving, Ernie turned and slammed his fist on the hood of his tiny sports car.

"Listen, none of this is Aunt Gully's fault," I said. But the thought wormed in, *We only had all those customers today because they couldn't go to Kahuna's.*

"The police questioned my Megan today." Ernie turned back to us, pinching the bridge of his nose. "My Megan, who wouldn't hurt a fly."

Ernie blinked in the bright light. He took a deep breath. "Well, the police let us go."

He spun back toward me. I tensed. "Heard I have you to thank, Allie. So, thank you. I wanted to come by and let you know before I go home."

"Ernie, they didn't"—Aunt Gully stepped around me—"arrest you, did they?"

"No, just invited me in for some garden-variety questioning. Twice over two days." Ernie rubbed his face and folded his arms. "Shut up in a little room all freaking day. Talked to some big shots from the state police. Asked me the same freaking questions over and over. What did I have against the YUM Network? Well, nothing. What did I have against Contessa Wells? Well, nothing. Same with Rick and Rio. Who're the lobster libbers? Hell if I know. What did I have against the mayor? Well, there they got a bit more interested in my answers." Ernie's laugh was bitter. "But the upshot is, I'm out. They can't figure out why I'd kill somebody with my own lobster rolls. I'd have to be crazy to do that, right? But then they saw the footage."

Ernie's head drooped and he seemed to shrink a few inches. His shoulders slumped forward. He looked beaten. Scared.

"When you pointed out that I ate my own lobster salad, that helped. They still questioned us for hours." That same humorless bark of laughter. "But they let us go. For now."

Ernie's eyes turned to me. Aunt Gully looked from Ernie to me as silence hung between us.

"Ernie, would you like a cup of tea?" she said.

"Nah, thanks, Gully, I gotta get home."

Ernie got into his sports car. The motor whined as he

threw it into reverse. The car skidded from side to side, then screeched down the street.

Ernie's words rang in my mind. *My loss was your gain.*

"Poor man," Aunt Gully said.

"Let's just be glad he didn't hit anything with that sports car. Or garden gnome." I returned Aunt Gully's gnome to its place.

The phone shrilled as we went in. Aunt Gully hurried to answer it.

"Wait!" I said, too late.

"News Channel 2!" she exclaimed. "The Providence station. You've been calling for hours?"

Aunt Gully exchanged pleasantries even though she'd been on her feet all day. I pulled the phone from her hand.

"Sorry, she can't speak to you now. Good night." I hung up.

Aunt Gully chuckled. "I should remind you about your manners, young lady." The phone shrilled again. Along with the awful grating ring, Aunt Gully's antiquated phone didn't have caller ID.

I lifted the phone and hung up, waited a few moments, then left the phone off the hook. "Just for tonight, Aunt Gully. And put your cell phone on silent so you can get some sleep."

"What if it's your sister or your dad?" Aunt Gully fumbled the phone from her tote bag. I turned off the ringer and put it back.

"They can call me."

Aunt Gully hung up her sweater and tote bag on the hooks by the kitchen door. "I'm going to soak for a while."

"Good idea, Aunt Gully." Nervous energy from the encounter with Ernie still coursed through me. I followed her upstairs, the sound of the phone beeping to remind us it was off the hook. After thirty mind-numbing seconds, it stopped.

Soon the sound of water tumbling into her claw-foot bathtub and the scent of her lavender bubbles wafted out onto the landing.

"I'm going to take a quick trip down to the cove," I whispered.

I slipped into a bathing suit, sweatpants, and a sweatshirt, grabbed a towel, and scrawled a note on the kitchen table. I held on to the screen door until the last moment, knowing the bang as it closed by itself would alert Aunt Gully. Aunt Gully wouldn't want me out alone so late at night, especially swimming alone.

But Ernie's visit had unsettled us both. She coped by relaxing in the tub, self-medicating with book-club brandy. I needed to move, needed to burn off my restless energy.

I scanned the street for Ernie's black sports car, then got in the van and drove through Fox Point to Orion Cove. It was my happy place, my escape.

Not many people knew of Orion Cove. Local kids mostly. A sprawling estate fronted on the cove's half-moon of sandy beach. Masses of rocks hemmed each end. High stone walls shielded the property off a gated private lane. The owner was a wealthy businessman who visited Mystic Bay only three times a year: once in high summer for a Fourth of July bash, one weekend at Halloween, and once in the winter for his Christmas getaway. The rest of the year the pristine beach was deserted, protected by a rich man's greed.

All Mystic Bay kids knew the path that skirted the towering stone walls of the estate and had no problem scrambling over the rocks. Of course, they weren't wearing a walking cast. Still, I managed. Hazy moonlight lit my way and made the wet sand shine. Even though it was cold, wet sand beneath my feet is one of my favorite sensations. I cursed my walking boot and finally ripped it off. I threw off my clothes, jogged into the water, and dove in.

The burning cold of the water made me gasp. I rolled to my back and let the black water cradle me. For a few moments my mind was blank, emptied of all the craziness of Ernie's visit. My body drifted with the waves, free of gravity, free of thought. Then I reached back and swam a few strokes. With shock deeper than the cold I realized why Ernie'd come to Aunt Gully's house. It hadn't been to thank me.

He thought one of us had poisoned the rolls in order to drive him out of business.

He'd looked right at me. *My loss was your gain.*

I dove one more time and then splashed up on the beach, the cold sand giving way beneath my feet.

My teeth chattered. Courting hypothermia by swimming this early in the season was nuts. "Stupid girl," I berated myself as I threw on my sweats and walking boot and ran back to the van. I cranked the heat. After a few minutes I stopped shivering and headed home.

As I drove past the turn for Fox Point, I passed Edwards Inlet, a public beach at the entrance to Fox Point's causeway. A gleam of red drew my eye to a fancy sports car parked under a light pole.

Chick Costa's red sports car.

I slammed on the brakes and pulled to the side of the road. What was he doing here? Wasn't he going back to his shack in Chatham?

I tapped the steering wheel. Why on earth was Chick Costa hanging out at night at Edwards Inlet? Had he gone for a nighttime swim, too? The thought almost made me put the van in drive. I didn't relish the thought of seeing that blowhard in board shorts. But still, my curiosity got the better of me. I turned off the engine.

Skirting the chain-link fence, I crept in the shadows at the edges of the parking lot, hoping my black sweats would help hide me. Chick's car was parked by the path to the beach. Another car was parked next to it. A Subaru wagon. Everyone in New England drove a Subaru wagon. I hurried closer and shined the flashlight on my phone on the license plate. KAHUNA2.

KAHUNA2? Kahuna one would be Ernie Moss. Number two: Megan Moss? Was she here with Chick? Voices carried from the beach. A man's voice. A woman's voice. Megan and Chick?

I scurried away from the cars, looking for a place to hide. The voices grew louder.

There was a Dumpster by the side of the bathhouse. Crouching low, I ducked behind it. I peeked around the rusty metal wall, trying to ignore the smell, praying that they didn't need to throw away any trash from their midnight picnic. Quiet little mouse Megan Moss meeting Chick Costa? Talk about opposites. But then I remembered the roses. Was Megan Moss having an affair with Chick Costa?

A slim woman passed through the curtain of gray haze from the light pole, her arms hugging her waist. The breeze whipped her hair around her face and carried the sound of her panting breath. No, she was sobbing. She moved slowly, as if each step were an effort.

A broad-chested man followed, stabbing the air with his finger. Chick's voice carried clearly. "You know it worked out anyway. What do you stay with that loser for? Don't you see? He's going to jail, Megan, and he'll take you with him."

Megan Moss!

"Chick, I told you I wasn't doing it. And I didn't do it. I wouldn't do anything to hurt Ernie. Ever." Megan gasped for breath. She leaned on the hood of the red car, shoulders shaking. "Why did you come back? You ruined my life!" She swung toward him, battering his chest with her fists.

My knees shook. This was no tryst.

"Listen. Megan." Chick grabbed her wrists. Megan collapsed, her body hanging limp from his hands. Chick dragged her slack body onto the hood of his car. Megan didn't struggle, just lay there, crying, then slid to the asphalt.

He leaned forward and whispered in her ear. Her weeping turned into a sharp keening sound that clawed in my own chest. I covered my ears, but I couldn't look away.

She struck at him again. She missed, but Chick raised his arm. I tensed. If he struck her, I was ready to spring.

Chick whirled, then turned back to her, his chest heaving. "Shut up! I'm the only one who can help you," Chick shouted. "The only one who knows."

Megan sat up. "I've shed enough tears over you, Chick." Using the bumper, she pushed herself upright. She took a shuddering breath. "Just tell me where he is."

"Where he is"? Did she mean Ernie?

Chick threw up his hands and stomped to his car door.

"I didn't come back for anything halfway, Megan. It's all or nothing. Got that? Call me when you're ready to see the light."

He got in his car, revved the engine, and pulled out, inches from where Megan stood. He slammed his brakes at the entrance to let a car pass. Megan scrambled into her car and the engine turned over.

I felt sick. What I'd witnessed was so intense and private. Cruel.

Megan Moss's car screeched across the asphalt, just missing Chick's car as she swerved from the parking lot. Chick's car turned on to the road, cutting off a car coming across the causeway from Fox Point. Car horns blared and engines roared as he sped toward Mystic Bay.

The red brake lights of the car following Chick burned into the distance. I hurried to the van. What was going on between Megan and Chick?

As I put the key in the ignition, I realized that I'd parked directly beneath a streetlight.

Chapter 21

The next morning I woke to the sound of laughter. Aunt Gully's and a deep, rich chuckle rose from downstairs. *A man in the kitchen at six o'clock?*

I threw on my kimono (compliments of Verity) and tightened the silky red belt. My body ached with tension. Sleep had eluded me as I replayed the confrontation between Chick Costa and Megan Moss.

Lorel's bedroom door was closed. I must have slept some. I hadn't heard her come home.

I tiptoed down the polished wooden stairs, skipping the third step from the bottom that would betray my presence with a loud noise like a shot.

I peeked into the kitchen.

A dark-haired man sat across from Aunt Gully at the kitchen table, his broad back to me. Aunt Gully looked at him over the rim of her teacup. Her expression was . . . flirty?

She glanced up. "Oh, good morning, Allie. Good thing you're decent. We have company."

The man turned in his seat. Leo Rodriguez.

"Good morning." Leo stood. "Sorry to intrude, but I was in the neighborhood and thought I'd see if your aunt was available. She was in the garden and was kind enough to invite me in."

"Oh." Conversation isn't my strong suit in the morning. Plus I was flabbergasted. Aunt Gully just let Leo in? Leo's vibrant male energy filled the small room: his broad shoulders, his wide smile, and his strong hands made Aunt Gully's teacup look like a toy. And wow, was he handsome. Before I could stop myself, my hand flew up to smooth my hair.

"What. Well." I slid into my chair.

"Leo brought doughnuts." Aunt Gully offered me the box.

Leo took his seat. Aunt Gully had served him my usual breakfast, scrambled eggs made with cream and fresh marjoram and thyme, plus she'd added some strawberries cut into a fan shape for garnish. Aunt Gully had totally lost her mind.

"Beware a man bearing doughnuts." Leo winked at Aunt Gully. Aunt Gully giggled.

"I heard what happened with Ernie Moss," Leo continued. My eyes went to Aunt Gully but she was smiling, unconcerned. "Kudos. You pointed the police in the right direction. You could've just let them believe Ernie's a suspect."

Did Leo know about Ernie's visit last night? Aunt Gully's smile didn't waver. My shoulders relaxed. That wasn't going to be a topic of conversation.

"Is this an interview? Because I don't give interviews before breakfast." I helped myself to a cinnamon sugar doughnut and took a bite. Heavenly.

"If we're eating, it's technically not before breakfast anymore. Right, Mrs. Fontana?" Leo's teeth gleamed like a toothpaste model's.

Aunt Gully's cheeks pinked. Good grief. Either she had it bad for Leo Rodriguez—and who could blame her because actually he was awfully good-looking—or she was in matchmaking mode. Ugh.

"You'll have to excuse me; I have to do my PT." I stood and hooked another doughnut, this one chocolate frosted with sprinkles. "Thanks for the doughnuts."

Lorel and I passed on the stairs. On the rare occasion she forgot pajamas, she'd raid Dad's sweatshirt collection.

"That doughnut looks good." Lorel yawned and pulled an old Bruins sweatshirt over her mussed hair. For a second, I considered telling her that Leo was in the kitchen.

"Yep." I hurried upstairs, stifling a laugh.

After my floor barre and a shower, I went downstairs. Lorel sat at the kitchen table, tapping on her phone, an untouched yogurt in front of her. She'd changed into a navy shirtdress, looking cool and collected as usual.

Aunt Gully hummed and packed her tote bag.

I waited but no explosion came. "Good visit with Leo?"

"Yes, nice interview with Aunt Gully," Lorel said. "We're lucky he fit us in since he's in town to cover Contessa Wells's funeral."

"I'll go over this afternoon to pay my respects," Aunt Gully said.

Lorel didn't look up from her phone. "Leo's planning a segment about how we're coping after the tragic events at the food fest. He's going to do a stand-up at the Lazy Mermaid and have a lobster roll."

"To prove it's not poisoned?" Despite his charm offensive, I didn't trust Leo Rodriguez.

"Such a nice young man." Aunt Gully wiped down her already immaculate pink Formica countertop. "I met him by the lilac bushes this morning. He told me they were his mother's favorites."

That clinched it. "Aren't the lilacs in the backyard?" I

put my hands on my hips. "What was he doing in the *backyard*?"

Aunt Gully straightened the dishtowel on the oven door, avoiding my gaze. "Admiring the lilacs, Allie. He didn't want to just knock on the door at this early hour, so he waited to hear if I was up. He was lured to the lilacs by their beauty."

I folded my arms.

Aunt Gully started digging in her tote bag. "You know, he's really very nice. Very nice."

Nothing was going to shake Aunt Gully's opinion. "Off to the Mermaid." I picked up the keys. "Are you coming down later, Lorel? Oh, that's right, you'll be there for the 'stand-up.'" *While I'm picking lobster*.

"Ready, Aunt Gully?" I noticed the receiver of Aunt Gully's old phone was still on Uncle Rocco's recliner.

I hung it back up. It shrilled immediately. "Lorel, could you get that? We've got to go."

Just as I started backing out, a Mystic Bay Police SUV pulled in behind me, boxing me in the driveway.

"Jeez!" I slammed the brakes. "Not again."

"God bless America!" Aunt Gully said. "I don't have time for all these social calls. I've got a lobster shack to open."

I turned off the engine and we got out.

Emerson Brooks, Mystic Bay's chief of police, heaved his stocky frame from the SUV. He settled his hat on his gray buzz cut and hitched up his belt as he walked around the vehicle.

"Good morning, Mrs. Fontana, Ms. Larkin," he said.

Aunt Gully's eyebrows flew up. The chief's wife was a friend. He'd coached Lorel's softball team. He was also Verity's uncle and a regular at the lobster shack. He usually called her Gully.

"Good morning, Emerson," she said.

The chief's eyes shifted to the SUV. "This is Detective Rosato." A woman stepped from the tall vehicle as she slid her sunglasses into her breast pocket, the movement efficient. She wore her brown hair slicked back into a bun, a dark pantsuit over a crisp white button-down shirt, and sensible low-heeled pumps. She gave us the tiniest of nods, her small dark eyes shifting from me to Aunt Gully.

Chief Brooks slid his finger under his collar. "From the state police."

Mystic Bay, and many towns in the state, were too small to have expensive, forensic investigative units. For more serious crimes, they called on the state to send officers with specialized expertise.

Serious crime. Like poisonings.

Like murder.

The woman in black didn't move or speak.

"But we have to open the Mermaid," I said.

"Please. It won't take long." Chief Brooks threw a look at Detective Rosato.

"All right." Aunt Gully met my eye. "Hector and Hilda will get things started."

Chief Brooks walked with us along the path to the front door. Detective Rosato followed right behind us, a bit too close. Just as Aunt Gully reached for the door, Lorel jerked it open.

"Hilda called." Lorel blinked. "Coach Brooks?"

"Hilda?" Aunt Gully asked. "What did she want? Is everything okay?"

Lorel looked from Chief Brooks to Detective Rosato. "Hilda said the police were at the Mermaid."

Chapter 22

Suddenly the dining room of Gull's Nest looked unfamiliar, as if I'd never seen it before. We took seats at the round oak table, gathering for the most uncomfortable dinner party ever.

My phone buzzed with a text from Hilda.

POLICE HERE.

Normally at this time Aunt Gully would be hanging up the flag at the Mermaid. Blowing her kiss to Uncle Rocco. Singing to her lobsters. The comfortable vibe of a typical day had been yanked out from under us. What were the police doing here and at the Mermaid?

"Emerson, is everything okay?" Aunt Gully asked.

"Everything's fine." Chief Brooks smiled a weirdly big smile.

"Allie, dear, will you put on the tea, please? Or would either of you prefer coffee?"

"Nothing, thank you, Mrs. Fontana." Detective Rosato's voice was pleasant, calm, and colorless, like the robot voice that answers the phone at the DMV. *Your call is important to us.*

"No, thanks." Chief Brooks looked like he wanted something stronger than coffee.

The phone shrilled. "Excuse me, I'll get it," Lorel said.

"Just leave it off the hook again," I said.

Lorel returned moments later. "The Hartford TV station," she said in a low voice.

Detective Rosato aligned a small leather notebook and a gold pen on the table. As she reached into her pocket, I noticed a bulge under her jacket. My heart rate kicked up a notch. I'd read enough crime novels to know what that was.

Of course the police want to talk to Aunt Gully; they have to question everyone. She's innocent of any wrongdoing. It wasn't her lobster roll that sickened the judges.

And killed Contessa Wells.

"What's going on?" My normally cool sister's voice cracked.

Chief Brooks threw a sideways glance to Detective Rosato. "We're, ah, talking to everyone who's involved in the, er, terrible events at the food festival."

Detective Rosato observed Chief Brooks as if he were an experiment she was sure would go wrong. Her dark eyes were steady, her expression bland, her body motionless. I'd never met someone who made me feel so uncomfortable by doing absolutely nothing. How old was she? Maybe her late thirties? Her skin was so smooth it was hard to tell.

After a few minutes of Chief Brooks's meandering conversation, Detective Rosato broke in and fired questions at Aunt Gully. "Mrs. Fontana, do you know Rick and Rio Lopez?"

"I haven't really met Rick," Aunt Gully said. "Well, I guess I did. If you watch their show, you know they come into the restaurant in disguise. Rio grew up here in Mystic Bay but I haven't spoken to her in years."

"How long have you known Ernest Moss?"

"Oh, ages. His older brother was in my class at Mystic Bay Elementary."

"Megan Moss?"

Aunt Gully paused. "Well, her family's from Mystic Bay, but I think the first time I met her was when she was a teen and we volunteered at the Ladies' Guild."

"Paul Pond?"

"We met Saturday at the festival," Aunt Gully shifted in her seat.

"Charles Costa?"

"Chick? His family summered here when he was a teen, but I don't think I ever met him then. Same as Paul, we met at the food festival."

"Contessa Wells?"

"Her family owns a big house on the hill but I never met her. Different circles. She left for Hollywood before I was born."

Chief Brooks kept running his finger under the collar of his shirt, uncomfortable and out of his depth while Robo Detective shot questions at Aunt Gully. A tiny line appeared on Aunt Gully's normally tranquil forehead, worry percolating under her normally cheerful demeanor.

I squeezed her hand and she squeezed mine back. I felt her strength. Aunt Gully was worried, but she wasn't beaten.

Detective Rosato shot a look at Chief Brooks that said, *That's how you do it.*

"We need to search your house and the shack," she said.

Aunt Gully blinked. "Today?"

Detective Rosato said, "Do we have your permission?"

"Well, yes, I suppose so."

Detective Rosato stepped into the kitchen. Her voice

was a low murmur as she made a call. She returned, clicking off her phone.

Lorel raised her hand. "Wait a minute—"

"We have a warrant, Lorel," Chief Brooks said quietly.

I frowned. "Shouldn't I, we, be there at the Mermaid?"

"Not necessary," Detective Rosato said.

"What else do you want to know, Emerson?" Aunt Gully said. I shared a glance with Lorel. The peppery way Aunt Gully said "Emerson" showed she hadn't lost her fighting spirit.

Chief Brooks swallowed. "Perhaps you can tell us a little bit, uh, about the events of the morning—"

Detective Rosato leaned forward. "Tell us what you did the morning of the food festival. Start when you arrived."

Aunt Gully surprised me by offering a concise summary in a steady voice. She was the only person sitting at the table who seemed comfortable. Well, maybe Detective Rosato was comfortable. Chief Brooks was smiling his weird smile but sweating as if he'd just finished running the Mystic Bay Five Miler.

"I understand you were the last to leave the food preparation area." Detective Rosato's dark eyes glittered.

Lorel stiffened. I practically choked. I remembered running into the church to see where Aunt Gully was. I tried to keep my breath steady, but in my mind I could see Aunt Gully running down the church hallway, a couple of minutes behind the other contestants.

Oh, God. Ever since I'd proved that Ernie couldn't have poisoned the lobster roll, a formless worry had hovered at the edges of my mind. What had Aunt Gully been doing while everyone else trooped out to the stage? She was alone with the lobster rolls. With dread, I remembered a word I'd read in Aunt Gully's mystery novels: opportunity. Aunt Gully had had opportunity.

My phone vibrated. Keeping it on my lap, I lowered my eyes. BRONWYN. It vibrated again. VERITY. HILDA. Hilda had called twice. I clenched my hands around the phone, willing them to stop shaking.

"Oh, that." Aunt Gully smiled. I forgot my apron and ran back to get it.

Detective Rosato gave a barely perceptible nod, her eyes wide and unblinking, like a cat ready to pounce.

Lorel twisted her hands. "Wait a minute, wait a minute. Shouldn't my aunt have her lawyer?"

"Would you like a lawyer, Mrs. Fontana?" Detective Rosato asked.

Aunt Gully shook her head. "No, I'm happy to help."

"Aunt Gully," Lorel said.

"Lorel, I have nothing to hide. I want to be helpful." That explained Aunt Gully's serenity. She was in helper mode.

"So you were the last person in the room with the lobster rolls?" Detective Rosato didn't miss a beat.

"No leading the witness!" I jumped to my feet.

Detective Rosato threw a glance at me. *Dismissed.* I sank back into my chair.

"I'm not sure if anyone went in after me. Lots of volunteers ran out to see Cameron Kim," Aunt Gully said slowly. "When the cooking was done, the network people told us time was up. We put our plated rolls on a large tray the counter."

"Each chef put four plates on their own tray?" Detective Rosa asked, Aunt Gully nodded. "Then each tray was covered with a cloche to keep the lobster rolls warm. We went to the green room. Well, they called it the green room. It's the kindergarten classroom by the exit to the playground. We started to go to the stage. But then I remembered I left my apron in the kitchen. I ran back to get it."

My heart dropped. Detective Rosato didn't change expression, but Chief Brooks swallowed hard.

"Was there anyone else in the kitchen when you went back?" Chief Brooks said.

"No, everyone else had left. Everyone rushed out to see Rick and Rio and Cameron and Contessa and get to the stage for the judging." Aunt Gully's eyes widened. "Wait, there was one volunteer leaving the kitchen as I went in."

"A volunteer," Detective Rosato said.

Aunt Gully straightened. "Someone, in black. Baseball cap. Maybe a woman, well, someone slight. Maybe a teen boy? I'm certain of one thing. She or he had a badge like everyone else. I didn't really look. I was in such a hurry."

Detective Rosato maintained the same expressionless expression, but something had shifted. Sure, lady, a volunteer in black. How many volunteers in black had worked at the food festival? Dozens.

"You were alone with the lobster rolls?" Detective Rosato pressed.

Aunt Gully swallowed. "Yes."

Lorel closed her eyes.

The police chief tugged his collar.

My heart dropped as it sank in. Aunt Gully was the last one with the lobster rolls. All alone with the lobster rolls right before they were served. Right before they poisoned four judges. Right before Contessa Wells died.

Chapter 23

The silence deepened in the dining room, a silence so deep that over the hum of Aunt Gully's refrigerator I could hear the ringing buoy off Seal Rock. It was a melancholy, lonely sound, a warning for mariners sailing too close to unseen danger.

Detective Rosato left the room to take a call.

I took a deep breath, trying to quell the panic surging through me. "You cannot believe for a single moment that my aunt—"

"This is ridiculous," Lorel said.

"Are you suggesting that I tampered with the lobster rolls? That I put poison in them?" Aunt Gully's voice rose to a shriek.

Chief Brooks reared back. "Now, now, Gully—"

Aunt Gully's normally pink cheeks reddened. "Oh, now I'm Gully! You've known me for how long? You coached Lorel in softball! I've been in the Ladies' Guild with your wife for thirty years!"

Chief Brooks hunched his shoulders. "Gully. Nobody thinks you did anything. We just have to check everyone."

"Are you questioning Paul Pond and Chick Costa and

the Moss—" I bit my lip. I knew they'd questioned the Mosses.

Chief Brooks blinked. "We have to investigate everyone."

Aunt Gully looked stunned, like someone slapped her.

The chief's words tumbled. "We're still interviewing people who were at the food festival. Some remembered seeing you go back to the kitchen after everyone else left."

Detective Rosato returned. "That's enough, Chief."

Chief Brooks stood, clutching his hat.

"Why do you have to search? What're you looking for?" Aunt Gully seemed to have reached a limit. I put an arm around her.

"You'd better have a good reason." As soon as I said it, I realized how stupid I sounded. Murder. Murder was the reason.

"Now, I know it's upsetting. But I'm sure everything'll be all right." He looked to Detective Rosato for confirmation. She kept her gaze leveled on Aunt Gully.

"Kahuna's is still closed," Chief Brooks said. "Everyone's being interviewed. Everyone's lobster rolls were tested."

Detective Rosato shot Chief Brooks a withering look and he pressed his lips together. Of course he had no idea what to do in a murder investigation. Nothing ever happened in sleepy Mystic Bay.

My phone vibrated with a text from Verity. WHY ARE THERE COPS AT YOUR HOUSE? THEY WONT LET ME IN. I hurried to the front window, ignoring the way Detective Rosato moved her arm, the slightest bit, toward the bulge under her jacket.

A Mystic Bay police cruiser was parked in front of the house. Verity stood by the Tank, which had recently been full of the dead woman's clothes. Good grief. What day was it? Tuesday? We were going to Contessa's funeral this afternoon.

Chief Brooks joined me at the window. "Verity." He winced. "I'll tell her to go home."

"Can I tell her?" I said.

"Please come back to the table, Ms. Larkin," Detective Rosato said. I complied.

She turned to Aunt Gully. "May we search the house and garden?"

"Yes. I've nothing to hide." Aunt Gully raised her chin.

"Can it wait?" Lorel put her arm around Aunt Gully. "My aunt's very upset."

"It's best if we do it now," Detective Rosato said.

Chief Brooks joined us.

"Wait a minute," I said. "Chief Brooks, did you get my call? My aunt's been getting anonymous letters from the lobster liberation group. For three days before the competition. And they posted a sign by the Mermaid and by Kahuna's. Maybe they had something to do with this."

"Sorry, Allie, I've been awfully busy. Is that true, Gully?" Chief Brooks said.

Aunt Gully's brow furrowed. "Yes, but I thought it was just kids playing a joke. They were letters saying 'Stop before we stop you' or something like that. Signed, the 'Lobster Liberation Group.'"

"Did you report it? Where are the letters?" Detective Rosato flipped open her notebook.

"I threw them away," Aunt Gully whispered.

Detective Rosato flipped her notebook closed with a movement that said, Nice try.

Great, now the police would never take the letters seriously.

"There was a poster, too. I brought it to the Plex," I

said. Detective Rosato's eyes flicked from me to Chief Brooks. "We're looking into it," he said.

Police techs swept into the house. They let Aunt Gully make a cup of tea and herded us into the living room. Aunt Gully clutched her mug until it went cold, sitting between Lorel and me on the couch. Poor thing looked beyond tired. We all flinched whenever a bang came from the kitchen. What on earth were they looking for? Voices floated in the open windows from the direction of the garden.

A police officer set a dining room chair by the doorway, sat down, and scrolled on her phone. Our keeper.

I texted Verity.

I'LL CALL AS SOON AS THEY ARE GONE.

WE HAVE A FUNERAL TO GO TO TODAY, she texted back. If only Verity knew how bad things were.

Anxiety tightened my muscles like trip wires.

My body ached to stretch. Dancers don't just like to move, we need to move.

Lorel must have been stunned since she didn't say anything when I slipped to the floor and started stretching on Aunt Gully's braided rag rug. The police officer glanced up, but after a moment turned her attention back to her phone.

Aunt Gully's head fell upon her chest and she snored softy. Lorel took the cup of tea from her hands and set it on the coffee table.

A few minutes of stretching helped me calm and focus. Sound helped me keep track of the searchers: heavy footsteps crossing the bedrooms above. The banging of the back screen door. The rumble of the garage door. Detective Rosato's voice floated through the open dining room window.

"Can I get my aunt's sweater?" Aunt Gully had left

hers on the back of a dining room chair. The officer looked up from her screen and nodded.

As I retrieved the sweater, I glanced out the dining room window. Aunt Gully's backyard was small, but lushly landscaped. Well, "landscaped" sounds intentional. It was full to bursting. An officer and Detective Rosato poked around the colorful flags and statues that were interspersed in the overflowing beds, trellises, pots, and plants in old coffee cans. They conferred, then the tech shook his head.

With a jolt I remembered what Aunt Gully'd told me about Leo Rodriguez. I squeezed next to Lorel on the couch.

"Monkshood." I whispered. "It's a plant, right? That's why they're searching the garden."

Lorel's eyes widened. "Did they find anything?"

"Of course not. Leo Rodriguez was poking in the garden this morning. That snake! Admiring the lilacs, my—"

Detective Rosato and Chief Brooks came into the room. Aunt Gully jerked awake.

"Mrs. Fontana, I'd appreciate it if you'd come down to the station later today and answer a few more questions. Say one P.M.?" Detective Rosato said.

Chief Brooks kept his head down.

Aunt Gully raised her chin. "I'm happy to help, but—" her voice wavered—"I have to open my lobster shack. Are they done searching there?"

Detective Rosato's phone rang. Once more she stepped into the kitchen.

My phone vibrated with a text from Hilda.

POLICE FOUND SOMEONE IN THE SHED. BADLY INJURED.

I gasped and showed the screen to Lorel and Aunt

Gully. Chief Brooks's phone buzzed and he stepped into the dining room to take the call.

Detective Rosato came back, her erect posture radiating command. "There's been a development."

"A development?" Aunt Gully whispered, her eyes huge behind her glasses.

"Who is it? Who'd they find at the Mermaid?" I said.

Chief Brooks came back into the living room. "Gully, I'm real sorry—"

Detective Rosato cut him off. "I'd like you to accompany us to the police services building for further questioning. You should call your lawyer."

Chapter 24

As Detective Rosato led Aunt Gully from the front door of Gull's Nest, Aunt Gully squeezed my arm. "You girls keep an eye on things at the Mermaid, okay? Everything'll be fine." Aunt Gully squared her shoulders but still looked so small getting into the Mystic Bay Police SUV.

"This isn't real," I whispered.

Lorel and I clung to each other and watched them leave.

"What do we do?" Lorel's eyes brimmed with tears. I shook my head.

"My God," Lorel said. "Leo was going to the Mermaid. He probably saw the police—"

"Is that all you think of!" I pushed her away. "What things look like? Aunt Gully's going to jail." *Breathe, Allie, breathe.* "Call Aunt Gully's lawyer. Have him meet her there."

Lorel shook herself. "John Dombrowski. Right."

"And let's get to the Mermaid. Right away."

After Lorel spoke to John Dombrowski, we hurried to Lorel's car and my sister sped—really sped—to the Mermaid.

A string of yellow police tape blocked the entrance. We couldn't pull into the parking lot, so we angled into a spot farther up Pearl Street. Then we ran back to the Mermaid, ignoring passersby craning their necks to get a better look at the police and emergency vehicles parked by the shed that housed the lobster tanks.

"Allie! Lorel!"

Hector jogged over to us, leaned across the police tape, and threw his strong arms around us. "How's Aunt Gully?"

We ducked under the tape. Hilda joined us and, sobbing, hugged us hard.

"The police took Aunt Gully in for questioning," I said.

"No!" Hilda clasped the small gold cross around her neck. "Anyone with a brain can see that she's innocent."

"Who is it?" Lorel said. "In the shed?"

Hector shook his head.

"We started prep work but we were mainly in the kitchen, not the shed with the lobster tanks. Then the police came and made us sit outside. Took them a while to get started. Then." He took a deep breath. "They found him. Some officer said 'body' but they took him away fast. They wouldn't do that if he was dead."

"So somebody was hurt badly?" I said. "How?"

Hector shrugged. "Cops won't say. They made us wait here. With our keeper." He looked back at the officer relaxing on a pink Adirondack chair, sipping from a thermos.

"Officer Petrie!"

Officer Petrie joined us, swaggering a bit with his hand on his utility belt. "You girls okay? I heard about your aunt." He shook his head. "That's messed up."

"Who was in the shed?" I swallowed.

Petrie jutted his chin toward the police vehicles. "No

way to know yet. Got a bunch of the staties here and they don't talk. Especially that one."

A Mystic Bay SUV stopped by the entrance to the parking lot and Detective Rosato got out. She ducked under the tape and crunched across the gravel into the lobster shed without a glance at us.

She must have just dropped off Aunt Gully, I thought. "I'm going to walk up to the Plex and see if I can wait with Aunt Gully."

"Save yourself a trip. They won't let you. You can sit in the waiting room or at one of the picnic tables between the park and the Plex." Petrie settled back into his chair. "Hope she has a good lawyer."

"I called Aunt Gully's lawyer. He's headed to the Plex now," Lorel said.

I rested my head on Hilda's shoulder and squeezed my eyes shut. I was not going to cry. I had to keep it together, find a way to help Aunt Gully. When I opened my eyes, my gaze settled on a red convertible sports car parked across the street.

Suddenly, I knew who'd been found in the lobster shed.

Chapter 25

A crowd milled just outside the yellow police tape. I scanned their faces, then tugged Lorel's hand. "I have to tell you something." To Hector and Hilda I said, "I'll bring you some coffee from the Tick Tock."

"No, thanks, hon." Hilda slumped into a blue Adirondack chair.

"Extra large black with two sugars," Hector said.

"Officer Petrie?"

"No, thanks."

I pulled Lorel with me into the crowd. To my horror, I saw Leo Rodriguez emerge from the Tick Tock Coffee Shop down the street. No doubt he'd soon be writing his story about Aunt Gully, the sweet little old lady murderer of Mystic Bay.

"Maybe I should talk to him," Lorel said.

"Are you nuts?" I tugged her arm. "What on earth can you say to him? Oh, don't you worry about another little old body dropping near Aunt Gully! Let's just get over to that red car."

Lorel followed me. She took the monogrammed navy blue silk scarf she'd tied to her purse and looped it over

her hair, managing to look even more glamorous and no-
ticeable.

I circled the red sports car. Scrapes marred its front
end. A "Chick's World Famous Lobsters" bumper sticker
was on the dented back bumper. It had to be Chick's
sports car.

Sidling up to the car, I slung my leg over the side and
angled myself into the driver's seat. My body slid along
the rich leather. For a moment the embrace of the car's
ergonomically designed seat made me forget the craziness of what I was doing.

"Allie! Allie!" Lorel clenched her teeth in a smile as
a couple with cameras nodded and passed her.

I patted the steering wheel, admiring the picture of a
rearing horse in silhouette in bright yellow at its center.

"Get in," I said. "You're more conspicuous standing there than sitting in the car. I'm not going to hot-
wire it."

Lorel's eyes darted side to side, but she obeyed. Her
eyes went wide as she slid into the seat. "Whoa!"

A jogger stopped and ran in place. "You got room for
one more?"

Lorel waggled her fingers and he ran on.

"Allie. Are you nuts!" Lorel hunched down in the seat,
her hand shielding her face. "What are we doing here,
Allie?"

"One, hiding from Leo." I slid down so the leather
headrest hid me. I hoped. "Two."

I took a deep breath and told her what I'd seen last
night at Edwards Inlet.

"That's horrible. So Chick's an even more disgusting
human being than we thought. It sounds like he wanted
Megan to throw the lobster roll contest. But to use poison? Do you think she did?"

"No," I said slowly. "Well, she said she didn't. She seemed hysterical and furious with him. Like she hated him. But the weirdest thing was what else he said. 'Stop. I'm the only one who can help you. The only one who knows.'"

"'The only one who can help you? The only one who knows?'" Lorel repeated. "That she poisoned the rolls? Do you think Ernie found out that Chick was using Megan to poison the lobster rolls? Why use poison? If he wanted her to throw the competition, she could've just used a lot of hot pepper."

I shook my head. "It sounded like something else. A secret. He said, he's 'the only one who knows.'"

"So she has a secret? That she's hiding from Ernie?"

"Maybe that's why Megan and Chick met at the beach and not at Kahuna's Cove." I told her about the roses I'd seen in the Mosses' kitchen trash.

"An affair? But you said it sounded like she hated him. Maybe they're breaking up?" Lorel straightened. "Or maybe it was blackmail? But what on earth could you blackmail boring old Megan Moss about?"

Something tugged at my memory, something Aunt Gully said. "Chick and Megan dated before Ernie came on the scene."

"Everyone's heard that story. Megan turned down the rich summer kid for the steady, but much older, local guy." Lorel turned her head.

"Yeah, doesn't seem like a big secret. The way Aunt Gully told it, it was all common knowledge."

"Ernie's awfully possessive of Megan. Maybe Chick and Megan were rekindling their romance and it set him off."

Last night, Ernie had been out of control and smelled of alcohol. "Maybe Ernie came here and tried to kill Chick?"

"And all of that made you want to get in this car, why?" Lorel snapped.

All right, maybe it was crazy. But there was something about Megan and Chick's relationship, something that made me think there was something in it worth killing for.

I just had no idea what it was. I needed to think.

"Okay, okay." I ran my hands over the steering wheel.

"So you think, what?" Lorel said. "You think the injured guy is Chick Costa?"

I nodded. "Ernie was angry and out of control and drunk last night. What if he saw Chick's and Megan's cars leaving Edwards Inlet together? There's only one road in and out of Fox Point." I remembered the screech of brakes. Could it have been Ernie in his sports car?

"Right when Chick was waiting to exit, Megan tore past him." I pictured the cars tearing out of the parking lot. "She cut off another car." I replayed the moment in my mind, heard the overpowered sports car engines. "It could've been Ernie's car. Maybe he realized it was both Chick's and Megan's cars and he followed Chick."

"Followed him? And?" Lorel's voice rose.

"Chased him. Ernie was kind of crazy last night. Maybe he managed to get Chick to pull over." I pointed to the rear of the car. "There's a dent on this car I don't remember seeing when Chick visited Aunt Gully's."

"And the two of them agreed to fight here at the Mermaid?" Lorel's voice had an edge. "Now you're crazy."

"Maybe Chick was on his way out of town. He'd have to pass by here. It's a direct route to the highway."

"Now you're really making things up."

I sighed. "I don't know. I just think that Chick's been up to dirty stuff. And I want to know why Megan was so upset. Maybe Ernie called Chick and asked him to meet at the Mermaid. Perhaps it was a bit of revenge on us. He thinks we're to blame for the poisoning, I'm sure of it." I chewed my lip. "Lorel, check the glove box."

Lorel wheeled on me so fast her blue scarf slipped from her hair. "For what?" she spat. "Brass knuckles? Nuclear codes? Maybe an assault rifle? No. Allie, you've lost your mind."

"To check the registration and—"

Lorel scanned behind the car. "I'm getting out of here just as soon as these nice normal-looking people pass by. Hopefully no one'll recognize us. Because we just broke into this car, because you imagined a whole scenario about this guy that is probably not even the slightest bit true. And if Chick was injured or murdered in the Lazy Mermaid, now our fingerprints are all over his car. God, Allie, way to screw up."

I felt sick. Of course Lorel was right. I was just so sure that Chick was, just, awful. That he was up to no good. Even if I wasn't sure exactly what he was doing.

Chick's car was pristine. No junk lying around, no food wrappers, no incriminating, well, anything. No bloodstains. The buttery soft leather gleamed. I ran my hands along the seat by my thighs. An envelope was tucked next to it. I could see the return address, a picture of a church, and the words "Aldersgate Family Services, Chatham, MA." I pulled the envelope up so I could see it better. A label on the front read Brian Lukeman.

"You're not going to read that!" Lorel slapped my hand.

"Okay, okay!" I slid the envelope back.

"Honestly, Allie, I don't know what's gotten in to you."

She climbed out of the car. After I scanned the crowd, I slipped out. Lorel stomped in front of me as we walked toward the Tick Tock. Leo Rodriguez and the news truck were nowhere to be seen.

"Let's get coffee for Hector and then go up and wait

for Aunt Gully. God, I cannot believe my aunt's being questioned. And my sister now thinks she's Sherlock Holmes and it's okay to break into cars and read people's personal stuff! What else can go wrong today?" Lorel huffed.

I pulled open the screen door to the coffee shop just as Chick Costa emerged.

Chapter 26

"Ladies." Chick carried a large coffee and an oversized muffin.

My mind whirled. If it wasn't Chick in the lobster shed, who was it?

"Good morning, Chick, how are you?" Lorel said brightly, her automatic good manners saving the day.

"Hi," I whispered, still in shock.

Chick stepped aside to let a family pass, angling his leather boat shoes away from a little girl's dripping ice-cream cone.

"Great, great." His face was unmarked. I lowered my eyes to the oversized gold signet ring on the beefy hand holding the coffee cup. His knuckles had angry red scrapes.

"Whoa, what happened to your hand?" I blurted.

Chick blinked. "Oh, nothing, just a flesh wound." He laughed. "Yeah, happened while I was jogging. Slipped in some gravel."

"Last night?" If Chick had had to protect himself from Ernie, he'd gotten the better end of the fight. My stomach churned. Maybe there hadn't been a fight. Maybe my whole crazy scenario was, well, crazy.

"I thought you were heading back to Chatham after the meeting?" I asked.

"Yeah." Chick took a long swig of coffee. "But I changed my mind. Stopped in a little place not too far from here. Took a run to unwind. Went to bed early."

Liar. I saw you at the beach last night.

"But the cops called, wanted me to answer some questions, so I came back."

"What time was that?" I said.

Chick gave me a hard look. Lorel's eyes went wide.

"Not exactly sure." He laughed. "They got me up early."

"Oh, so you came back this morning."

Lorel angled behind Chick's shoulder. Her intense expression begged me to Shut Up.

"Yup. No rest for the wicked. So since I'm here, I'll pay my respects at the funeral this afternoon. Sorry, girls. Gotta jet." He turned to wink at Lorel. She smiled at him.

Chick melted into the crowd.

"Ugh."

"He's gross, I know," Lorel said. "But your imagination's working overtime."

"Oh, yeah? I didn't imagine his argument with Megan last night."

We bought coffee and headed back to the Mermaid.

"Allie!" Lorel stopped short.

"What?"

Lorel turned to me, her hand to her neck. "Where's my scarf?"

We retraced our steps but didn't see it. As we arrived back at the Mermaid we both looked up as Chick's car roared away from the curb.

"Oh, no," Lorel said. "I think it fell off in Chick's car!"

Chapter 27

"If Chick puts me together with that scarf, I'll kill you," Lorel hissed. "It has my initials on it!"

"I don't think he's smart enough." I hoped. My cheeks burned. What else could I mess up today? "With his ego, he'll just think you want a date." We ducked under the police tape at the Mermaid.

Hector and Hilda were still in the Adirondack chairs with their silent keeper, Officer Petrie. Petrie bent over his phone. Although he wore earbuds, the tinny sound of a computer game leaked out.

Lorel gave Hector his coffee, glared at me, then pulled out her phone.

My phone. I'd forgotten all the texts from this morning. Bronwyn had texted that there was something big happening at the Mermaid. Guiltily, I erased it. I didn't want Bronwyn getting into trouble.

Verity's texts were all CALL MEs.

Bronwyn coasted up the sidewalk on her mountain bike. "Hey, Allie." Bronwyn wore a khaki skirt, tan Mystic Bay Police polo shirt, helmet, and biking gloves. I joined her at the police tape.

She waved at Officer Petrie, who responded with a friendly chin jut.

"How're you managing with your wrist in a cast?" I said.

"I'm managing." She smiled. "How about you? With that boot?"

"I'm managing."

"Do you have a few minutes?" Bronwyn whispered, throwing a look at Officer Petrie.

I turned to Hilda, Hector, and Lorel. "Be right back."

Bronwyn and I walked away from the Mermaid, Bronwyn pushing her bike, past the Tick Tock. Her face resumed its earnest look.

"What's up, Bron?"

"I'm on a break from work. Listen, I shouldn't be talking to you. At all." She exhaled. "But. I heard some of the detectives talking about your aunt."

I grabbed her arm. "What did they say? Oh, Bronwyn, I don't want you to get in any trouble, but what did they say?"

"Allie. It's absolutely ridiculous! They're all state police, not from around here. They don't know your aunt. Chief Brooks is totally in over his head. Detective Rosato, she's so, I don't know, awesome but also kind of . . ." Bronwyn groped for words. "Scary."

"Like a robot," I said. "Did you see Aunt Gully?"

Bronwyn shook her head. "No, she's been taken into an interrogation room. Well, the interrogation room. There's only one. Her lawyer's there."

I heaved a sigh. At least she wasn't alone.

"Well, it's crazy thinking Aunt Gully would hurt anyone. I mean, they must have other suspects." I remembered the letters and posters. "What about the lobster libbers?"

We turned onto the dock by the yacht club, away from the crowds on the sidewalk. From here I could see downriver to the dock and the rear of the Lazy Mermaid property. By this time of the day, it should be busy with customers sitting at picnic benches and lobster boats dropping off their catches. Now it was empty.

"Chief Brooks had me doing research on that," Bronwyn said. "The two signs, yours and the one at Kahuna's, were pretty much the exact same sign. But Kahuna's sign was covered with a big *X* of red paint."

"Why the red paint on Kahuna's sign and not the Mermaid's? Like maybe it was two different people who posted the signs?"

"Or two different messages," Bronwyn said. "The whole lobster libber thing isn't going anywhere. There're some Web sites for groups that do want to 'Save the Lobsters'"— she made air quotes—"but not a lot. Frankly, they just don't have the numbers or the appeal of Save the Whales or Dolphins or other cute animals."

Lobsters weren't referred to as "bugs" by a lot of lobstermen for nothing. "There's nothing cute or cuddly about lobsters," I said.

"And none of those Web sites are up to date." Bronwyn leaned on her bike. "Too bad your aunt doesn't have security cameras."

"She's too trusting." The wind picked up and tossed my hair around my face. "Kahuna's? Did they have cameras?"

"Nope."

A sleek ocean racer glided past. "You know what? There are a lot of boats down by the marina next to Kahuna's," I said. "Some customers were chatting about security cameras on their boats. Maybe they, or the marina, got some footage of the person who put up the sign."

"I'll check that, but still, I think the search for the lobster libbers is a dead end. Besides." Bronwyn threw a guilty glance up the street toward the Plex. "The lead investigators think it's some big conspiracy against YUM."

"Conspiracy? With lobster rolls? That's ridiculous." I shrugged. "But what do I know? I'm a dancer, not a detective."

Bronwyn smiled.

"Bron," I said, "the news reports said the poison was monkshood?"

"It was the root. Grated. It's very poisonous."

"Where do you get it?"

Bronwyn shrugged. "Someone grew it? Though you can get anything on the Internet. It's extremely toxic. Even just touching the leaves has paralyzed people and animals. It wasn't hard to figure out."

"Really?"

Bronwyn nodded. "It was sprinkled across the top of the lobster rolls."

"Wait a minute. We saw photos of the lobster rolls up on big screens at the contest," I said. "Believe me, Ernie and Megan would've said something if they saw their lobster roll with—stuff—sprinkled on it."

"The TV producers took the photos from the behind-the-scenes footage shot in the kitchen when the competitors plated their lobster rolls," Bronwyn said.

"Oh." Again, I saw Aunt Gully hurrying from the church, tying that blasted pink apron behind her, trying to catch up. Laughing. "So Robo Detective has my aunt admitting that she was the only one alone with the lobster rolls. After they were finished and photographed. Alone in the kitchen with them."

"A very small window of opportunity," Bronwyn said. I grabbed Bronwyn's arm. "Except that Aunt Gully saw someone else there, someone in a black T-shirt and a cap. And, and a volunteer's ID badge." I took a deep breath to calm myself. "Did they find Aunt Gully's fingerprints on the cloche?"

"Those big silver covers?" Bronwyn asked. "Megan Moss's prints, but not Ernie's. Lots of smudgy prints, probably from the volunteers who carried them. And your aunt could've worn gloves."

"She didn't have gloves," I said. "But she could have used her apron to lift the cloche."

"Yes."

"Where would she keep the monkshood? In her pocket?"

"That's why they searched the Mermaid and Gull's Nest. Looking for it."

I frowned. From the dock, I could see the rear wall of our lobster shed, hung with buoys, still colorful despite being weather-beaten and faded by the sun.

"They won't ever find it because she didn't have it."

"Just playing devil's advocate." Bronwyn waved at the piers. "She could've thrown it off the dock. Heck, you guys live a block from the ocean. Hard to find something that's tossed in the ocean."

"I know you're playing devil's advocate, Bron, but I want to go redhead on somebody."

"Make it Detective Rosato, not me, okay?"

A small white lobster boat chugged upriver. The *Sadie Mae*. It belonged to one of Aunt Gully's lobstermen chums. He was probably dropping off lobsters and had no idea about the drama taking place at the Lazy Mermaid.

Bronwyn clicked the strap on her helmet. "Listen, Allie, I'd better go."

"Thanks, Bron. I appreciate it."

Bronwyn pedaled up the street toward the Plex.

For a few moments I leaned against the railing of the dock, feeling the waves move the wooden structure under my feet in a gentle sway. It was all so plausible. Aunt Gully was the last one with the lobster rolls. She had opportunity.

But motive?

I looked up toward Pearl Street, jammed with tourists who'd come to Mystic Bay to try the best lobster rolls in America. Now both of Mystic Bay's lobster shacks were closed. I heard Ernie's bitter words: "My loss is your gain." If Kahuna's were closed—permanently—that would mean a lot of business for the Lazy Mermaid.

But how could those police detectives think for a moment that my gentle aunt could hurt another soul just to get business for her shack?

The groan of an engine and shouts made me turn. "No!" The *Sadie Mae*'s bow swung about and crashed into the Lazy Mermaid's dock.

Chapter 28

I ran as fast as I could back to the Mermaid. I pushed past tourists who stood outside the police tape, craning their heads and slurping ice cream as they watched the latest disaster unfold as if for their entertainment. Disgusted, I hurried to the dock, gasping as pain flashed through my ankle.

Hector, Hilda, Lorel, and Officer Petrie were already there. Lorel pulled a life ring off the side of the dock pilings and slung it toward the boat.

The *Sadie Mae* was half submerged, its bow just barely above water. Aunt Gully's friend Hugh O'Hare clung to the roof of his wheelhouse and caught the life ring with his right arm. He swung the ring over his head and pushed it down under his arms. It was a tight fit on his stocky torso. I heaved a sigh as it took his weight just as water surged around him and the boat slid backward.

Moments later, the *Sadie Mae* sank with a gurgling bubble of water. Lobster pots, line, and a red cooler bobbed to the surface. Hugh splashed toward the dock while Lorel, Hector, and I pulled the end of the line attached to the life ring.

The water off the dock wasn't very deep. The white

shimmer of *Sadie Mae* was visible as it settled to the bottom of the river, just beneath the surface. As we all leaned over the dock's edge, Hugh called out.

"Hit something!" He splashed in a circle. "I'm standing on it! Hell's bells! It's a freaking car!"

Chapter 29

I joined the crowd craning to see over the edge of the dock. The Micasset was usually about eight to ten feet deep here. Some days, depending on the tides and weather, the water could be cloudy, but today it was clear. I looked down onto the top of a black car. My heart pounded. The car that boxed me in last night was black.

"Ernie Moss's car," I gasped.

Several people screamed and shouted for help. "What if someone's down there!"

Officer Petrie spoke into his shoulder mic.

Lorel tightened her grip on my arm. "What if it was Ernie in the Mermaid?"

An even worse thought made me clutch my chest. "What if it wasn't? What if Ernie's down there?" I whispered.

"I'll check." Bit Markey had been standing at my shoulder but I hadn't noticed him. He slipped through the crowd of bystanders.

I hurried after him. "No, Bit!"

Bit dove off the dock.

"Don't you go, too." Lorel pulled me back as Bit surfaced.

"Bit Markey, you get back here," Officer Petrie bellowed. Bit's answer was a wave. Nervous laughter rippled through the crowd.

Bit was a good swimmer. But as I watched his dark head and skinny arms circle the boat and then the car, I slipped off my flip-flop and bent to loosen the fastenings on my boot. If he showed the slightest distress, I wouldn't let anyone stop me from helping him.

Bit dove. The crowd on the dock inhaled and bent forward as one, watching the dark head disappear under the water. Bit splashed back to the surface, then dove again. Officer Petrie grumbled and shouldered through the crowd, holding the life ring we'd just used to haul up Hugh O'Hare.

Bit surfaced, shook his hair out of his eyes, and stroked smoothly to the ladder. He clambered up in seconds. Some people applauded. Something colorful trailed from his hand, a strand of plastic flowers.

"No bodies," he said. "It's kinda dark, but I didn't see anybody in there."

"In there? Did you go in the car?" Lorel gasped.

"Yeah, the windows were open." He held up the strand of flowers. Officer Petrie took it from Bit's hands. Lorel and I exchanged glances. It was the lei Ernie'd worn at the lobster roll competition. His badge still hung from it.

"It was on the rearview mirror," Bit explained.

"Bit, you gave me a heart attack." I hugged him tight, not minding his sopping-wet clothes. "You nut."

Bit grinned and blushed.

"Come with me, Bit," Officer Petrie said. "Gonna get you warmed up."

Bit cut through the crowd, followed by a wave of murmured "attaboy"s, back slaps, and a smattering of applause.

I bent to retighten the fastenings on my boot.

"What on earth is Ernie Moss's car doing there?" Lorel whispered.

"Was it Ernie Moss in the Mermaid?" I said.

After the discovery of the submerged car, the police cleared everyone from the Lazy Mermaid parking lot except for Hugh and Bit. These two actors in the most recent Lazy Mermaid disaster sat in the Adirondack chairs as EMS evaluated them. Bit was wrapped in a blanket simultaneously enjoying a hot chocolate and ice-cream cone from the Tick Tock. Hugh sipped from a flask passed to him over the police tape by a friend.

Hector, Hilda, Lorel, and I canceled deliveries from our bakery, distributors, and lobster providers. The police declared our dock off-limits to lobster drop-offs until the boat and the car were removed. "Perhaps two days," Officer Petrie told us.

"How on earth did that car get down there? How could somebody drive off this dock? There's hardly room," Lorel said.

Officer Petrie considered our dock. "That sports car's little. Almost a toy. Ernie looked funny in it sometimes, you know, almost like one of those clown cars."

"You'd have to have nerves of steel. It's so narrow." I shook my head. "Or maybe somebody pushed it?"

Lorel and I hurried up to the Plex, but as Officer Petrie said, we weren't allowed to see Aunt Gully. My stomach churned thinking of her in a cell, picturing her handcuffed to a wall. I hated the thought of her being alone.

"Let's wait outside," I said.

Bronwyn walked with us. "Aunt Gully's okay. I was just talking to her. The minute I hear anything new, I'll let you know."

She ran back inside. Lorel and I sat at a splintery picnic table. As usual, Lorel lost herself in work, scrolling on her phone. I texted Verity to let her know where I was, then I paced on the sparse grass.

The Tank roared up to the curb. Verity slammed the door and hurried over to us.

"It's time for the funeral. I got someone to watch the shop."

"Verity, you won't believe what's been happening—" I began.

"Fill me in on the way. We've got fifteen minutes to get to the Ancient Burying Ground."

"The funeral!" I looked down at my clothes. Not only was I not dressed for a funeral, my T-shirt and jeans were damp from hugging Bit Markey.

"Don't worry, I've got just the thing," Verity said. "Nobody's going to notice you."

Perhaps no one would notice me because I was with Verity, her highlighted dreads pulled into a demure low bun. She wore a black sheath dress that hugged her dramatic curves. A black pillbox hat with a half veil covered her forehead and eyes. A pearl choker completed her look. She looked dangerous, like a sexy black widow who'd just murdered her millionaire husband.

Lorel frowned and folded her arms.

I hesitated. "I don't know. I might get to see Aunt Gully."

"Really. Playing dress-up at the funeral of the woman Aunt Gully's accused of murdering? Yeah, doesn't strike me as a good idea." Lorel's voice dripped with disdain. "Seriously, Allie."

"How's Aunt Gully?" Verity said.

"They won't let us talk to her, but Bron said she's okay," I said.

"Look, you might as well come with me. You can't do anything here. You don't have time to go home and change. I brought you a dress and shoes. Well, a shoe since you've got your boot thingy." Verity angled her body between Lorel and me. "Come on. This is the funeral of the century."

On any other day, I would be curious about this movie star's funeral. But a bigger part of me felt that I couldn't sit still and wait, that I had to get to work to discover something that could clear Aunt Gully.

"I'm going," I said. Lorel scowled. "I know it's crazy, Lorel. But maybe if I talk to people, I'll be able to help Aunt Gully. I've got to find out who's really responsible so the police'll let Aunt Gully go. On cop shows the police always watch funerals "

Verity nodded vigorously. "The murderer always shows up to celebrate."

Lorel threw up her hands. "Go play detective," she fumed. "I'll be the grown-up and handle things."

Verity and I hurried to the car.

"Have no fear," Verity said. "Believe me, with the outfit I got you, you'll blend right in."

Chapter 30

Blend in to what, Verity hadn't said. Maybe the same black widow's support group she was dressed for. On the way over to the Ancient Burying Ground, I told her everything that had happened as I shimmied out of my clothes and into the black silk shirtdress Verity had chosen for me.

Verity almost swerved off the road several times as I described last night's and today's events.

"At least Ernie wasn't in the sunken car," she said. "Why would he drive his own car off the dock?"

"Maybe he didn't. Why would he? Maybe Chick did it?" I couldn't believe Chick's story about his midnight jog. "It must be Ernie that they found in the lobster shed. But why drive his car into the water?"

"Yeah, that's weird."

My mind whirled with ideas. "So people wouldn't be able to find him? At least until we opened the Mermaid," I said slowly. "Or someone just wanted to be mean because Ernie loved his car?"

"Well, actually, I love my car." Verity patted her steering wheel. "It would kill me if someone drove the Tank off a dock."

"What about my hair?" My red hair made me stand out in a crowd.

"Behind you," Verity said.

On the rear seat was a black straw hat with a broad brim.

I put it on. Sheer black organza and black roses encircled the brim, which bent with a flirty dip. I frowned. I looked like I was going to a goth garden party.

"What? It was all I had in the shop!" Without taking her eyes from the road, Verity fished in her handbag and handed me some black sunglasses. "The sunglasses'll help."

I slid them on. "Maybe Lorel's right. This is a monumentally bad idea."

"We're going to find suspects and clear Aunt Gully," Verity said. "And then buy the rest of Contessa's designer clothes and jewelry tomorrow."

The Mystic Bay Savings and Loan clock flashed 2:55 as the Tank lumbered through town. We passed Christ Church, a classic white clapboard building set high on a hill. "I thought that was the Wells's family church?"

"The service is graveside." Verity swung the Tank onto narrow Cemetery Lane by the burying ground. Riding in the vintage DeSoto was more like riding in a boat than a car.

We cruised past row after row of cars double-parked along the burying ground's crumbling, low stone wall.

I winced as Verity rolled the Tank onto someone's lawn. I slid on the black silk Louis heel Verity had brought for me. It was tight, but better than wearing the flip-flop I'd worn earlier.

I angled the broad brim of my hat to shield my face as we passed a group of reporters. Leo Rodriguez, as usual, was at the center of things. Verity trailed me as I scurried between lichen-covered headstones to the far side of the cemetery.

Here among the oldest residents of the burying ground, we had a good view of the white marquee where Juliet would sit with other mourners, which was where the news cameras were trained. The ground was slightly higher here, a perfect spot for us to watch the crowd. I wasn't sure what I was looking for, but I intended to watch for anything suspicious, anything that could help clear Aunt Gully's name.

A black hearse parked at the entrance of the cemetery, followed by a limousine.

With practiced, economical movements, two men in somber black opened the back of the hearse. Sprays of white mums, roses, and lilies burst forth as they slid Contessa's coffin out of the hearse.

At the same time, a tall man with a thick silver mane of hair emerged from the back of the limousine—Mac Macallan, the director of Broadway by the Bay. Tall, with regal carriage, Mac exuded old-fashioned, masculine grace as he helped Juliet Wells from the vehicle.

Mac bent toward her, nodding sympathetically. Either he was sincere or he was indeed a very good actor. Juliet stepped forward, adjusting the veil on her own black hat as she scanned the crowd.

The burying ground was full of people, those closer to the grave dressed in black. Farther out from the white tent, the clothing and atmosphere got more colorful and relaxed, more festive. Several people in shorts and T-shirts filmed with their cell phones.

Juliet's face lit up when she saw Verity and me. She made a beckoning gesture.

"Oh, God, what do we do?" Verity whispered out of the side of her mouth.

People in the crowd turned to see what was going on.

"Too late to hide behind a headstone," I said. We picked our way through the headstones to Juliet.

"My friends." Juliet took our hands in hers. The tear holder thingy she'd shown us before swung from a chain around her neck.

"These people don't know how to dress." She waved dismissively toward the crowd. "Nobody has a sense of drama anymore. Death is the ultimate drama. It deserves respect."

Verity and I looked at each other then back at Juliet.

"My condolences," I stammered.

"So sorry for your loss," Verity said. She curtsied.

I almost laughed, but there was something so over the top about Juliet that I understood why Verity did it.

Juliet smiled. "You're some of the only people in this whole town that I've ever spoken to. Except for Susan and Mac and the good father here." She turned to the Reverend Priddy, the rector of Christ Church. He looked like a man preparing to defuse a bomb.

Susan emerged from the limousine, dressed in a black sweatshirt, wrinkled black pants, and black sneakers for the occasion. When she saw us she rolled her eyes.

"Oh, Susan, my flowers," Juliet said.

Susan reached into the limo. Verity and I exchanged a look at the strange bouquet: orange lilies and yellowish-green palm branches tied with an elaborate black bow.

"Carry them for me, please, Susan."

"Victory. Hatred," Verity muttered under her breath.

"What?" I whispered, but Verity had turned away.

Juliet whispered to me. "Well, the show must go on." She took Mac's arm, pressed a handkerchief to her dry eyes, and stepped into the entrance to the burying ground. She waited for every eye to turn to her. The crowd quieted. A small combo started playing.

We followed, stepping slowly and carefully over the uneven ground.

Juliet wore a black shirtdress with a very full skirt and her hat was practically a carbon copy of my own. Television cameras swung to us. *Please, earth, just swallow me now.* Susan walked just behind Juliet, carrying the bizarre bouquet.

There were three open seats in the front row, reserved for Juliet, Mac, and the ever-present and unhappy Susan. My eyes flicked along the melancholy faces under the tent.

Who looked guilty?

Mayor Packer and his wife, Bliss, sat in the front row. The mayor's face looked thinner and with a shock I noted a cane tucked next to his leg. Bliss Packer sat ramrod straight, martyrdom etched on her lovely, bored face.

A row behind, Finella Farraday leaned forward to whisper into Bliss's ear.

Chick Costa, a navy blazer over his yellow polo shirt, sat two rows behind the Packers. I pulled my hat brim farther over my face. Another person I didn't want to see. His head was bowed, but I was pretty sure he was just checking messages on his phone.

Verity and I headed to the back row. Rio Lopez sat in the aisle in a wheelchair. My breath caught. Rio's body curled into one side of the seat as if she didn't have the strength to sit upright. She looked so fragile and weak. The poison must've taken a terrible toll on her. Rick's arm draped protectively over the back of Rio's chair and two stocky men stood behind her. Bodyguards or nurses? Rick stood and gestured to empty seats in the row.

Rio smiled as we edged in. One seat had a sign that read RESERVED FOR GINA FONTANA. I blinked. Hardly anyone used Aunt Gully's given name. The other two chairs were reserved for Megan and Ernie Moss, more confirmation that the man found at the Mermaid was Ernie. Verity and I sat next to Rick, picking up the programs on the seats of the chairs. Two other empty seats were reserved for CHARLES COSTA and PAUL POND. Chick had decided to get a better seat, Paul had probably gone back to Maine as he'd said. I scanned the mourners but didn't see his distinctive white hair.

"How are you?" I whispered to Rick.

"Survived," he said. "Hell of a thing. We're lucky to be here."

"Lucky to be anywhere," Rio leaned over. "You're Mrs. Fontana's niece, right? Allegra?"

"Yes, but call me Allie. This is my friend Verity Brooks." Verity lurched across me to shake hands.

The small group of musicians played the final notes of the processional.

"Don't leave without talking with us, okay?" Rick whispered.

People fanned themselves with their programs in the warm spring air. A sudden hush fell, punctuated by birdsong and a few coughs.

The reverend began with the words of the Book of Common Prayer, the old-fashioned cadence poetic. I tried to resist, but I couldn't help checking my phone for news of Aunt Gully. There were no messages. I let the soothing words of the service wash over me.

"Ashes to ashes, dust to dust." Reverend Priddy spoke into a hushed silence, then beckoned Juliet to join him She approached the open grave, carrying the strange bouquet. Mac followed a discreet distance behind her. She circled the grave so she faced the seated mourners under the marquee, playing to the VIP audience.

The spiky palm branches she carried jarred against the mound of soft, feminine white and pastel-hued flowers. Something metal on the black bow of the bouquet caught the sunlight. Checking behind me to make sure I wasn't blocking anyone's view, I stood to see better. Juliet was no longer wearing the lachrymatory.

The Reverend indicated a small pile of dirt. Juliet took a handful and scattered it into the grave. Then she kissed the bouquet and also let it fall into the grave. A smile curved her red lips, then she turned to Mac and leaned heavily on his arm, her black handkerchief pressed to her mouth. The audience/mourners stirred but Mac wrapped an arm around her waist and escorted Juliet back to her seat without incident.

Verity tugged my arm.

I hadn't realized I was still standing. I sank into my seat. "Remember that thing Juliet wore around her neck? The tear thingie?" I whispered.

"Lachrymatory? Yeah?"

"She tossed it into the grave with the flowers."

Verity shrugged. "A symbol? Maybe she's tossing away her tears."

A Broadway by the Bay singer took the microphone and delivered a stunning version of "Memory" from *Cats*. Sniffles turned to loud weeping as the singer gave the song the full Broadway treatment. Some people on the outskirts of the funeral applauded as the singer held the song's final note.

Mac announced a reception at Broadway by the Bay, and everyone processed out, accompanied by the combo playing "My Heart Will Go On." Juliet led the black-garbed flood of mourners through the gates of the Ancient Burying Ground.

"Want to go to the reception?" Verity said. "Check for guilty people?"

"Yes, but it depends on how things are with Aunt Gully," I whispered. "I'll check in with Lorel but first let's talk with Rio and Rick. Maybe they saw something at the food fest."

I leaned toward Rio. "How are you feeling?"

"Funerals," she said. "They take it out of me." Rio looked even paler than before, her skin pulled taut over her high cheekbones.

Rick stood slowly, unfolding his lanky frame from his seat, leaning heavily on the handles of Rio's wheelchair.

"Let's head back to the van," Rick said. "You guys want to walk along?"

"Sure."

One of the security guards undid the brakes on the wheelchair.

Rick pushed the wheelchair while the two men flanked us. Verity and I looked at each other as they hemmed us in. With a pang I realized that Rick was using Rio's wheelchair for support. Sweat stained his blue button-down shirt in the soft May air. Rick breathed heavily as he pushed Rio over the bumpy, uneven ground.

"Are you going to the reception?" I asked.

"No, the doctors told us they'd let us out for just a little while." Rio craned her neck to look back at us, her long black bangs falling into her eyes. She brushed them aside. "I have to say, you guys know how to dress for a funeral."

We pulled up to a black van with LIFT ASSIST stenciled across the back.

"Yeah, you're rocking the mourning thing. Oops, sorry," Rick said to Rio's look. "I always say the wrong thing. That's what I get for having a big mouth."

"It's okay." I smiled. "We are a bit over the top. Verity owns a vintage store and had to loan me something. I don't have any black dresses."

"I love vintage," Rio said. "I'll have to stop by your place, Verity."

Verity grinned. "That would be great. So, you're feeling better?"

Rio took a breath. "Yeah. You know, I just wanted to say how sorry I am about the whole thing. I don't mean what happened to us, or Contessa or the mayor. Yeah, that's all awful. I mean how your aunt got frozen out by YUM. We heard about the meeting with Stan Wilder."

"I appreciate that." I looked at Verity, mentally willing her not to say anything about Aunt Gully. I didn't want to talk about her being questioned by police. "YUM's a feel-good network, right? That's what Stan said. There's nothing feel-good about people getting poisoned."

"It's the weirdest thing," Rio said. "Who'd want to poison four judges? I mean, we're all so different."

I jumped in. "The day of the lobster roll competition, did you notice anything strange?"

Rick shrugged. "We've done a lot of contests. This one ran like a top. Top-notch. It's funny. I saw you that day. Your red hair stands out. You ran to the church door before your aunt came out."

My stomach dropped. Great. He'd noticed the one thing that would tie me to the poisoning, that I now realized I hadn't mentioned to Chief Brooks or Robo Detective.

"I remember you looked uncertain when you ate Kahuna's roll," I said.

Rio nodded. "The Godlobster looked great. But the stuff, monkshood? Bitter. Ugh. But we eat a lot of unusual foods, so we plowed ahead."

"Who'd do such a thing? I still can't believe it," Verity said.

"Someone who wasn't a fan, right, Rio?" Rio shook her head as Rick chuckled. "We've heard the theories. Maybe a psycho fan?"

That was one I hadn't heard.

"I've only been in Mystic Bay twice," Rick said. "Once the first time on our real estate scoping trip, when we went to the Mermaid, and then we came back for the judging. Before that, Rio hadn't been here since, what? You were a kid working at some place called Scoops by the Bay."

"Scoops by the Sea," Rio said. "Maybe it didn't have anything to do with us. Someone was making a point. Against the network. Or the town."

"The police were looking into the lobster liberation movement," I said.

Rick laughed. "Some crank who wants to save the lobsters does not a movement make."

"Some people were upset about Ernie's plan to widen Pearl Street so more tourists could get through town to Kahuna's," I said.

"That would help you, too," Rick pointed out, as if reading my mind. "But poisoning a bunch of lobster rolls on TV in order to stop traffic? That's really crazy."

"Though it worked," I said. "Kahuna's is closed. The Lazy Mermaid's closed."

"Well, that's because of the body. And the car in the water. And the sunken boat," Verity said.

I groaned.

"A body at the Lazy Mermaid!" Rick and Rio glanced at each other.

"Not a body, an injured man," I said, but Verity was on a roll.

"And Ernie Moss's car was driven off a dock and we think he's the one attacked at the Lazy Mermaid. And now they're blaming Aunt Gully for the poisonings."

Rio's mouth made a red-painted O.

I threw a look at Verity. "The police are questioning Aunt Gully."

"That's terrible!" Rio gripped the handles of her chair so tightly her knuckles were white. "Is Aunt Gully okay?"

"They have her locked up at the police station," Verity said.

"No way! She wouldn't hurt a soul. That's it." Rio straightened her back. "We're going to the police station, Rick."

"That's really sweet—" I began.

"I've had bad stuff happen in my life. You have to face the bad stuff. And fight." Her bony hands balled into fists. "Your aunt." Rio coughed, then took a deep shuddering breath. "She's one person I owe a lot to."

"Small but mighty. That's my Rio." Rick kissed Rio's hand.

Rio's ashen skin and dark under-eye circles alarmed me.

"Um, shouldn't you be getting back to the hospital?" Verity asked.

Rick shook his head. "Things were getting too crazy at the hospital. Come see us at the inn later. The doctors are letting us recuperate in a suite there with private nurses."

"After we visit the police station," Rio said.

"Aye, aye, captain." Rick saluted, then signaled one of the security guards. He opened the back door of the van and lowered the lift. Rick kissed Rio's cheek as the man made sure Rio's chair was secure. As the lift raised Rio and the wheelchair, Rick said, "And away we go!"

Rio laughed, but my heart twisted. Poor Rio was in a wheelchair. It was torture for me to not be able to dance. To not be able to walk . . .

As the other man helped settle Rio in the van, Rick leaned tiredly against the door frame. "The doctors say that she'll eventually regain her strength. But the"—he twisted his lips—"poison, God, I can barely say it! It hit her hard, because she's just skin and bones to begin with."

"Just like it hit Contessa hard."

Rick nodded. "We'd better go. Do you need us to drop you anywhere?"

"No, thanks." We started walking back to the Tank. My phone buzzed.

"Hi, Lorel."

"Allie." Lorel's strained voice made me stop. "The police are looking for you."

My stomach dropped. "What did you tell them?"

"The truth, Allie!" Lorel snapped. "That you're with Verity. That you were going to the funeral. Bronwyn told me they've been questioning volunteers from the food fest and somebody mentioned you running into the church to find Aunt Gully. And it doesn't look good because we kind of forgot to mention that when the police were at Gull's Nest."

"So much was happening, I just forgot. Because I didn't do anything!"

Lorel sighed. "Honestly, I forgot, too."

A Mystic Bay Police SUV threaded its way through the mourners streaming down Cemetery Lane from the Ancient Burying Ground. I couldn't get pulled into the police station now. I had to find out who poisoned the rolls and clear Aunt Gully.

"I'll call you back." I pulled Verity back toward Rick and Rio's van.

"Verity, we have to ditch the Tank. Rick! Can we still take you up on that ride?"

Chapter 31

Verity and I climbed into seats in the center of the van. She stifled a scream and fanned herself as I explained the situation.

"Why didn't you mention to my uncle and that robot detective that you went into the church to find Aunt Gully?" she whispered.

"I totally forgot about it!" I glanced at Rick and Rio, who talked quietly behind us. "I was in the church building for maybe one minute."

Verity shook her head. "Now you look guilty. Even Rick noticed you going into the building."

"Thanks a lot, Verity." Then another thought struck me. "What if they want to talk to me about something else? What if it's about Ernie Moss?"

"What would you have to do with Ernie Moss?" Verity's eyes widened. "Maybe they want to know about that business with Megan and Chick at Edwards Inlet."

"I may be the only one who knows about that. And besides, all I care about is proving Aunt Gully innocent. The police are totally barking up the wrong tree thinking she's guilty. I'm going to talk to all the judges and all the contestants. I can't waste time sitting in jail."

Five minutes later, the van dropped us at the Jake. We said goodbye to Rick and Rio and scanned for police cars. None, not yet. We joined the mob of mourners jammed into the Jake's ballroom overlooking the bay and huddled behind a pillar near the bar.

"Verity, what did you mean back there in the cemetery? You said something weird when you saw Juliet's ugly bouquet."

Verity shuddered. "That bouquet. Remember when I took that adult ed class on the Victorian language of flowers? How every flower meant something back then? In the Victorian language of flowers, that bouquet sent a message."

I took two glasses of wine from a server's tray and handed one to Verity, then snagged several mini crab cakes from another. Avoiding the cops was making me hungry.

"Orange lilies symbolize hatred. Palm branches mean victory," she said. "It was like Juliet was carrying a sign saying I HATE YOU, CONTESSA. I WON.

"Well, people don't call Juliet the Crazy Lady for nothing." I scanned the room. With the police on my tail, I'd have to ask questions fast. Detective Rosato could march in and slap handcuffs on me at any second.

Mac Macallen tapped a microphone on a small dais. Behind him was a black-and-white glamour shot from one of Contessa's films. Her face beamed over the crowd, her eyes shining with life force, intensity, and charisma. She commanded attention.

"What movie was that from?" I whispered.

"The Princess of Wall Street," Verity breathed.

Chatter died down as Mac spoke. "Sadly, Juliet Wells was"—he hesitated—"overcome with emotion, understandably, so she's unable to be with us this afternoon. I know we all were devastated—are devastated—by the sudden loss of one of our own, an artist of the highest caliber and standards."

"His way of saying 'don't cross her,'" one actress near me whispered.

"A woman committed to her craft, her art," Mac continued.

"She got me fired from *Company*," another actor muttered.

"Let's raise a toast to Contessa Wells. Her artistic legacy will shine on, kept alive in the hearts of her fans." Mac raised his glass. "To Contessa!"

"Contessa!"

"Boy, when I kick the bucket, I want Mac to memorialize me. He made Contessa sound like a tap-dancing Mother Teresa." I peeked around the pillar. "Okay. Operation Free Aunt Gully commences. I've got to talk to everyone who was at the lobster roll competition."

"Who's first?" Verity asked.

I jutted my chin toward the deck where Mayor Packer was holding forth.

"He looks better than Rick. Definitely better than Rio," Verity whispered.

"Remember what Rick said. Size mattered. The big guys could withstand the poison better." Still, Mayor Packer'd been affected. His tie didn't look like it was choking him. I'd seen him at events before. He'd tell the servers to make their way back to him on a regular cycle. Now he held a glass of what looked like tonic water and leaned on a cane.

"You go ahead," Verity said. "I'll watch for the cops. And find more of those crab cakes."

I sidled up to the group with the mayor and forced myself to nod as they talked about building codes and tax rates. Just as I was wondering how I'd get a word in, the mayor jovially waved off the crowd and took my arm.

"Allie, how's your aunt coping with that business about the man in the shed?"

He led me to a table in a quiet corner of the patio.

"You've heard?" I said.

The mayor held up his phone. "Gotta stay plugged in with this job."

I decided to say it. "Ernie."

The mayor nodded. "Yes, it was Ernie Moss. Looks like he was in a fight, then hit his head on the edge of the tank. Lost a lot of blood. Touch and go." He propped his cane against the wall and sat heavily in a chair. I sank into the seat next to him. *It was Ernie.*

"This darn monkshood makes you weak. It paralyzes the muscles." Mayor Packer gestured toward his wife, who sat at the bar. "Bliss says it was a good weight-loss tool for me, but let me tell you, getting poisoned's a hell of a way to lose weight."

"Did you know that Aunt Gully was taken in for questioning about Contessa's death?" I said.

Mayor Packer blinked. "Now that I didn't know. That's ridiculous. Those state police, Allie, they don't know the folks here. I'll give the police chief a call."

"Thank you, Mayor." I took a breath. "Do you have any idea who's responsible for the poisoning?"

Mayor Packer looked over the bay. "Well, I had plenty of time to think in that hospital bed. But all I have are questions. Hard to believe anybody could do such terrible things. But people do bad things all the time, for their own reasons.

"Who would benefit if one of us died? Rick? Rio? They're big stars. Maybe somebody had a beef? Jealousy? You know Rick and Rio are trying to get approval for a spa. I think it's a great idea. Some folks were lobbying Rio to build it in Green Haven instead of here in Mystic Bay."

He shrugged. "Contessa? Did her sister benefit by losing her financial and emotional support? Or was there jealousy from another star? Did someone want her role in *Mame*?"

He took a sip of his tonic. "Who'd benefit if the YUM Network show didn't air? Who'd benefit if YUM looked bad? Who'd benefit if lobster shacks closed? A conspiracy. I heard there were some of those 'save the lobster' signs on the Mermaid and Kahuna's?"

"And Aunt Gully got threatening letters from lobster libbers," I said.

"You see?"

It seemed so long ago that we got the letters and I found that sign. I thought it was ridiculous. But it was the beginning of this whole terrible mess.

"All I know is"—he raised his glass—"I'm glad to be alive."

"Thanks, Mayor." As I crossed the gleaming wooden floor, I remembered one thing he hadn't mentioned: Ernie Moss trying to change his mind about the new traffic pattern for Pearl Street.

I also hadn't thought that anyone could be trying to kill Contessa. I sidled up to Mac Macallen.

"Allegra Larkin!" He kissed my cheeks. "My favorite dancer. How's the ankle?"

"Getting better."

"I'd love to bring more dance companies here to the Jake. I'm hoping your company will come next season."

"I'd love that!"

"It's so great to see you. Even under such unfortunate circumstances." Mac grimaced. "Just a short time from opening night on *Mame*. Good thing our understudy's fantastic. Kate Kimmel." He nodded toward an elegant blonde in a navy blue sheath dress, surrounded by several Broadway by the Bay actors. "Kate's been in California for a week dealing with family stuff. Her mom had a stroke. She just got back last night."

That meant she wasn't here for the lobster roll contest and couldn't be responsible for the poisoning.

"Even though she's a less well-known name, with all the publicity from the, er, tragic events, we're sold out," Mac said. "We might even have to add shows."

"Did other actresses try out for the part?" I asked.

"No. We wanted Contessa. She'd reached out to me a couple of years ago. Said she wanted to spend some time at the old family home. Said it would be good for her sister. Her sister needs a lot of care. Contessa was a good sister to Juliet. God knows it couldn't have been easy."

Bliss Packer leaned against the bar. The bartender slowly poured bourbon into her glass. She rattled her ice cubes. "Oh, for heaven's sake, just top it up," she said.

"Hi, Mrs. Packer."

"Oh, hi, Lorelei, right?"

"Allie."

"That's right, the dancer. Call me Bliss. 'Mrs. Packer' makes me feel like my mother-in-law." She grimaced and took a sip.

"How's the, er, mayor doing?"

Bliss Packer waved her glass toward the patio where the mayor was again surrounded by a group. "He always bounces back. Not that it was easy. I wouldn't say it was touch and go. But this stuff, monkshood? Sounds like something out of one of Contessa's horror movies, doesn't it?" She drank. "I just hope they get the bastard who did it."

I guess she didn't know about the police questioning

Aunt Gully. "Me, too. Um, do you have any ideas about who might've done it?"

"What do I look like, Miss Marple?" She finished her drink in one gulp and again shook the ice cubes in the now empty glass at the bartender. He refilled her glass.

"But I have my ideas." She scanned the crowd, her lips pressed together.

"I heard Ernie Moss—"

Bliss Packer wheeled toward me. "What've you heard?"

I stepped back, but I guess she didn't expect me to say anything. "Ernie Moss thinks he's some kind of great businessman. He owns a smelly lobster shack, for God's sake."

My back stiffened. Bliss must be too drunk to remember that my family owned a lobster shack, too.

"Ernie thinks that makes him a person of importance." Heads turned as her voice rose. "Like he can give orders to my husband, the mayor. I have no doubt that he's behind this business. Oh, his wife can boo-hoo and fall to pieces about her Ernie's lobster roll having poison in it. Well, Ernie would've danced a hula if my husband died instead of Contessa Wells. Oh, he had a motive, all right. Ernie's been trying to influence the board of selectmen to vote his way. My husband stands between him and his blessed highway to Kahuna's."

"But doesn't it make him look bad?" I said. "To have his lobster roll poison those people?"

Bliss swayed toward me. "Oh, come on. It's brilliant. Who'd believe he'd poison his own lobster roll? He could reopen under another name. You're his alibi, right?" She smirked. "You played right into his hands."

She took another drink. "Genius. Nobody was watching him every minute. Nobody." Bliss sneered. "He could've paid somebody. Some volunteer, right? There were plenty of them all over the place in their little black T-shirts. Security was a joke. And Ernie has plenty of money to pay somebody off. That tacky Kahuna's Kove's one of the most expensive houses on Fox Point."

Paying someone to poison the lobster rolls? "But—"

Bliss cut me off. She waved her glass at the bartender. "Genius."

Bliss slinked toward the bathroom. The bartender offered to refill my wine glass but I waved him off.

Did Ernie pay someone to poison the rolls? Could someone else have done the same? Chick? Paul Pond? The lobster libbers?

Paul seemed so decent. I couldn't imagine a scenario where he'd hurt someone to further his own business. Chick, on the other hand. I scanned the room, but didn't see him. Maybe he went back to Chatham.

Could it have been as easy as paying one of the volunteers to poison the rolls?

Maybe someone who got a bad review from Rick and Rio?

A disgruntled actor who had a beef with Contessa?

I kept coming back to that night at Edwards Point. The sound of Megan weeping. The way Chick held her wrists, her body dangling limp, like a puppet. Could he have forced her to poison the rolls? Chick had something on Megan. But what? I had to find out.

Verity materialized at my side and handed me a plate of hors d'oeuvres.

"If Juliet used the money I paid to fund this shindig, I say it's money well spent. Look at these mini spring rolls."

"Verity, we have to go to the hospital."

"What! Do you feel okay?"

I shook my head. "I have to talk to Megan Moss."

Chapter 32

"The Mayor confirmed my suspicions. Ernie was the guy they found in the lobster shed," I said as Verity and I cut through the crowd. "I'm sure Megan will be by his side at the hospital."

"Did you find out anything to help Aunt Gully?" Verity asked.

I remembered what the mayor had said. "All I have is questions. Let's find a ride." We hurried out the front door.

"We could call Lorel," Verity said.

"She'd just drive me directly to the police station. I need to ask more questions first."

A Mystic Bay cruiser pulled into the parking lot. "Oh, great. Duck."

We scurried around the building as the cruiser pulled up to the front doors. Bliss Packer slinked out, talking on her cell. The officer called to her and she went over to the car.

"I was just talking to Bliss." I groaned.

Bliss waved the officer off with a shrug. He parked and headed toward the doors.

"Now what?" Verity asked.

"Let's cut through the administration building. There's an exit through the dance studio to Gruber Farm Lane."

We scurried across the parking lot. Nobody was at the reception desk of the administration building. The underpaid staff would be taking advantage of the free buffet and open bar at the reception.

Since the administration building also housed the dance studio, I'd been here many times. We cut through the dance studio to a parking lot that flowed into a narrow lane shaded by dogwood trees and bordered on one side by a picture-perfect stone wall.

"Now what?" Verity said.

"Let's just get as far away as we can."

We hurried down the lane. Hurrying was no problem for me, although I cursed my boot as it slowed me down. Verity huffed next to me, sweat beading her forehead. She stopped to kick off her pumps. Though she'd earned a black belt in karate as a teen, now Verity's idea of exercise was shopping.

"Just call Lorel." Verity fanned herself with her clutch purse.

"You know what a rule follower she is. She'll take me right to the police herself."

"Maybe not this time." Verity dialed. I grabbed her hand.

"No! I'll call Hilda." Hilda was a perfectly law-abiding woman, but she would understand that I was avoiding the police so I could help Aunt Gully.

"Look!" The police car slid through the parking lot behind us. "Quick!" I tugged Verity's hand and jumped up on the wall. Well, I jumped up. Verity climbed to her knees, then clambered up and knocked us both over.

* * *

"Ugh!" I pushed myself up to a sitting position, brushing dirt from my dress. I took stock. Nothing broken or twisted. Luckily I'd avoided landing on my injured ankle.

"Ouch." Verity sprawled facedown in patchy grass.

We scooted to our knees by the wall and watched the police car cruise past.

"That was close," I said.

"I'll say." Verity jutted her chin at a mushy brown pile. "That's a cow pie."

We squealed as we checked ourselves for contact with it.

"I cannot believe this." Verity brushed at her skirt and straightened her hat. "I wish we were back in that nice, clean, cow-free building eating that nice food."

"And drinking nice wine." I fanned myself with my hat. "Come on, Verity. Courage."

"Courage, my Aunt Fanny. Let's get Hilda over here pronto."

Ten minutes later, Hilda's green VW Bug pulled into the lane and we hopped in.

"Hilda, you're a lifesaver." I tucked my full skirt around my legs and closed the door.

"Bless you," Verity said. She pulled a leaf from the netting of her half-veil.

"Now, I don't know where you girls want to go"—Hilda glanced in the rearview mirror—"but there's a police car at the Mermaid."

"And probably one at Gull's Nest," I said.

Hilda's VW sputtered as it took the curves of a hill past a vista of fields and stone walls.

"Hey look, we're going by the Happy Farmer," Verity said. "Hilda, would you please pull in? I'm parched."

"Yes, please, turn right here, Hilda. We need to regroup." I figured nobody at the Happy Farmer would know or care that the police were looking for me.

In addition to fruits and vegetables, the Happy Farmer sold honey and candles from their bees, butter and milk from their cows, and organic treats from their bakery. They also bottled their own spring water. Verity hurried in.

The Happy Farmers worked their image pretty hard. All the men wore long beards and man buns. The women wore their hair in braids, often looped on their heads. This patch of land had long been an outpost of the counterculture. Over the years, whatever the culture was, the Happy Farmers were counter to it.

I turned to Hilda. "So what's happening?"

Hilda brushed a smudge of dirt from my cheek then threw up her hands. "What isn't happening? First your aunt's taken by the police. And now they want you!"

Hilda's big brown eyes filled with tears. I squeezed her hand.

"And it's just awful to think someone was injured in our building like that," Hilda said.

"Officially, it's Ernie Moss," I said. "I talked to the mayor."

"What was he doing in our lobster shed?" Hilda exclaimed. "Do the police think you had something to do with that?"

I shook my head. "No, I think it's about the mess at the food festival."

Hilda eyed my dress. "So I'm guessing you went to the funeral."

"I thought maybe I could find out something that would help Aunt Gully."

"She's innocent." Hilda's round face beamed with certainty. "It'll come out. We must have faith."

"Sometimes faith needs a little help, Hilda. Could you drive us to the hospital? I want to talk to Megan Moss. I'm sure she's at Ernie's bedside. She might be able to explain what's going on. And prove that Aunt Gully's innocent."

"Anything to help Aunt Gully." Hilda smiled. "Besides, playing detective with you girls is more fun than waiting at the police station."

Verity opened the back door. "Geez, you'd think these happy farmers would actually be happy." She handed Hilda and me glass bottles of artisanal spring water. "They're all crabbing about the spa. Going to take away their grazing land, they said."

"We almost landed in some of their cow pies." I took a sip. "But that isn't their land. It's the Jake's."

Hilda turned back toward town. "They let their cows roam everywhere."

Minutes later, Hilda's VW passed construction equipment parked by the side of the road. A chain-link fence closed off a rutted dirt lane. "That's the old Gruber place, right?" Hilda slowed. "Rick and Rio want to build a spa out here."

NO TRESPASSING signs were posted on the gates.

Hilda pulled back onto the road. "Nobody's lived there in years." Several tumbledown buildings hulked just past walls topped by rusty barbed wire.

"Rich people at a fancy spa aren't going to want cows wandering all over," I said.

Hilda shook her head. "Too bad for those Happy Farmer cows."

"And those Happy Farmers," Verity said. "Oh! I've got it. Maybe the Happy Farmers poisoned the lobster rolls. They wanted to stop Rio's spa. If the spa goes in, they won't be able to let their cows roam on her property."

"I don't know, Verity," Hilda said.

"Wait a minute. The Happy Farmer had a booth at the food festival! And—" I shifted in my seat. "Look at all those fields. I bet monkshood grows there!"

"Wait a sec. Don't you think they'll benefit from having the spa next door?" Hilda said. "They sell organic food. The spa will serve organic food. Seems like win-win to me, and they'd like to be on Rio's good side."

Verity folded her arms. "Stop making sense, Hilda. I liked my theory."

I laughed. "I like your theory better than the cops' theory. That Aunt Gully poisoned all those people to ruin Kahuna's and have all the lobster business in Mystic Bay to herself."

"That kind of makes sense," Verity said, busily looking in her handbag.

I stared out the window. "I know. It does."

"Don't talk like that! It's ridiculous!" Hilda patted my knee and swerved.

"Thank you, Hilda."

Hilda steered her VW into the hospital parking lot.

"If only we could convince the police of that," I said.

Chapter 33

Once again a TV news truck hunkered in front of Mystic Bay Hospital. A police cruiser was parked next to it.

I slid down in the front seat and directed Hilda to the back parking lot. I didn't want to go through the front door, right in front of reporters who'd just been at Contessa's burial service. In our vintage black dresses, Verity and I couldn't be any more conspicuous.

Hilda parked.

"What's the plan?" Verity lay across the back seat.

"Well, if Aunt Gully were here, she'd call Mrs. Yardley, who would probably let us in. But I don't have her number."

Hilda fished in her purse. "I have a friend who works in Maternity. I'll see if she'll meet us at a back door and bring us up to Ernie and Megan."

"Thanks, Hilda."

While Hilda called, I scanned the parking lot for police cars. I couldn't wait to talk to Megan.

"She's so invisible," Verity said.

"Are you reading my mind again?" I said.

"If you're thinking of Megan Moss."

I sighed. "I cleared Ernie and now the police have glommed onto Aunt Gully."

"Well, I hate to say it, but she has a better motive than Ernie or Megan ruining their own lobster business. I mean—" Verity covered her mouth with her hand. "Sorry."

"It's okay. You're right." I took off my hat. "But after what I heard Megan and Chick talking about—"

Hilda hung up. "What did you hear Megan and Chick talking about?"

I told Hilda what I'd heard at Edwards Inlet.

"That's terrible." Hilda tsked. "My friend said she'll take us to see Megan. We have to meet her at the loading dock."

We climbed cracked cement steps to a loading dock. Two women in scrubs surreptitiously smoked cigarettes at a picnic table on a sparse patch of grass. A dented metal door opened at the top of the steps and a woman with curly blond hair leaned out.

"Hilda!"

"Katie!"

Katie wore cheerful scrubs, pink pants and a top with teddy bears.

Hilda hugged her. "Do you know Allie and Verity?"

We all said hello as Katie led us through fluorescent-lit hallways. Katie walked with a cheerful bounce and everything she said seemed to have an exclamation point at the end. "There's a lull upstairs in babies coming, so I'm happy to see you!"

We headed toward the same elevator bank we'd used to visit the mayor.

"Things had quieted down when Rick and Rio and the mayor left! Well, the mayor, eh." Katie waggled her hand back and forth. "With Rick and Rio—whoa! We had people trying to sneak into their room! A staffer tried to take pictures of them in their beds, can you believe it?"

Hilda shook her head.

"We were just getting back to normal, and then Ernie Moss came in, and the news trucks are back! It's nice that you're here! Poor Ernie was unconscious. Now he's sleeping, but Megan's all by herself." Katie's voice modulated. "All alone. My friends in ICU say she needs someone to sit with her."

"We're happy to do that," Hilda said.

"What're you going to say to Megan?" Verity whispered.

"No idea." My stomach churned. I had no right to stick my nose into what was very personal and painful business. But I had to. I had to help Aunt Gully.

My heart rate kicked up. Asking Megan about Chick would mean admitting I'd witnessed that terrible scene on the beach.

"Has Megan eaten, do you think?" Hilda turned to Verity and me. "Let's bring her a sandwich from the cafeteria."

"Great idea!" Katie said.

I froze. Walking into the cafeteria where lots of people could see me didn't seem like a great idea. What if there were police officers there?

"I'll go. You guys wait," Verity said.

"Can we step in here a moment?" Hilda nodded toward an empty lounge.

"Be right back." Verity hurried down the hall and a few minutes later she returned with fruit salad, a turkey sandwich, water, and some cookies.

As we rode up in the elevator, Hilda and Katie chattered about kids, pets, and knitting club while my stomach lurched.

"I'll tell Megan she has friends waiting to see her."

Katie went down the row of ICU cubicles and ducked into one. I felt like a fraud. "Friend" was stretching it.

"Oh, I do want to see how Megan is," Hilda said. Hilda had no qualms about being there. After hearing that Megan was alone and needed sustenance, she kicked into the same helper gear that Aunt Gully did.

A television, computer, chairs, and couch were set up in a quiet corner for visitors. I took a deep breath, trying to steady my nerves as we took seats.

Verity unwrapped the cookies and nibbled one. "Oops, sorry! I eat when I'm nervous. I'll go get some more. Be right back."

Down the hall, Katie and Megan Moss emerged from one of the ICU cubicles.

Hilda hurried toward Megan. I followed slowly.

Megan turned her head. Her eyes were wide, searching, tired. She looked lost.

"Oh, hi." She raised a hand. "Allie, right? And, and, Hilda."

"Hi."

Katie waved good-bye and walked to the elevators.

Hilda went to Megan and put an arm around her, murmuring, "How are you?"

Megan sagged in Hilda's arms. "Tired."

"How's Ernie?" I whispered.

Megan's arms wrapped around her stomach. "Still barely conscious, but the doctors said they're optimistic. They've upgraded him."

"Good." Hilda led Megan to the couch. "Come sit for a moment."

Megan didn't protest. I offered the sandwich and fruit.

Megan took them gratefully. "I've been too stressed to eat and then all of a sudden I realized I was starving. I was getting dizzy."

"When did you eat last?" I asked.

"I don't remember." Megan started to open the fruit cup, but her hands shook so badly I unwrapped it for her. Tears spattered Megan's cheeks and she wiped them with the back of her hand.

"You guys are so kind." She made a little hiccup sound, then started weeping.

Good grief. Hilda pulled Megan to her shoulder and let her sob. She patted Megan's back and rocked her, and made soothing, clucking noises. "There, there."

What on earth could I do? I unwrapped the sandwich and put it on the table next to the fruit cup. What would Aunt Gully do? I texted Verity.

GET SOME TEA. WITH SUGAR.

A few minutes later, the storm of Megan's sobbing passed. Hilda pulled tissues from her purse and handed them to Megan. Megan wiped her face. "I'm a mess."

Verity's pumps clacked as she arrived with the tea and cookies. I took the tea from her and handed it to Megan. "Try this."

Megan sipped. After a few moments, palest pink bloomed in her cheeks. With a shock I realized that even in the harsh fluorescent light, under the lank hair and with no makeup, Megan Moss was beautiful. It was the nonflashy beauty of a statue of a Madonna, with a smooth curved face and thin but shapely lips. Her large, almond-shaped eyes were spring ocean blue, her skin pale and smooth as milk. Her ears were pretty, small, and shell pink.

But Megan's nails were bitten to the quick, and her shoulders slumped forward, as if she didn't have the energy to stand up straight. *To stand up for herself.*

Megan nibbled the sandwich while Hilda kept an arm on her back, making encouraging noises that blended into the constant beeping of machines in the rooms, the soft nearby swish of a respirator. The whisper of the stiff crinoline under my skirt as I shifted on the couch.

I said the first thing that popped into my head.

"How's Lucia?"

"She was . . ." Megan's voice was so soft I had to lean close to hear her. "Really great. When Ernie didn't come home last night . . ." She sniffed and Hilda handed her another tissue. "I waited and waited. Called and called his cell phone. He didn't answer. Lucia waited with me. She called the police. They went out and looked for him, his car. Nothing until this morning."

Verity's brow wrinkled. "I didn't think the police looked for adults unless they're missing for twenty-four hours?"

Megan shook her head. "That's not the policy here. I don't know about other places. But they didn't find him. Until today."

She turned to face me. "Why was Ernie at the Lazy Mermaid?"

"I was going to ask you, Megan. I've no idea why he'd be there, especially at night when we're closed." I took a deep breath. "Do you think he was meeting someone?"

Megan leaned away from me. Her hand holding the tea shook and she set the cup on the table. "No, I don't think so."

Hilda and I exchanged looks. Verity shifted on her vinyl chair. Megan was lying. But why? Could she be protecting Chick? Or was she protecting Ernie?

Or was she lying because of what happened at Edwards Inlet? I took a deep breath. "Megan, have you ever heard of"—I recalled the envelope in Chick's car—"Aldersgate Family Services in Chatham?"

Megan's hand flew to her throat. "What did you say?" she whispered.

A loud beeping alarm sounded. Nurses rushed into one of the glass cubicles. Ernie's.

"Ernie!" Megan jumped up, her knee knocking the teacup over. She looked down at me. "Allie, come see me later."

She ran to Ernie's room.

Hilda fished more tissue from her purse and mopped up the tea. "Allie, what was that about?"

Chapter 34

"What's Aldersgate?" Hilda said as we got into her car.

"I'm not sure, but it has something to do with Megan and Chick." That was as far as I was going. Hilda didn't need to know I'd searched Chick's car.

Thankfully, Hilda's phone rang just as mine buzzed with a text from Lorel.

COME TO THE PLEX. NOW.

"Great, Lorel wants me to turn myself in."

Hilda hung up. "There's a rally to release Aunt Gully."

Verity grabbed my arm. "Don't go, Allie. How're we going to prove Aunt Gully's innocent if you're arrested?"

My mind churned. I was dying to see Aunt Gully, but I wasn't ready to turn myself in to the police.

Hilda's deep brown eyes were sending me beams of command. "Of course you're going to talk to the police."

"Of course." I felt bad lying to Hilda. "Hilda, will you drop me and Verity at the Tank so I can change?"

"Everything will be fine." Hilda patted my knee. "You have nothing to hide."

No police cars guarded the Tank, thank goodness. I

waved good-bye to Hilda then shimmied back into my jeans and T-shirt.

"What's the plan?" Verity said. "I'd go with you to the rally but I've got to get back to the shop."

"Drop me behind the park," I said. "I'll talk to you later."

"Please don't get arrested. We're going to Juliet's tomorrow."

"That's the plan. Come to Aunt Gully's for dinner tonight."

"If you're not in the slammer," Verity muttered.

"I'll talk to Lorel and see what the situation is with Aunt Gully." Suddenly I had the strangest feeling. "It's weird, Verity. I feel like I want to talk to the police. That I could help them." That somehow I knew something, had heard something that was important, that would prove Aunt Gully's innocence.

Verity dropped me off. Skirting the Plex, I cut through backyards until I could see its front door. A small crowd of people gathered on the sidewalk and steps. I stood at the back of a group across the street, peering through the branches of some bushy rhododendron.

More than a few in the crowd were curious tourists, making a side trip to Mystic Bay Village to get some great seafood while enjoying prime water views. They were disappointed by the closure of both the Lazy Mermaid and Kahuna's but would go home with good stories about the murder, the poisonings, the injured man in the lobster shed, the sinking of the *Sadie Mae,* the submerged sports car, the daring young man who dove in to check the car for life, and the little old lady lobster shack owner who was arrested and now had a mob of gentle townspeople and tourists with nothing better to do demanding her release.

Crowds on the sidewalks flowed down to Pearl Street.

A line of hungry visitors stood outside the door of the Tick Tock. Ernie Moss's bitter comment resonated: *My loss is your gain.*

Bit Markey stood at the top of the steps with—I couldn't believe it—Aggie. And Hector. Hilda hurried up the street.

"Hey hey ho ho. Let Aunt Gully go!" Bit chanted. Aggie pumped a clenched fist.

Bit held up a poster. FREE AUNT GULLY was lettered in all caps in black marker. His lettering was precise and even, a neat job, except for a splotch of red paint on one corner of the poster.

My heart beat faster. Where had I seen that poster before? Where had I seen paint that shade of red?

Could Bit Markey be a lobster libber? I snorted. A man in Bermuda shorts and a UCONN T-shirt turned and grinned. I faded back into the rhododendron. But Bit's red paint was the same shade, and the sign was the same size, as the signs posted at the Lazy Mermaid and Kahuna's.

Chief Brooks stepped from the front door of the Plex to a smattering of boos. He raised his hands.

"Now, folks. Everything's okay. We're just talking. Mrs. Fontana's a good citizen who wants to help the police in their investigation and she's going home."

The crowd cheered.

Aunt Gully and Lorel emerged from the Plex. Aunt Gully shook Chief Brooks's hand, then hugged Bit Markey. Lorel smiled, but it was a shoot-me-now smile. This wasn't the kind of attention she wanted for the Lazy Mermaid.

I surged forward with the crowd. I wanted to get a closer look at Bit's sign.

Someone grabbed my arm.

I whirled.

"Miss Larkin, would you mind coming with me?" Detective Rosato said.

"Wait, Bit, wait!" Detective Rosato frog-marched me across the street. "Just a minute, please, Detective Rosato. I'm not trying to run from you, really."

Bit Markey walked back toward Pearl Street, sandwiched between two friends. "Bit!"

Bit turned and jogged toward Detective Rosato and me.

"Hi, Allie." He looked back at his friends. One gave him a thumbs-up.

Good grief. "First of all, that's a great sign," I said. "Thanks for making it."

Bit smiled. "Nik and Karma say the People have to take action or the Man'll crush our spirits."

I tried not to roll my eyes. How had Nik Markey and Karma—just Karma—produced such a great kid?

Detective Rosato didn't move, but waves of impatience rolled off her.

"Listen. Where'd you get that poster board?" I asked.

"Dumpster-diving at the Ellicott place," Bit said. "They're remodeling it. Sometimes there's great stuff there."

The Ellicott place. Right across from Kahuna's.

"That's true," I said. "Like that great crystal doorknob you gave me."

Detective Rosato shouldered in. "We have to go."

"Please, wait, please. Bit, could I, could we have the sign?"

"Sure!" Bit's skinny chest puffed out. I took the poster by the edges, hoping I wasn't smudging any fingerprints.

"I'm sure Aunt Gully'll want to keep it." Right after I get the cops to check it for fingerprints.

Detective Rosato put her hands on her hips and looked away. The gesture exaggerated the bulge under her jacket.

"Thanks, Bit."

Bit ran back to his friends. They slapped his back.

"Very touching," Detective Rosato said. "Do you have time for an interview or do you have more social calls to make?"

So Detective Rosato wasn't a complete robot.

"No, but I think you're going to want to do some Dumpster-diving."

Chapter 35

Detective Rosato declined my invitation to go Dumpster-diving at the Ellicott house. She hustled me through the front doors of the Plex, past the incredulous face of my friend Bronwyn, and into an interview room.

"Interview of Allegra Larkin. Six P.M."

"Honestly, how can you even think my aunt would poison all those innocent people? For heaven's sake, she's on the church Ladies' Guild! She volunteers at the food bank! She took care of me and my sister after my mother died." Sweat broke out across my back and chest. I had to make the detective understand what a wonderful woman my aunt was. How innocent she was.

"My aunt had no reason to hurt any of those people!"

"Think about this." Detective Rosato turned to me, her eyes black and glittering like Mystic Bay on a moonless night. "There are two lobster shacks in Mystic Bay. One's long established. One's new.

"One's well-known, practically all over the world. What would make someone choose your aunt's new restaurant over the world-famous, highly regarded, longtime favorite of so many? Or more to the point, what would make a diner not want to go to Kahuna's? Maybe if they heard something so bad about the food, they wouldn't set foot there."

Ernie's sweaty face loomed in my mind. *My loss is your gain.*

The thought dragged my heart down like an anchor. Although I knew Aunt Gully would never hurt another soul, Detective Rosato had a plausible motive for her to poison Kahuna's lobster rolls.

"We've been interviewing attendees at the food festival. You were heard to say"—she read from her little notebook—" 'I'd do anything to help Aunt Gully win this competition.' Is that true?"

"That I said it or that I meant it? Both." As soon as the words were out of my mouth I regretted it. And I remembered the person I'd said them to—Finella Farraday.

My jaw dropped. "You can't think I meant poisoning or murdering someone."

Detective Rosato said nothing.

"Finella's been out to get my aunt ever since she bought property Finella wanted!" No wonder Finella was so helpful to the police. A hot blush crept up my chest to my face. Going redhead wouldn't help Aunt Gully. I forced myself to take a deep breath, trying to center myself. I contracted my muscles and then relaxed them.

Detective Rosato's face didn't move.

I felt steadier. "It's a figure of speech, as you're probably aware." I leaned back and folded my arms. Two can play this game.

Detective Rosato set a laptop computer on the table and turned the screen so we both could watch.

With a shock I saw myself hurtle through the crowd at the food festival and vault onto the stage. I watched myself hurry to Contessa and kneel next to her. My back was to the camera for several moments as I tended to her.

I watched myself look up and scoot aside as Hayden Yardley joined me. Once more, I could feel the relief as he knelt next to me. An EMT joined us.

Detective Rosato leaned forward. Small gold studs gleamed in her ears. She pressed the keyboard, freezing me in profile.

I blinked, pulling myself back. My hand was at my throat.

"You were alone with Contessa Wells for a short time."

"Yes, I was afraid she'd choke. I went up to roll her to her side."

Detective Rosato watched me. My mind raced. What was she waiting for? So I was alone with Contessa Wells. Alone with Contessa Wells. Realization broke upon me.

"Do you think I killed her? What would I have done? Strangled the poor poisoned woman?"

Detective Rosato closed the laptop.

"Where were you last night, from ten until midnight?"

My gut twisted. If I told the truth I'd have to admit that I'd trespassed at Orion Cove. That I'd witnessed that awful scene between Chick and Megan. That—

"Do you think I attacked Ernie Moss?" I exclaimed. A worse thought crossed my mind. "Do you think Aunt Gully attacked Ernie Moss?"

"Your aunt was home alone last night. She said you left for a while."

"Me attacking Ernie Moss? Ridiculous!"

"Is it?" Detective Rosato's lips twitched into something that almost looked like a smile. "You're athletic. Look at the way you jumped up onto the stage. You're a dancer, in excellent shape."

I raised my leg, showing her my walking boot.

"That didn't slow you down much." She inclined her head to the laptop.

Breathe, Allie. Don't let her upset you. Think before you talk.

"Come on, Ernie Moss has a hundred pounds on me." I realized I had to tell her the truth because I was sure Chick had attacked Ernie. I was the only one who could explain why.

"I went for a swim." I tapped my finger on my chin, silently adding "at Orion Cove." "I stopped at Edwards Inlet. It's the public beach."

"Don't public beaches close at sundown?"

I swallowed. "Yes."

She didn't say anything. Neither did I but I was thinking furiously. I didn't want to tell any details about Megan. That seemed personal. But Ernie and Chick . . .

"I think I saw Chick Costa cut off Ernie Moss's car. Leaving Edwards Inlet."

Detective Rosato's chin rose a fraction. She was interested.

"Are you sure?"

"Not one hundred percent," I said. "I mean about Ernie's car. But I'm sure I saw Chick's. I mean, that red car is hard to miss."

"Are you sure about Chick Costa's car because you were meeting him?"

"Ugh! Are you kidding me? No. Absolutely not."

Detective Rosato's lips curled in something close to a smile.

She nodded toward the counter where Bit's poster lay. "What's so interesting about that poster?"

Chapter 36

After I told Detective Rosato about the signs and letters, she opened the door. "You may go."

"Thanks." *Just go, Allie, before she changes her mind.*

I hurried outside, texting Verity to come and get me. I filled my lungs with cool, salty air. The sky was tinged with pink—red sky at night, sailor's delight—and a soft breeze breathed off the river. Simply not being in the stuffy interrogation room with Detective Rosato made me happy to be alive.

Minutes later, Verity pulled up and I got in the Tank.

"So they let you go?"

"Crazy, huh? Guess who I owe my police interview to? Finella Farraday."

"What!"

I filled Verity in. "There's something about her. That lobster pick. I think she's been out to get Aunt Gully all along. I wonder if she sent the letters?"

Verity shrugged. "Let's not talk about her. She ruins my appetite. Your aunt called me. She's making lazy man's lobster."

Although my mouth watered, I nodded toward Pearl Street. "One stop before we go home."

* * *

The Tank's engine growled as it crested Brook Street. Uncle Rocco's nephew Frank had a summer home on the hill across from Kahuna's. We parked and looked down at the sagging police tape crossing Kahuna's front door. My eyes went to the Ellicott place across the street, to the Dumpster on the side of the old house.

"Aren't you hungry? I'm starving," Verity said as I fished the key from under the mat at the back door.

"Cousin Frank has security cameras." We went inside.

"Everybody in the world has security cameras. My landlord put them in, though I think he did it just to spy on me."

I flopped into the large leather recliner in front of the big-screen TV.

"Now you're watching TV?" Verity asked.

Cousin Frank had his security system plugged into his cable. "If I can figure this out, maybe we can see who put the sign at Kahuna's. And most importantly, put the red paint on it." Something about the red paint disturbed me more than anything.

"Did you tell the police about Cousin Frank's camera?" Verity perched on an arm of the chair.

"I'm going to remember tomorrow. I want to look first." I clicked on the television. "See, I wonder. Why the red paint on Kahuna's poster and not on the Mermaid's? There's got to be a reason why the lobster libbers—or whoever—used red paint on Kahuna's sign and not on the Lazy Mermaid's."

"Maybe the lobster libbers forgot. People forget," Verity said.

"I'll grant you that. But, I don't think so." SEC SYS flashed onscreen. That must mean security system. I pressed play.

"And you think the letters and the signs are connected?

What about the tires?" Verity said. "You said you thought Finella was responsible."

"Maybe?" The letters were so secretive. So restrained. The signs were so public. So untidy. "I'm not sure." Maybe Aunt Gully and Lorel were right. Would Finella really do something like that?

I rewound to Friday, the night before the food festival. Cousin Frank had several security cameras. One gave a view from his second-story deck down to the river. Kahuna's parking lot and the Ellicott place were visible in the background.

"That was Friday right?" Verity leaned close to the screen. The images were grainy. We watched cars pull in and out of Kahuna's, jockeying for position on the narrow street. After Kahuna's got really busy, cars parked in no-parking areas and on sidewalks.

I fast-forwarded, watching the clock.

Two people walked to a tiny black sports car. "Is that Megan and Ernie?" Verity pointed.

"Pretty sure. That's how Ernie walks." I puffed out my chest and swung my shoulders and arms.

"And Megan." Verity hunched forward and imitated Megan's short, quick, tentative steps.

"So they left early."

"Yeah, they probably figured they'd need a good night's sleep before the food festival."

"Okay." I fast-forwarded again. "Kahuna's closes at midnight. Staff cleans up. Everyone leaves." The last car left the parking lot.

"Now what?"

I pressed play. "We watch." My stomach growled. "I hope it goes fast."

Part of me hoped I'd see Finella Farraday posting the sign. Wouldn't that be a treat for her yacht club friends?

Ten minutes of hazy footage later a car pulled into the parking lot. A sports car.

"Look!" Verity said.

A stocky figure got out of the car carrying a large poster board. He hurried to the Kahuna's sign. Within moments he hung the poster board and jumped back into the car. The car rocketed out of the parking lot and up Pearl Street.

"Heading to the Mermaid," I murmured. "He lied. He said he came down early the day of the food festival, but there he was the night before."

"That was Chick Costa," Verity said. "Even grainy, you could tell. Not Finella, sorry."

"Yup."

"Chick Costa is a lobster libber? A guy who owns his own lobster shack?"

I clicked off the TV. "A fake lobster libber." I thought of the way he'd pressured Megan. "Do you think he made the signs to throw suspicion onto lobster libbers? Megan would poison the rolls but the signs would make police think the libbers were responsible?"

"Does that mean he sent the letters to Aunt Gully?" Verity asked.

"I don't know how he could've done that from Chatham. But who else would? Megan Moss? And what about the paint? He didn't make the red X."

Verity took the remote from my hands. "Maybe he went back later. We're not going to find out tonight. Let's get to your aunt's and gorge ourselves. We'll come back."

Chapter 37

Aunt Gully and I exchanged stories of our police interviews and celebrated our freedom with a delicious dinner: lazy man's lobster, lobster mixed with seasoned bread crumbs and baked golden brown under the broiler; green salad; potato salad; and a lemon tart from the Tick Tock.

Hector and Hilda and a line of well-wishing neighbors and friends streamed in and out of Gull's Nest until Lorel shooed them away.

"Aunt Gully needs her rest." Lorel acting like a mother hen? What happened to my big-shot executive sister?

"Beauty sleep, right, sis?" Dad teased. He was on Skype with Aunt Gully.

"How the police could think you two were guilty! Ridiculous!" Esmeralda's lovely round face leaned in to the camera.

My dad beamed behind Esmeralda. He'd bought my explanation that I'd spoken to the police. Technically true. Nobody had the heart to tell him I'd eluded the police all day. Dad looked relieved. Esmeralda kept a protective hand on his arm. Perhaps it was good that he had her, even if her theatrical mannerisms drove me crazy.

"Besos. Besos." She threw us kisses. The air was so festive in Aunt Gully's little dining room, Lorel and I threw *besos* right back at the woman who stole our dad away. Even for just four months, it was too long. I couldn't wait until Dad returned.

I escorted Aunt Gully up to her claw-foot bathtub and started running the water. "In, young lady."

"I'm not fighting tonight," Aunt Gully said. I poured her lavender-scented bath crystals and hung her powder-blue chenille robe on the hook by the bathtub.

"My lazy mermaid." She shook her head. "Allie, I just want the police to find the person who did these terrible things. Poor Ernie Moss! Do you think the same person poisoned the rolls and then beat up Ernie?"

"No idea, Aunt Gully."

She took her Maeve Binchy novel from the shelf, then put it back, and pulled down another.

"This is a Nora Roberts night." She closed the door.

I joined Verity and Lorel in the kitchen.

"I thought you said the police searched the house?" Verity said. "Don't they usually make a mess? This place looks even cleaner than usual."

"Aggie watched the whole thing from her kitchen window. When the police left, she and a bunch of neighbors came over and tidied up." Lorel closed the dishwasher.

"We'll have to do the same at the Mermaid tomorrow," I said. "They'll let us open tomorrow, right?"

Lorel shook her head. "I spoke to Coach Brooks. Chief Brooks." She rolled her eyes. "He said he'll check in tomorrow morning. The crime lab people had to finish processing the scene where Ernie was injured."

"What about the car and boat at the end of the dock?" Verity said.

"Hugh and Megan'll need to hire a crane to recover the boat and the car," Lorel said. "I imagine their insurance will cover it. Better not be ours. It'll cost a fortune."

"Maybe the police will raise the car," I said. "It's evidence."

Lorel pulled out her phone. "Maybe. I'll call Chief Brooks now."

With all the business we'd missed, the Lazy Mermaid was hardly making money. "I hope we're open while the crane's at work. We'll have crowds that'll want to watch that."

Lorel's eyebrows rose. "Good point, Allie. I can get word out on social media."

Verity put her arm around Lorel. "Lorel, why don't you just hang with us tonight? We're going to have a Contessa Wells Memorial Film Festival."

"We are?" I laughed.

"Yes, we're going to watch *The Gypsy's Daughter*," Verity said.

"Have I seen that?" Lorel said.

"Probably," I said, "I've watched that campfire dance scene a million times."

Lorel shook her head.

"You haven't seen it?" Verity put her hands on her hips. "It's just one of the most famous dances on film."

"Contessa played Adalia, a Gypsy girl who falls in love with a prince disguised as a traveling musician," I said. "He falls for her as she performs her Gypsy dance. The high point is when she does this amazing bunch of spins in a circle around the campfire."

Verity started spinning wildly. I joined in, my precise tight turns contrasting with Verity's wild circles, until my ankle told me to stop. I perched on the countertop.

Verity stumbled into the table, upsetting a basket of

Lazy Mermaid aprons. "Whoa, dizzy. I don't know how you do that, Allie."

I laughed. "And the crazy thing is, Contessa does the whole thing spinning to the left."

"So? Is that a big deal?" Lorel asked.

"We train to spin both ways, but usually people favor one side or another. Most people, and I'm one, are more comfortable spinning to the right. Clockwise. Contessa did all her spins to the left, counterclockwise."

"Like a goofy foot surfer?" Verity put the aprons back in the basket.

"Kinda, yeah."

"Then what happens?" Lorel said.

"Her frenemy Rosalia's consumed by jealousy," I said. "She watches Adalia do this amazing dance, sees the prince totally fall for her."

Lorel grinned and leaned back against the sink.

As Verity and I hummed the music, I slid off the counter. My arms traced serpentine shapes in the air, my wrists turning, playing pretend castanets, as I remembered Adalia's dance. It was magic, the way Contessa's body had painted gorgeous shapes in the air to the Gypsy guitar soundtrack.

Verity spun around. "And just when it can't get any more smoking hot, you just want to swoon, she ends with that cool pose."

We both flung our right arms up, our left hand on our hip, heads tossed back. Lorel clapped.

"The camera zooms in on Adalia's earrings, an expensive gift from the prince pretending to be a traveling musician," I said.

"And when Adalia's returning from a secret meeting with the prince. Woo-hoo!" Verity crowed.

"What? What happens?" Lorel said.

"Rosalia jumps out of the shadows and rips one of the

earrings from Adalia's ears and pushes her into the camp-fire!" I said.

Verity spun by me. I pretended to rip the earring from her ear. She fake shrieked, clutched her ear, and fell onto a kitchen chair, writhing in pretend pain.

"She should have gotten an Oscar for the role," I said.

"It wasn't really acting." Verity got up, clutching her lower back.

"What?" Lorel asked.

"I read it on a movie Web site. Contessa was working on that film with her sister, Juliet."

"Juliet, the crazy sister that Contessa took care of?" Lorel's eyes were wide.

"Yeah, she's still in the house at Rabb's Point," I said. "Juliet played Rosalia. Well, Juliet was supposed to pull off a stunt earring that would break away easily—"

Lorel's hand flew to her ear. "Oh my God, are you telling me—"

Verity's eyes glittered. "Yep. Juliet ripped Contessa's pierced earring right out of her ear. Contessa never wore earrings again."

Lorel's eyes went wide. "And after that Contessa took care of Juliet? That woman was a saint."

"I just remembered something." Lorel rooted in Aunt Gully's bag. "You had Aunt Gully turn off her cell phone yesterday when you took the phone off the hook. I'd better check her cell for anything important. Huh, she's got four messages." She took the phone upstairs.

Verity yawned.

"Verity, why don't you sleep over? We'll put sleeping bags in front of the TV."

"Great idea." Verity stopped. "Oh, wait." She swept her hand over her dress. She was still wearing the black dress she'd worn to the funeral. "I don't have any pj's."

"You left some the last time you were here. Make some popcorn and I'll check."

I checked my closet. Verity had left some men's striped silk pajamas. I gathered a terry-cloth robe and fuzzy slippers. As I slipped into my own pajamas and kimono, I heard the microwave hum.

Aunt Gully emerged from the bathroom, smelling of lavender.

"How're you feeling, Aunt Gully?"

"Like." She tilted her chin and started to sing "Climb Every Mountain."

"Sweet dreams, crazy lady."

While Verity changed, I grabbed a bottle of wine and two glasses. Then we unrolled two sleeping bags, ancient old things we'd used at Girl Scout camp years earlier. Aunt Gully was a true New Englander. She held on to things for years "just in case."

"Just like old times." Verity sighed as she sank onto the musty sleeping bag.

"Except now we have wine instead of lemonade." We clinked wineglasses.

Lorel came back downstairs, wearing Dad's faded Bruins sweatshirt. "Aunt Gully's out like a light." A soft snoring wafted down the stairs.

We offered Lorel the popcorn bowl. "So what were you doing today while I was at the Plex with Aunt Gully?" she said.

"It's kind of a long story." I threw Verity a look.

Lorel scooped a handful of popcorn. "I'll get a wineglass."

"You're still coming with me to Juliet Wells's house, right?" Verity whispered.

"Yes. It sounds like the Mermaid'll be closed again."

I slumped against the couch. "I just want things to get back to normal. For me, for Aunt Gully, for Lorel. For you."

"With the haul from the Wells place"—Verity's eyes glittered—"it'll be better than normal."

"Here's to better than normal." We clinked glasses.

"What do you think happened," Verity said, "with Ernie at the Mermaid?"

I sipped my wine. "All I know is Ernie was a mess when he left here. My theory? I think he drove home—"

Lorel came back with her wineglass. "When he got home, Megan wasn't there and Lucia didn't know where she was."

"How do you know that?" I asked.

"Aunt Gully's voice mail," Lorel said. "Aunt Gully's cell phone was full of calls from Lucia. That woman has got to start answering her cell."

"So Lucia couldn't get through. What did she say?"

"She shouted, 'Ernie found the roses'!" Lorel said.

The roses. Verity and I exchanged looks.

Lorel sipped her wine. "Lucia said she didn't know where Megan was. In the next call Lucia said Ernie came home and blew up because Megan wasn't there. Then Ernie went out to look for her. Then Lucia said Megan came home and didn't know what happened to Ernie. Not a good night at Kahuna's Kove."

My mind whirled. Had Megan known the car she cut off at Edwards Inlet was Ernie's?

Lorel said slowly, "I wonder if Ernie noticed Aunt Gully's van when you were parked at Edwards Inlet."

"And he suspected that I'd poisoned the rolls to help Aunt Gully." I nodded. "So at this point, jealous Ernie Moss sees roses that were a gift for his wife. He sees his wife with Chick. Reason to blow his jealous top." My mind flashed back to Ernie's furious red face. His barely restrained temper in the porch light of Gull's Nest last night. The smell of alcohol.

"And if he sees your van, what does he think then?" Lorel said.

"He thinks . . ." The word surfaced from all the news interviews with YUM. "Conspiracy. That we were all conspiring against him. Us, Chick, Megan," I said. "At this point he's ready to blow."

"So that jerk Chick Costa cuts him off. What does Ernie do?" Lorel said.

I remembered the angry sound of a car horn blaring.

"He follows him. Now he has road rage on top of everything else," I said. "There were dents and scratches on Chick's car."

"Their beloved cars," Verity said. "That was one fight that was going to happen."

"But why at the Mermaid?" Lorel said.

"Because Ernie's mad at us," I said.

"But Ernie was following Chick." Lorel's brow furrowed. "You said Chick cut off Ernie."

"They were on Shore Road, right?" I followed the curving road in my mind. It led to a cut-through called Marsh Road. "Maybe they turned onto Marsh Road. It's quiet. Dark. They were still jousting with their cars at that point."

Verity ate a handful of popcorn.

"But if you want to pull over and duke it out, you need a place to do that," Lorel said.

"Kahuna's is the first parking lot you come to. But even if Chick pulled in there, Ernie wouldn't want to stop at his own restaurant. Think about it. By this time, I think they knew who the other one was. You know how tight the road is. The next parking lot they would've come to past Kahuna's would be—"

"The Mermaid," Lorel said.

A soft knocking on the door made me jump.

"Oh, God, don't be the police again." Lorel sloshed wine on Dad's sweatshirt.

Verity whispered, "And there's still a murderer on the loose."

"Don't say that." I hurried to the front door and looked out the peephole.

"It's Lucia." A slight figure stood to her left in the shadows. "And Megan Moss!"

Chapter 38

A few minutes later, Lucia and Megan were seated on Aunt Gully's couch.

Lucia kept an arm around Megan. Megan's pale, exhausted face contrasted with Lucia's bright red lipstick and glossy hair.

"Ernie told me what happened." As Megan recounted Ernie's actions, Lorel, Verity, and I shared glances. Everything Megan reported was pretty much everything Lorel, Verity, and I had deduced.

"What's this? A party I wasn't invited to, in my own home?" Aunt Gully's pink fuzzy slippers swished down the stairs and across the floor.

Lucia burst into tears and jumped up to embrace her. "Oh, how I felt when I couldn't reach you last night! So lost!"

"What happened?" Aunt Gully hugged Lucia, then the two women sat on either side of Megan.

I got three more wineglasses from the corner cabinet in the dining room. After we got Aunt Gully up to speed, she leaned forward and refilled everyone's wineglasses. "This story calls for more than tea," she said.

"Ernie regained consciousness," Megan said. "He told

me what happened last night. When Chick's car cut Ernie off, Ernie saw red. He went after Chick and rammed his car."

She stared into her wineglass but didn't drink. "When they got to the parking lot of the Mermaid, Chick pulled in and they just went at it. Of course Ernie's bigger, but Chick works out."

Megan continued in a monotone while Aunt Gully rubbed her back. "Ernie said they wrestled and rolled in the gravel. Then Chick ran into your lobster shed. Ernie said, well, let's just say he said Chick was a coward. When Ernie followed him into the shed, Chick jumped him. And that's the last thing Ernie remembers. His head struck the edge of the lobster tank and he lay there all night. Ernie has a terrible concussion. Bled a lot, too. I heard there was blood all over. No wonder people thought he was dead." Megan's hands shook as she set her glass on the table.

Lorel and I shared a look. We'd have to make sure we cleaned that up. I didn't want Aunt Gully to have to perform that upsetting task.

"I wonder if Chick thought he killed Ernie?" I asked.

Megan shrugged.

"But the car? Why did Chick drive Ernie's sports car into the river?" Lorel asked.

"Chick." Megan shook her head. "Chick wanted to hurt Ernie. Chick told me, 'Ernie won. He won you.' As if life were a competition. Love was a competition. That's how he sees everything. Winning and losing. It didn't matter that I didn't want to be won. I wanted to be loved." Her voice trailed off. "To love."

Lucia patted Megan's hand. A sympathetic silence settled over us. Suddenly, Megan was more than a woman wiping tables at Kahuna's. She was a woman who had loved. Who wanted to love. Who had secrets.

"Maybe Chick saw trashing Ernie's car as another way to hurt Ernie. He could have driven Ernie's car to the end of the dock," Verity said. "And pushed it in."

The Lazy Mermaid dock was a bit wider than most, but still, that was a hair-raising thought. "Maybe Chick drove his own car behind it and nudged Ernie's car into the water," I said. That would account for the dents on Chick's and Ernie's cars.

"Sounds like Chick had a very busy night," Aunt Gully said.

Our little group sat quietly, the carriage clock on the mantel ticking next to Uncle Rocco's photograph.

"Megan." I took a deep breath. "What is Aldersgate in Chatham?"

Lorel shot me a look of horror.

Megan sighed. "A community services agency. They"—she looked at her chapped hands—"specialize in adoptions."

"And who's Brian Lukeman?" I said. "That name was on an envelope from Aldersgate in Chick's car."

"Brian Lukeman." Megan said the name so softly it was almost a breath. Then she burst into tears. Aunt Gully and Lucia hugged her from both sides. Lorel handed her tissues. After a few moments Megan's tears subsided. "I've been waiting for years to say that name. I'm not sure but I think maybe Brian Lukeman is my son."

"Your son?" Lucia gasped. Aunt Gully squeezed Megan's thin shoulders. Verity grabbed a handful of popcorn.

I handed Megan another tissue.

"Thank you." Megan wiped her eyes. "And Chick's," Megan whispered. "Years ago, being pregnant and unmarried was a big deal. Not like today. My parents were very strict; they would've disowned me if they'd known."

At my incredulous look she said, "No, really. And I." Her hand went to her abdomen. "I loved the baby. Chick told me he'd help. My parents thought we were a match made in heaven but they didn't know about the baby. I didn't know anything then. I just knew I was . . . in trouble."

Lucia murmured and patted Megan's hand.

"Chick took me to Chatham to meet his family. That's what we told my parents. They thought I was going away for the summer to work at a camp. I gave birth at his home. This mansion, right on the water." Tears striped Megan's cheeks.

"They had maids in black dresses with white frilly aprons." She sighed. "The doctor took the baby away. Told me it would be placed with a fine family. I signed some papers. Their chauffeur drove me back home."

Megan took a choked breath. "Never saw Chick or his family again. Seems I wasn't the right sort for their son.

"Then I met Ernie. He was a rock. We married but couldn't get pregnant. We tried fertility treatments, but Ernie couldn't have children. And I searched my heart. I realized I didn't want to have children. I wanted the child I gave up. I just wanted to make sure he was okay.

"There are different laws in different places, but here and by Chick's home, after a child turns twenty-one, adoption records are open and searchable. I got in touch with Aldersgate. They told me they had no records with my name. No record of my giving birth. Chick's family had erased me.

"I got in touch with Chick last August. Chick told me

the adoptive family, the Smiths"—Verity snorted—"had moved out of state and they'd lost touch."

"But Chick's name," Lorel said. "They'd know his name."

"Then when the competition was announced, Chick had a proposal for me." Megan's lips trembled.

"Oh my God. He used your child as leverage. He said if you threw the competition he'd tell you where to find your son," I said.

Megan's eyes brimmed. She nodded.

"But you didn't." Aunt Gully sounded sure.

Would Megan have been so desperate to find her child that she'd poison four people? The YUM footage replayed in my mind. I was pretty sure Megan, like Chick, hadn't gone near Kahuna's completed lobster rolls after they were plated. The cloche had gone down on ordinary, regular Kahuna's Godlobster rolls. The poisoning must've happened when the cloche-covered rolls were in the kitchen, during that window of time when Aunt Gully returned for her apron. The volunteer that Aunt Gully'd seen. That person was the key.

"Of course not." Megan's voice strengthened. "That would be crazy. The only person I wanted to kill was Chick. A few months ago he broke up with"—she waved the tissue—"oh, wife number four, I think it was. He decided he wanted me back. Ha. His first love. Letters. Calls. Flowers. He had to win, you see. Had to beat Ernie. I didn't matter a bit years ago. I don't matter now."

"Did he ask you to use poison?" I said.

Megan shook her head. "No, he just said to make sure the rolls, as he put it, stank."

"Megan, has Detective Rosato questioned you yet? Have you told her this?" Lorel asked.

"I spoke with the police, but I didn't tell them any of this. But Ernie spoke to the police tonight. He was too exhausted to say much besides Chick's name. Now I know I have to tell the truth. I want to tell the truth. I'm meeting the police in the morning. I'd better go."

Megan embraced me. "Allie, I never could've gotten that out of Chick. Now that I have a name, maybe I can find my son."

After Lucia and Megan left and Aunt Gully and Lorel went to bed, Verity and I slid into our sleeping bags. After Megan's real-life drama, we were too excited to watch *The Gypsy's Daughter*.

"Know what this means?" Verity said. "That Chick Costa's the killer."

"I'd like to see Chick fry." I plumped my pillow. "But why poison? Why not just use ghost peppers? Or too much salt?"

"What was he doing with that lobster libber stuff?" Verity finished the last bit of wine in her glass.

"Think like Chick," I said. "You think your old girl-friend's going to agree to poison her husband's lobster rolls because you dated her years ago and had a child with her. *A child you hid from her.* But in his Chick way, he's going to be nice, because he's decided that he wants his old first love back. He's going to pin the poisoning on the mythical lobster libbers."

"Hmm. That's good."

"That's one theory." I curled up in my sleeping bag. "Or the conspiracy against YUM."

"A conspiracy against the YUM Network?" Verity said. "Who on earth buys that?"

"It kind of makes sense," I mused. "All those judges getting sick, somebody dying at an event they sponsor."

"And who'd do that? Another network?" Verity said. "YUM's wonderful. You'd have to be a total weirdo to want to hurt them."

"Agreed. And look what happened. They make the whole thing go away by just not doing the show," I said slowly. "Maybe it was an accident, killing Contessa. Maybe Chick just wanted to make people think it was food poisoning . . . or maybe he didn't even do it."

"Let's look at this systematically," Verity said, counting off on her fingers. "Okay, what if you had it in for one of the judges?"

I shook my head. "Then Chick's out. I don't think he knew any of them."

"We know Ernie fought with the mayor over the plan for widening Pearl Street," Verity pressed. "Would somebody kill over that? And would you take out four judges if you really only wanted to kill the mayor?"

"Bliss Packer thought so." I remembered Bliss twisting her beautiful pearl necklace. "But it's so extreme. Ernie has a violent temper, but he doesn't seem the type to brood and plan revenge. Someone planned this. They had to get the monkshood for one. And it made Kahuna's look bad. I don't think Ernie'd make his own business look bad just to increase parking and access for that very same business.

"Though Bliss hated Ernie. And she could pay someone to do her dirty work. But that would mean poisoning her own husband to make someone else look bad." Would Bliss do that?

Verity sighed. "Okay. Could someone have been after Rick and Rio? That spa they're building. Maybe somebody wanted to stop it."

I yawned. "The Happy Farmer people? They had a booth at the food fest. But I think Hilda's right. The spa's a win for them. And I can't think of anyone with a grudge against Rick and Rio. Well, maybe one of the restaurants that Rick gave a bad review to?"

"What about Contessa Wells? Who wanted to kill

her?" Verity's voice was soft in the darkened living room.

"Well, she had a pretty bad reputation at Broadway by the Bay." I stretched my arms over my head. "Got some people fired over the years. Made lots of people unhappy, stressed, embarrassed. But that's par for the course in theater. I don't know if anybody hated her enough to poison three other people to try to get to her." I rolled over. "Her sister hated her." That was certain.

"Agreed. But she's nuts," Verity said.

"And did you see those locks on the doors at the Wells House?" I shivered.

"Maybe she got Susan to help," Verity said.

We both burst out laughing.

"Well, we know Susan has a black shirt. She wore it to the burial." Verity yawned again.

Aunt Gully's lace curtains rippled at the open windows. The sound of the waves filled the room, as if the ocean were breathing alongside us.

"We're back to Chick," I said. "What if the killer was hired? Chick has plenty of money. He could have paid somebody to poison the rolls. He was angry about Megan shooting him down and refusing to throw the contest. He's a competitive maniac. He was going to make Kahuna's look bad, really bad. Didn't the news say it was food poisoning at first?"

Verity's voice trailed. "Oh, I'm too tired to talk about murder any more."

"Yes. As long as Aunt Gully isn't in jail and I'm not in jail, I'm going to get some sleep."

The sound of Verity's breathing soon filled the dark room, but my mind raced. The black shirt. Aunt Gully saw somebody with a black shirt come out of the kitchen. Maybe a woman, maybe not. She's sure the person was slight, with a ball cap. Volunteer badge.

I tossed in my sleeping bag, replaying over and over images from the last few days. *Who poisoned the judges? Who killed Contessa Wells?*

As I listened to the buoy ring off Seal Rock, I knew I wanted to view Cousin Frank's security tape again.

Chapter 39

The next morning, the first order of business was scrubbing the lobster shed. Verity, Hilda, and I got down on our hands and knees and scrubbed Ernie Moss's blood from the rough wooden floors. The smell of the bleach we used made me feel like I'd pass out.

Lorel, of course, wasn't scrubbing on her hands and knees but was with Aunt Gully, negotiating our reopening with the police. Since Ernie was improving and it wasn't a murder scene, we were allowed to get back to business, but our parking lot would be closed off to create a safety perimeter while the recovery operation for the *Sadie Mae* and Ernie Moss's car proceeded. Our lobstermen would meet Hector at the town dock and he'd ferry the lobsters back to the Mermaid in Aunt Gully's van.

The insurance company arranged for Micasset Marine to raise Ernie Moss's car and the *Sadie Mae*. I'd seen Micasset's teamwork raise a sunken yacht off the riverbed after Hurricane Sandy. The huge equipment would draw a crowd. Lorel and Aunt Gully wanted to reopen the shack in time to catch the action.

Lorel rolled her eyes when I asked Aunt Gully about going with Verity to Juliet Wells's house.

"Of course," Aunt Gully said as she chopped onions for her clam chowder. "When you're done, come back for lunch. I'll like to see some of those clothes. Lorel can help with the lobster while you're gone."

The thought of Lorel picking lobster made me smile.

"Hope life returns to normal soon." Lorel sighed.

Verity and I went back to her apartment so she could change. Today she chose an outfit more appropriate for hauling boxes of clothes: cigarette pants and a white silk shell topped with a striped blazer that nipped in at the waist.

In deference to Verity, I popped a slim navy blue sweater over my Lazy Mermaid T-shirt. She pulled a wide black belt off a rack and handed it to me with a red and blue patterned Pucci scarf.

"Nice!" she exclaimed.

The only thing ruining the sophisticated effect was my booted foot.

"I can't wait to get this off." I nodded toward a pair of canvas espadrilles that tied with ankle ribbons. "Dibs on those when my ankle's better."

"They're yours." Verity tucked an envelope into her purse. "Oh, Allie, a buy like this is a dream come true."

As we drove to the Wells House, life in the town seemed to have returned to its usual rhythm. Tourists strolled the coffee shops and headed to the waterfront to take in the views. Shopkeepers set out signs advertising specials. Cars jockeyed for parking places near the green.

Sunlight sparkling on the bay lifted my spirits. Aunt Gully was free. The police didn't seem interested in me, at least at the moment. Megan Moss had hope of finding her lost child.

Contessa Wells had died and a killer was on the loose, but it felt like the whole food festival disaster was falling behind us.

At the Wells House, we hurried to the door and Verity pushed the bell.

"Won't Susan be happy to see us?" she said.

I stifled a laugh as the door opened.

A slim Latina woman in a starched white nurse's uniform answered. "May I help you?"

"Hello. Where's Susan?" I said.

The woman's forehead wrinkled. "Susan?"

"Miss Wells's nurse," I said.

"We're here to see Miss Wells. She invited us," Verity said.

"Oh," the nurse said. "I'm sorry, the funeral was very hard on Miss Wells. She's resting and can't be disturbed."

Verity and I shared a look. Resting? Did that mean sedated?

"She asked me to come today. I have an appointment." Verity's hands were gripped together in a praying gesture. "Please."

"Perhaps she'll contact you tomorrow." The door started to close.

"Or could I see her later this afternoon?" Verity said.

The woman sighed. "Perhaps."

"What happened to Susan?" I repeated.

The woman shrugged. "The nurse who was here before? She was with a different nursing company." She pointed to the logo on her blouse. Harbor at Home Nursing. "We just took over the contract."

My heart beat faster. Something I had heard . . . the nursing care changed every couple of weeks. Who told me that?

"Good-bye." The woman closed the door.

Verity, mouth open, didn't move as the door shut firmly

inches from her nose. On the other side of the door a bolt drove it home.

"That's strange," I said.

Verity pointed at the glossy black door. "I'm not letting this woman stand between me and the buy of the century."

I pulled her away. "I have another idea."

"What's your idea?"

"Let's find Susan." I pulled out my phone.

"How? We don't even know her last name. You think she'd help us get in?"

"I think Susan would do things to help Susan. We just have to make it clear that we can do something for her. She wore a sweatshirt with the name of her company." I closed my eyes, trying to remember. "Home or Heart something." I swiped on my phone, searching for home nursing care companies. "Yes!" I pressed call.

"Heart's Ease Homecare," a woman's voice said warmly.

"Hi. My name's Allie Larkin."

Verity shook her head wildly, whispering, "Mary Smith, Mary Smith."

I waved her off. "A very nice nurse named Susan was working for Miss Wells in Mystic Bay. Miss Wells asked me to bring Susan a gift. I was wondering if I could have Susan's address."

Verity high-fived me.

"We can't give out employees' information. But if you'd like to drop the gift here, I'll make sure she gets it. She's supposed to stop by the office this morning."

It would have to do. "Could you give me your address, please?"

We drove to the offices of Heart's Ease Homecare, which was located in a sooty brick building near the railroad tracks in Bridgeton. Pots of pansies struggled to brighten the entryway.

"Now what?" Verity jutted her chin at a package store across the street. "Do we buy a bottle of vodka and leave it for Susan? And hope she gives us a call?"

"No. We wait until she comes to get her gift."

"Well, I'm going to need sustenance."

The only signs of life on the street were the package store and a gas station with a Dunkin' Donuts inside. We bought a half-dozen doughnuts and some coffee, then plunked ourselves in the front seat to wait.

Four doughnuts later, Susan's car wheezed into the parking lot.

"Stay calm. We don't want to spook her," I said.

"Susan!" Verity jumped from the car. I shook my head and hurried across the parking lot.

Susan slammed her car door. "You two. I should've known. So there's no gift?"

I slid a twenty-dollar bill into her hand. "Listen, we just want to know something."

Susan tucked the money in her bag, then shook a cigarette from a package and lit up. "What d'you want to know? I can't tell you about her health. That's privileged information." Susan patted her purse.

I looked at Verity. I didn't have any more cash on hand. "All I've got is doughnuts."

Susan laughed, setting off a coughing fit. When she finished choking, she said. "You two. Better than TV."

"Did you take Miss Wells to a town hall meeting?" I asked.

"Yes."

"Um, did anything unusual happen there?" I pressed.

"Aside from her waving a stick and putting a curse on them all?"

Susan's good humor wasn't going to last long.

"Why do Miss Wells's nurses change every couple of weeks?" I said. "Isn't it better if a patient has consistent care?"

Susan glanced at the office window, then back at me. "You ever stayed in the hospital?"

"I had my tonsils out when I was eight," I said.

Verity shook her head.

Susan dragged on the cigarette, her eyes narrow.

"Everyone's supposed to make sure information gets passed on. Sometimes it does." She blew out smoke. "Most times it doesn't. Your Miss Wells had different nurses booked every couple of weeks. She has very interesting delusions. When she does, she gets worked up. Like yesterday when the police lady visited."

"Detective Rosato?" I whispered.

Susan laughed. "She marches in, all official. Oh, Juliet gave it to her with her stupid questions. 'Did Contessa have any enemies?' Juliet just laughs and says 'Evidently.' Real dry. Oh, sometimes she's a pistol.

"Then she got . . ." Susan looked away. "She had one of her bad days."

"Bad days?" I asked.

Susan looped her lank hair behind her ear, revealing red scratches on her cheek. Verity and I gasped.

"Your friend did this. She went for the cop, too, almost pulled out a fistful of her hair."

Susan tossed away her cigarette and went in to the office.

Chapter 40

Verity and I cruised back to Mystic Bay.

My mind tumbled. "I don't understand why Contessa didn't want her sister to have consistent care. And what did she mean by delusions?"

"And how am I going to get into Juliet's house?" Verity said.

I patted her shoulder. "We'll go back in a little while. Give Juliet time to settle."

"Want to go back to the Mermaid?" Verity said.

I couldn't get the image of Chick hanging the poster at Kahuna's out of my mind. He definitely hung the sign. But did he return to paint the red *X* on it? Why didn't he do it at the same time?

"No," I said. "Let's go back to Cousin Frank's to watch the rest of that tape."

"If we're going to watch that tape, I'll need more than doughnuts. We can get chowder at the Mermaid."

"Let's stop here." I pointed to a small storefront, Mystic Bay Soup. Verity ordered chowder and I got the ginger apple curry soup.

At Cousin Frank's we ate as we picked up viewing the tape where we'd left off.

Security lights lining the roof of Kahuna's sprawling shack glared on tape, but the parking lot was pitch-dark. A bright light over the shack's sign made a circle of light at its base. A few cars passed but no one stopped.

"Seriously," Verity said as we watched the grainy footage, "your aunt's chowder's much better than this. And this is pretty good."

A flicker of movement caught my eye. "Look!"

We leaned toward the screen. A shadow stepped into the pool of light and morphed into a slight figure wearing a baseball cap.

"Is that a man or a woman?" The figure walked up to the poster Chick had tacked to the Kahuna's sign. The right arm raised and made a slashing movement, like a swordsman in an old movie. I imitated it. Painting the *X*. Then the figure hurried toward the main restaurant building.

A car slid by. "Hiding from the car?" Verity whispered.

"Exit stage right," I whispered as the mysterious figure headed from the Kahuna's parking lot toward the Ellicott house. The figure melted into the darkness and disappeared.

"The lobster libber," Verity breathed. "Not Chick, was it?"

"No." I sighed. "Didn't look like Finella Farraday, either."

"Yeah, she's tall and snooty. She even walks snooty."

For a few minutes longer, Verity and I watched, barely blinking, afraid to miss a split second that might show the same slight shadow. Nothing more appeared on the screen.

"Sure didn't walk like Chick. Maybe it's just someone who didn't like Kahuna's?" But still something felt off. "Did they even see Chick's poster? I still don't know why they defaced Kahuna's sign and not ours." I clicked off the tape. "Let's go."

We gathered our soup cartons.

"Looks like you found the lobster libber." Verity grinned. "I'm proud of you. You're doing all this legwork the police should be doing. Honestly, Allie, if the dancing thing doesn't work out maybe you should be like Bronwyn and get into police work."

I put the key back under the mat. I'd have to let Cousin Frank know he'd probably be getting a visit from the police.

"Chick wanted people to think the lobster libbers were after Kahuna's and the Mermaid," I said. "To play into his plan to destroy Kahuna's and win back Megan. He must've really thought Megan would throw the competition for him."

"But it turns out there really was a lobster libber," Verity said. "We just saw him—or her."

I shrugged. "Maybe? But Bron said there really aren't any groups like that. At least any big, organized ones. I have to tell the police."

Something about that big red X reminded me of something — the red splotch on the sign Bit Markey had made. In my mind it melded into Ernie's bloodstains on the floor of the lobster shack.

"I just hope Robo Detective takes you seriously," Verity continued.

As we got into the Tank, a police cruiser and van parked by the Ellicott place. Two officers circled the Dumpster where Bit Markey had found the poster board.

"Maybe she is."

Chapter 41

The Tank joined a slow-moving stream of traffic crawling down Pearl Street toward the Plex. Tourists jammed the sidewalks and spilled into the street, forcing cars to inch past the Mermaid. Sawhorses blocked the entrance to our parking lot. A marine crane towered above the pier. Its pungent diesel fumes rolled in the window.

"Oh, they're moving the boat and the car! Hang on." I jumped out of the car and moved the sawhorses, then motioned Verity to pull in. She eased the Tank onto the grass next to the Adirondack chairs while I replaced the sawhorses.

In the middle of the gravel parking lot, a flatbed truck squatted. On the bed was a black sports car. Ernie's. Crewmembers used chains and straps to secure the vehicle to the truck bed. Dents and scrapes marred the front and rear of Ernie's car. Ernie wouldn't be happy when he saw this.

The guttural grinding of engines and tang of diesel smoke filled the patch of grass where customers would usually enjoy fresh food, sunshine, and a relaxing view of the river. Now guys in hard hats and work boots choreographed heavy machinery into a recovery mission. From just beyond the yellow caution tape, dozens of tourists watched the men and machines at work.

An extra line of caution tape cut off the dock area. The floating crane, three stories tall and groaning like a metal beast, swung slightly. The cable dipped and pulled taut. The crane jerked as *Sadie Mae* rose from the river streaming water. Behind the barricades, people raised cell phones to record the action.

Those who weren't recording held small paper cups. Bit Markey walked through the crowd offering the cups and spoons from a tray.

"What's that, Bit?" I asked.

"Aunt Gully's chowder. She sold out of lobster rolls. Hector's stuck in traffic getting down to the town dock for lobsters so she's been cooking extra chowder." He pointed to police tape making a narrow path to the door of the Mermaid from Pearl Street. "Customers can't stay and eat since there's a safety perimeter. But so many people're here watching, she wants them to—"

"Have a taste of the Lazy Mermaid." Aunt Gully joined us. She also carried a tray, which was empty. She wiped perspiration from her forehead.

I took the tray from her hands. "Bit, would you please get Aunt Gully some water?"

"Oh, I'm fine," Aunt Gully protested, but Bit dashed to the Mermaid. She leaned against the Tank with Verity and me. We watched the crane operator maneuver *Sadie Mae* onto the barge. "They'll take it over to the marina. Hugh says his insurance'll cover repairs."

Across the parking lot, a broad-shouldered man wearing a navy blazer and khaki pants spoke with Lorel. He turned. Hayden Yardley. His sunglasses were pushed to the top of his head, holding back his wavy brown hair.

He tapped a tablet computer a few times, then took photos of the boat as it swung onto the barge.

"Hayden Yardley's here?" I asked.

"Yes. He works for Hugh's insurance company," Aunt Gully said.

Hayden strode toward us. Verity checked her hair in the Tank's side mirror. I smothered a laugh. We'd known Hayden since first grade. Verity'd had a crush on Hayden's brother, Patrick, the bad boy of Mystic Bay High School, but she said that both Yardley brothers were hotter than any other guy in Mystic Bay.

I couldn't argue. While Patrick had been a dangerously handsome heartbreaker, hanging with the hard-partying lacrosse crowd, Hayden had been quieter, competing on the sailing team and painting scenery for the school plays.

"Hi, Hayden."

Hayden smiled, "Hi, Allie, Verity. Aunt Gully."

Bit brought water for Aunt Gully on his tray.

"Thank you, Bit."

"Chowder?" Bit held out the tray to Hayden.

"You bet. Thanks." Hayden took a cup and a plastic spoon and dug in.

"Aunt Gully, lots of people are asking if they can buy soup to take home," Bit said.

"Oh, I just thought it would be nice for them to try it," Aunt Gully said.

"Well, your chowder has worked its magic." Hayden put his empty cup and spoon in a trash bin by the Adirondack chairs. "I'd love to buy some to take home."

"We have some to-go containers in the storage room," I said.

"Oh, I'd forgotten," Aunt Gully said. "Let's make a sign that says CHOWDER TO GO."

We all headed to the shack.

Hayden jutted his chin toward Bit. "Doesn't that kid go to school?" he asked quietly.

"He's homeschooled." I made air quotes. "Aunt Gully says he's better off here. I agree."

I held the door and Bit, Aunt Gully, and Verity entered.

"Allie." Hayden took my arm. "How're you doing? I mean, that thing with Contessa Wells. That was intense."

I let the door to the shack close. "It was. But I think I'm okay."

"I remember doing CPR on people when I was with the volunteer fire department." Hayden shook his head. "If you ever need to talk, you can always give me a call." He pulled a leather card case from his pocket and gave me a card.

"Thanks." I nodded at the carved mermaid outside the shack. "If you ever want to talk, you know where to find me."

We laughed.

"How's your ankle?" Hayden said.

"Getting better. But the jury's out. Ballet's pretty tough on the body, so keep your fingers crossed for me."

He smiled, the same open smile he'd had since elementary school.

Behind us I heard a commotion. Police dragged aside the sawhorses. Diesel smoke plumed as the barge and the crane chugged away from the dock. As soon as the yellow police tape dropped to the ground, people streamed into the parking lot like champagne after the cork has popped.

"Ah, Hayden, could you spare a few minutes?" I said. "We could probably use you in the kitchen."

Hayden opened the door. "After you."

Several hours later every single cup of chowder, bottled beverage, and bag of chips had been sold. Aggie had brought over four coffee cakes and we sold every piece of that, too. Hayden looked at his watch and reached for his blazer.

"Gotta get back to the office," he said. "This was fun, Aunt Gully. Maybe I can help out some weekend."

Aunt Gully gave him a hug. "Come back any time, Hayden Yardley."

"Oh, Allie, do you have a minute?" Hayden said.

"Sure."

Verity waggled her eyebrows at me as Hayden and I went into the parking lot.

Hayden and I walked across Pearl Street, where he unlocked his four-door sedan. Patrick Yardley rode a Harley motorcycle. How different the brothers were.

"I didn't want to say anything earlier, but the police asked me to talk to them. They asked me"—he looked away—"if I'd seen you causing any harm to Contessa Wells. Specifically giving her any—" He looked back at me and said in a low voice, "They used the term 'substances.'"

His words stunned me. Hayden gently put his hand on my shoulder.

"I'm sorry, Allie. This has been hard for your family. Your poor aunt. Everybody knows she wouldn't hurt a fly. I told them they were crazy if they thought you did anything to hurt Contessa Wells."

"I spoke to them myself the other day. My own police interview," I said.

"You Larkin women. Well, they let you out."

"For now."

Hayden gave me a hug and I hurried back to the Mermaid.

Chapter 42

As I walked to the shack, I passed a group sitting on the Adirondack chairs.

One woman brushed crumbs from her hands. "Best. Coffee cake. Ever."

Another said, "No. Best. Chowder. Ever."

The guy with them tossed his trash into the bin. "Stick to the chowder and the dessert. This is the place where they have the poison lobster rolls, right?"

The first woman laughed. "No, that's the shack down the street."

The reassuring warmth of Hayden's hug evaporated. My fists clenched. Was that going to be the legacy of the food festival disaster? Even though the police had let me and Aunt Gully go, would rumors follow us forever?

I pulled open the screen door of the Mermaid and let it bang shut behind me. Aunt Gully worked at the register and Hector wiped the counter. Lorel spoke on the phone. Bit Markey's, Hilda's, and Verity's laughter rang from the kitchen. I grabbed a broom and started sweeping.

The television hanging near the ceiling blared the

news. "Police are asking for the public's help in finding this man: Charles 'Chick' Costa of Chatham, Massachusetts."

"Whoa! Listen, everybody!" I fumbled for Aunt Gully's remote and raised the volume as Chick Costa's photo flashed onscreen.

"Costa is the owner of the landmark Chick's World Famous Lobsters shack. As we reported earlier, he was among the contestants in the Mystic Bay Food Festival, where all four judges were sickened with a poisoned lobster roll and one judge, Broadway and screen star Contessa Wells, died. Costa is wanted for questioning in relation to an assault that occurred in Mystic Bay two nights ago, on Memorial Day. If you have any information on his whereabouts, please contact the police."

If Chick wasn't at his shack, where was he?

Chapter 43

"So where's Chick Costa?" Hilda said.

"Probably hiding out on his yacht," Lorel said.

"So the police are after Chick for beating up Ernie." I folded my arms. "He deserves a lot more than jail time."

Hector looked around the room. "Well, none of you look surprised. Spill!" We filled him and Hilda in on Megan and Lucia's visit last night.

"Megan told us she was meeting with the police this morning. She must've reported what Ernie told her about what happened in the lobster shed," I said.

"If only they could get him for the poisoning, too." Lorel's brow wrinkled. "You remember what it was like in that kitchen at the food festival. Total chaos. Maybe they reviewed the tapes and saw him do it."

"Chick wouldn't do his own dirty work," I said. "Aunt Gully, remember you said you saw someone coming out of the kitchen. When you went back to get your apron?"

Aunt Gully's voice wavered. "How I wish I'd looked at that person better. But I was in such a tizzy! I wanted to get my apron and get back fast. It was a slender person. Black hair. Oh, and a baseball cap!"

Verity said, "The baseball cap!"

I nodded. "The baseball cap."

"What baseball cap?" Hilda said.

I explained what we'd seen in the security video at Cousin Frank's house.

"Was the lobster libber a Sox or Yankees fan?" Hector asked.

"Couldn't tell. Chick made the signs because he wanted us to think lobster libbers were here." I hesitated, deciding not to say any more about Megan's painful relationship with Chick. "But then we watched the security tape at Cousin Frank's—"

"Oh my God, you have to call the police!" Hilda said. "You've cracked the case of the lobster libber!"

I frowned. "Not really. We know who it's not. It's not Chick Costa."

Aunt Gully stared out the front window to the street, tapping her lips with her forefinger. Her thinking pose.

"Couldn't even tell if it's a man or a woman." How slight the figure was, I thought. "Boy or girl. I'm just sure it wasn't Chick Costa."

"But it could be an accomplice," Hilda said. "The police have special equipment. They can blow up the images. Then they'll be able to tell who it is."

"I'll let the police know," I said.

"And go to Juliet's," Verity muttered.

Aunt Gully turned from the window. "Yes, you girls go have fun." She shooed Verity and me out the door. "Come back to the house when you're done and show me those wonderful clothes. I'll have supper for you."

Chapter 44

As I got in the Tank, I reached into my bag for my sunglasses. "Ouch!" A jolt of pain made me jerk my hand out. I pulled the lobster pick from the bottom of my bag. "Finella Farraday!"

"I wish she'd been the person who made the *X*," Verity said. "We'd have her on tape."

My mind raced, "Finella might not have poisoned the rolls, and she might not have put up the signs or painted the *X*, but I still think she sent the threatening letters and slashed Aunt Gully's tires. She was right there in the parking lot at St. Pete's."

Verity sighed. "But how to prove it? We've got nothing."

"All we have is a fancy lobster pick." I turned the glittering pick in my hands. I stared down Pearl Street. My gaze focused on a news van parked down the street.

"Leo Rodriguez and his news team sure like the Tick Tock." I tapped the shiny lobster against my lip.

"I know that look." Verity started the engine. "Do you want to go stick that lobster pick in Finella's tires?"

"Yes. But I won't. The decent thing to do is to give it back and I think Leo Rodriguez should deliver it for me."

I rooted in Verity's glove box. "Do you have an envelope?"

Verity leaned into the stash of boxes and bags in the backseat and found a manila envelope. I wrote on the envelope and showed it to her. She laughed. "Perfect."

As we rolled down the street, I prayed that the window of the news van would be open. It was.

Verity slowed the Tank. I tossed the envelope in, then we rolled toward Rabb's Point.

Chapter 45

"I wonder who Chick paid off," Verity said.

"Sorry?" Lost in thought, I stared at the sailboats on the bay as Verity steered the Tank into Rabb's Point.

"It's a conspiracy when you work together to kill someone, right?" she said. "We saw Chick's accomplice, with the baseball cap. Same one Aunt Gully saw at the food festival."

"I guess." Something was bothering me, but I couldn't explain it. I just felt more and more anxious. Where was Chick?

"Did I tell you Lorel left her scarf in Chick's sports car? Her monogrammed scarf?"

"Ha! What a hoot if he's at Gull's Nest trying to return it to her," Verity said. "You know, Chick's red sports car's easy to notice. You'd think someone would've seen it by now."

"Chick used to summer here. He must have sailed. If I were Chick, I'd be getting away in a sailboat right now," I said.

Verity considered. "Makes sense. But where would he get a boat?"

"He probably still has friends here. And even if they're not here, he could always just 'borrow' a sailboat."

"Oh my God, Allie! I'd better tell my uncle. This can't wait. I'll tell him about the video, too. Then he can look for Chick's accomplice." Verity pulled over and, for once, her uncle answered her call.

"Uncle M, my friend Allie and I have information that might crack the food festival case." She told him about the video and my belief that Chick might escape on a boat.

Her uncle's voice boomed from the phone.

Verity winced. "Okay. Bye." She leaned her forehead against the steering wheel.

"What did he say?"

"He said to mind our own business. We have to let the police do their job. We have to stop playing Jessica Fletcher," Verity muttered.

"Maybe when we're done at Juliet's, I'll try to get Detective Rosato," I said. "She actually listened about the Dumpster at the Ellicott house."

We pulled into the drive of the Wells House. The house faced west. Red-tinged sunlight reflected off the windows. For a split second it looked as if flames sparked within the mansion.

Why did I feel so uneasy? I couldn't shake the feeling that I'd forgotten something. I threw a glance down the driveway, but no one was there.

"Buy of the century!" Verity said. Her enthusiasm was infectious. I shook off my unsettling thoughts and helped Verity grab some boxes from the trunk.

"More great stuff," Verity said. "We just have to get inside."

I remembered the angry red scratches on Susan's cheek. "Let's just hope Juliet's not in a scratching mood."

"She likes us. Remember? I give her cash"—she patted her purse—"and you play ballerina with her. If she does get crazy, just distract her with some fancy footwork until I can get the boxes outside."

I pushed the bell.

Verity hummed as she bounced on her toes. Overhead, gulls wheeled, their cries loud in the leafy oasis of the Wells estate.

Verity pressed the bell.

"Hmm, wonder if Juliet drove the new nurse away." Verity rapped loudly on the door.

"There's a car over there." A Volvo wagon was parked not far from the front door. "I think that was here this morning."

Verity turned the knob. "What the heck? It's open." She pushed open the door.

"You can't just walk in!" I grabbed her arm.

"Hellloooo!" Verity called into the house. "I'm not leaving until I get my stuff," she whispered to me.

"Didn't you say Juliet called you? The number must be in your phone," I said.

"Oh, yeah." Verity pulled the door almost shut, then dialed Juliet's number on her cell. A shrilling came from deep in the house.

"It's a house phone."

The phone rang over and over. No footsteps hurried to answer. No voices called out. Verity ended the call.

"Maybe we should go in." I pushed the door open. "The Volvo must belong to the nurse. If her car's here, she should be here. Someone should answer."

As we stepped into the foyer I trailed my fingers along the doorjamb. An additional lock, the type you can only open with a key, met my fingers. A large security system box on the wall was dark.

"Something's not right," I whispered.

"There you are!" Juliet trailed her arm on the gleaming mahogany banister as she swept down the stairs. She paused halfway down. She had looped a white chiffon scarf over a worn sweatshirt embroidered with two cats in a teacup.

"Come on up, girls."

Verity and I exchanged glances. Where was the nurse? I stepped slowly into the foyer. "Good evening, Miss Wells. We were here earlier and spoke to your nurse—"

"Oh, her. She's having some Madeira by the fire." Juliet started back up the stairs.

"We could come back." Something felt so off. Verity turned to me, her eyes wide, but she went to the stairs. I followed.

"Madeira by the fire," I whispered to Verity. "Isn't that from the movie? The Gypsies drink madeira by the fire?"

"She's just quoting the movie," Verity said. "Listen, she's an old lady. If she does anything weird we can take her, right?"

The banister gleamed under my fingers. "If we have to make a quick getaway, slide down the banister. It'll be faster than running."

"Come along, girls!" Juliet trilled from the top of the stairs. Her eyes were wide and glittering, circled with dark eyeliner. I tried not to stare, but Juliet's wig was askew. Now I realized that what I'd thought was her real hair, cut into a sleek long bob, was a wig. Long tendrils of thin salt-and-pepper hair trailed from one side of the displaced wig.

A small overnight bag was open on a table.

"Just put the money in there," she said. Verity complied.

I swallowed. My mouth had gone dry. "Miss Wells, are you going on a trip?"

Juliet laughed and waved us down the hall, her peals of laughter bright and brittle as broken glass.

"Start in there." Instead of leading us back to the huge closet off the master bedroom, Juliet waved into the door she'd closed on our last visit. Verity and I walked past the fireplace under the gaze of the large portrait of Contessa Wells in her famous Gypsy costume. A small fire crackled within. Papers and letters littered the floor, spilled from two small boxes.

"All the things in the closet and the bureau can go. Clear it all out." Juliet left the room.

Verity handed me two boxes. I set to work on the bureau while she went into the closet. Unlike our previous visit, Verity and I worked in uncomfortable silence.

I slid open drawer after drawer, but unlike the pristine silks we'd bought before, most seemingly never worn, the clothes in these drawers were faded and gray. A bottom drawer rattled as I pulled it open. It held dozens of bottles of pills. I slammed it shut.

I slipped into the closet with Verity.

"The clothes here aren't like the others," I whispered. "I think they're Juliet's, not Contessa's."

Verity nudged aside several pairs of worn sneakers. Then she walked deeper into the closet. She unzipped a dust-covered garment bag and a glamorous dress of gold organza spilled out. "Here toward the back, the clothes are nicer. It's like she put the nicer clothes away and never wore them again."

Verity dragged a finger across a dusty shelf. "We'll start here and move into the other bedroom. I forgot trash bags. I'll see if I can find some in the kitchen. We'll bag up this junky stuff. Put the good stuff in the boxes."

I returned to the bedroom as Verity headed downstairs. Instead of packing boxes, I stood before the portrait of Contessa. Why did Juliet have this portrait in her own suite, a portrait of her sister in her most famous role?

The woman in the portrait was a force, a presence, vibrant as the red walls of the room.

The acrid smoke smell made me cough. I peeked into the hallway. No sign of Juliet. I took a packet of letters, tied with pink satin ribbons, and turned it over. "Contessa" was written on the envelopes in a heavy, masculine hand.

She was burning her sister's love letters. That made more sense, given their relationship.

A gleam in the ashes drew my eye. A photo.

Using the black metal poker I dragged the photo from the hot ashes onto the marble surround of the fireplace.

Contessa's face looked up at me from the melted remains of her food festival pass.

"What are you doing?"

I gasped and turned, stumbling back against the wall. Juliet stood in the hall.

"Oh!" The poker slipped through my fingers to the marble with a clang. "I saw the photo—"

"My dear departed sister." Juliet grabbed the ID badge and threw it back into the ashes. She picked up the poker.

"Did you see the letters?" She didn't seem upset that I'd been digging in the fireplace. "All these love letters."

She picked up a packet and held it to her chest, closed her eyes. "My husband was quite a letter writer."

Juliet's mascara spilled toward her cheeks like black tears. "And then she took him from me, too." The edge to her voice, the crazy makeup, the oversharing. I tried to tamp down the panic that rose inside me. *She's only an old lady. A crazy old lady holding a poker.*

"She seduced my husband." Juliet dropped the letters. "She wanted to crawl inside my skin and become me. And she did. My sister was a monster, a horror." Juliet lifted the poker with two hands and slammed it on the ID badge, swinging wildly, over and over.

I yelped and stumbled back against a side table, throwing my arms up to protect myself. Juliet threw more letters into the fireplace, her chest heaving, then grabbed the mantel to steady herself.

I was too shocked to move and was even more shocked when she turned to me. I edged away, my back against the wall until I bumped into an antique wall mirror.

She looped her thin hair behind her ear, pushing the wig farther out of place.

I remembered pushing aside Contessa's hair, her hair tangling in her scarf, when I helped her at the food festival.

Suddenly I knew why Juliet kept the portrait of Contessa in her room.

Chapter 46

"You're not Juliet," I whispered. "You're"—I pointed at the portrait—"Contessa."

Her shoulders heaved, mascara streaked her face. "I am Contessa Wells. I am Contessa Wells."

I looked away from the crumpled face of the woman in front of me, fearful of what I saw in her eyes. Hatred. Insanity. Self-pity. Her hand still gripped the fireplace poker. Reflected firelight sparked on her rings. Rings on her hands, bracelets on her wrists. No earrings.

Suddenly I was back at the food festival, looking for Aunt Gully in the church hallway. That rhyme Aunt Gully had hummed now made sense. *Rings on her fingers and bells on her toes, she shall have music wherever she goes.* Aunt Gully had noticed, unconsciously, this woman's rings when she saw her leave the kitchen at the food festival.

"You were at the food festival." I pointed at the ID badge smoldering in the ashes. "You wore your sister's security badge. No one noticed because you looked alike and wore a hat."

She snorted. "They barely looked. The badge came in

the mail. My sister never saw it. But I had things to do at the food festival. I helped Susan take a nice nap that day. I have so many lovely pills to choose from."

My mind whirled. I remembered the Contessa who danced in the *The Gypsy's Daughter*. Her magnificent spins around the campfire. I had recognized her when the woman here, calling herself Juliet, had spun aside on my last visit with Verity. The way she moved, even decades later, in a body changed by time, was unmistakable. Somehow, on some level, I'd recognized her.

"What happened?" I whispered.

"Everyone said I'd be a star after *The Gypsy's Daughter*," she spat. "But when my sister ripped the earring from my ear it was clear that her jealousy would consume us both. If I'd left then, I would have been free of her. But I was a fool. I tried to help her. Kept her close. Hah! Close enough for her to start drugging me. I'd be high for days. She told people that I was Juliet, the unstable one, the jealous one. The addict. She made me an addict. Everyone saw me, everyone believed it.

"We always looked so much alike. The only thing she couldn't do was dance like me, so she told people she'd been injured. Oh, the sympathy poured in. She could still dance well enough, but never like me. She left Hollywood and moved to Broadway. Fewer people there knew her."

"And she put you away," I whispered.

"She put me away. After all, I was crazy. Different institutions, all across the country. Nice ones, only the best, but still. In every place, they nodded with sympathy but I knew how I sounded. Crazy. Always going on about how my sister had stolen my life. How my sister had stolen my identity. How I was the real Contessa Wells. The ravings of a madwoman."

"She kept you drugged?" I whispered.

"I've had every drug you can imagine." The real Contessa's voice rose. "The only time it's bad is when I know what's going on. When the drugs stop. When I know what she took from me. What she stole!" The last words were a scream.

"I want to smash her face!" She swung at the mirror. I dodged aside as the poker shattered glass and clattered to the floor.

I backed along the wall toward the door, my heart hammering in my chest.

"Wait! Wait!" she beseeched, hands clasped.

"You are Contessa Wells," I whispered. "I believe you."

"No one else does," she whispered.

Hurry, Verity. Where was she? Maybe Verity's presence would make this woman, Contessa Wells, stop.

"I've told nurse after nurse after doctor after doctor who I really am. 'Sure, lady, you're Contessa Wells.' They never believed me. And if one did, they were soon gone."

"But now you're free." I didn't want to move, to set her off further. Curiosity vied within me with disgust and pity. "You painted the red *X* on the sign at Kahuna's. It's the same paint as this room."

She nodded. "That place's ruining the town. I had Susan take me to the town meeting. I saw Ernie Moss. Ernie Moss is a bully. The way he talks to his wife." She shook her head.

"How did you do it? At the food festival."

"Easy." She laughed. "Walked in, flashed my badge at some dumb kid who had never heard of Contessa Wells. No one noticed me. You're a performer. We know how to stand out, how to blend in. When they announced the show was starting, everyone streamed out of the kitchen.

I hung back. Lifted the cloche. Sprinkled some of my secret ingredient"—her lips curled—"on the lobster rolls. My, they looked delicious. I headed out just as some woman came running in."

Some woman. Aunt Gully.

"You used monkshood," I said.

"My nurses always encouraged my gardening. It's good therapy." She smiled. "When I heard my sister was a judge at the festival, I saw a way to get rid of her and that awful bully at the same time. Two birds with one stone."

My mouth was so dry I could barely speak. "Other people were hurt."

Contessa waved her hand. "Only one person really mattered. My sister." She moved to the shattered mirror, her face reflected in the remaining shards. "It doesn't matter that I killed her. I still see her face in the mirror. The *hate lives*."

Shock rendered me immobile. *It doesn't matter that I killed her.* Did she really just confess?

Behind us, through the open window, came the sound of car doors slamming. A police radio squawked. Contessa ran to the window.

Verity peeked around the corner of the door frame, her eyes huge, her chest heaving.

Contessa whirled and ran to the doorway. Verity jumped back.

"What did you do? Why did you call the police?" she shrieked. Verity flinched. "Stupid, stupid girl!"

The woman I now knew to be Contessa Wells ran into the hallway. "Enough! I've had enough! It ends now."

For a moment my body refused to move. I stepped shakily toward Verity. "Did you call the police, Verity?"

Verity panted, a hand to her side. "The nurse. I found her. In the kitchen. On the floor. She won't wake up."

Enough, I've had enough, rang in my ears. *It ends now.*

Contessa hurried down the hall away from us. She ran through a narrow door in the wood paneling at the end of the hallway.

"Did she just say she killed her sister?" Verity said.

I nodded. "Verity, let the cops in. I think she's going to the roof."

I hurried through the same door Contessa'd run through. A narrow, steep spiraling cast-iron stairway curled upward toward a dim square of light. I ran up. My boot caught on a step, knocking me to my knees. I ripped off my boot and kicked off my flip-flop. I hurtled up the rest of the stairs, suddenly very afraid. The Wells House was famous for its architecture, especially its ornate widow's walk at the top of the house. That's where this led, I was sure. Three stories up.

Enough, I've had enough, rang in my ears. *It ends now.*

At the top of the stairs, I pulled myself up on rusty metal handles into a small, glass-windowed cupola. A twinge of pain shot through my ankle with each step.

High above Mystic Bay, the first embers of sunset smoldered along the horizon to the west.

Contessa's figure was silhouetted against the reddening sky, standing at the low cast-iron railing that ran around the edge of the roof. The widow's walk.

Contessa reached out her arms to the sky, her scarf streaming behind her. I thought of how her sister's scarf had streamed behind her also, in the gentle morning breeze at the food festival. But tonight, stronger wind gusts from the bay buffeted us. I leaned forward into the wind, fearing that I'd see her body cartwheel into space.

The tarred roof surface was uneven. I stumbled on one of several small low vents that made an obstacle course across the roof. It was lunacy to be up here, but I was with a woman who had long ago shaken off reality's grasp.

"Stop. Please. Come back inside." I raised my voice to be heard over the wind, but I tried to keep my tone calm and reassuring.

Contessa turned to me. Her chest heaved and I remembered her age. She swung a leg over the low railing. I lunged forward. "No!"

"Don't come closer." She held up a warning hand. I stopped, my body taut with adrenaline.

"I'm tired of living. I'll just pull you down with me." She pulled off her wig and let it drop from her fingers. Shouts rose from below. "I will. I don't care. "

Where were the police? Surely Verity had told them where we were. I needed them to come now, before she threw herself off the building. I was alone with this broken woman three stories above an unforgiving gravel drive and I didn't know what to do.

Aunt Gully. She'd know what to say to this woman, but I could think of nothing.

More shouts rose from far below. Police radios squawked. Contessa unwound the scarf from her throat, raised her arm, and watched the wind snatch it away. The rescuers were too late. Nothing they could say to this woman would change her mind.

Contessa spoke clearly. "There's nothing left. Nothing worth living for." She leaned over the edge of the roof.

I thought of Contessa's dance. I said the one thing that came into my mind.

"Beauty. Beauty is worth living for," I shouted.

She straightened and turned.

I hummed the music of her *Gypsy's Daughter* solo. Slowly I stepped toward her on the hot, sticky black tar-covered roof. My bare feet burned as I swayed into her dance, slowly spinning, turning my arms into the elegant shapes she'd made, as much an artist as anyone who held a paintbrush or the bow of a violin.

She turned toward me, giving me her full attention.

"Brava, my child, brava!" Contessa clasped her hands. Her balance point shifted away from the edge.

She pulled her leg back over the rail and stepped toward me, her body bent forward against the slight pitch of the roof. Her arms swung side to side just as they had in her film. I could practically see her full Gypsy skirt swirl around her. Together we hummed and moved to the music only we could hear. As we danced, I maneuvered myself between Contessa and the rail, praying that she didn't hear the footsteps clanging up the metal steps.

A body curled up from the stairs into the glass cupola. Detective Rosato. She stepped forward, and as she did, I threw myself more deeply into the music we hummed. I had to fully embody the dance to keep Contessa's attention. One flicker of my attention toward the police would break the spell, could send her hurtling toward the rail.

I maneuvered Contessa back toward the stairs and threw myself into the final pose. Contessa mirrored my movement. She burst into laughter. Detective Rosato and another policeman dashed forward. Contessa focused on me so intently that she seemed unaware of them even as they grabbed her arms.

"Wonderful! Wonderful!" Contessa cried. "My theater the sky! My audience the stars and the ocean!"

Detective Rosato caught my eye.

"Thank you, Miss Wells." I bent into a deep *révérence*.

Detective Rosato jutted her chin at the policeman holding Contessa's other arm. They slightly loosened their hold.

Contessa put her hand over her heart and curtsied back.

"Wonderful performance," Detective Rosato said to

Miss Wells. She nodded to another police officer. "Make sure she gets downstairs safely."

We watched them descend the stairs.

"What did I just see?" Detective Rosato asked.

"A performance by Contessa Wells."

Chapter 47

Detective Rosato and I descended the slippery metal stairway to the second floor. I pressed my hand against the walls, trying to take the weight off my throbbing ankle. At the bottom, I put the walking boot back on but a shock of certainty pierced me. My ankle was reinjured, months of healing and rehabilitation ruined.

Detective Rosato held my arm at the bottom of the stairs. "So the woman who died at the food festival was—"

"Her sister, Juliet Wells." Suddenly I was exhausted.

A tiny line appeared between her eyebrows. "Were they twins?"

"No, but only a few years apart. This woman's the real Contessa Wells. Her sister"—it was so crazy I could hardly explain—"stole her life." I broke away and limped to the staircase. "Is Verity okay?"

"Your friend downstairs? Yes. She reported a medical emergency." Detective Rosato didn't realize I knew what the medical emergency was.

One look at the grand staircase and I threw my leg over the gleaming wooden banister. My ankle couldn't take any more stairs.

"Wait!" Detective Rosato shouted.

The slide down the banister was faster than I'd anticipated. I slowed myself at the bottom to step carefully to the marble floor. Detective Rosato's footsteps clattered down the stairs behind me.

Verity stood by the kitchen door, wringing her hands. I stopped at the threshold.

"You okay?" I said.

Verity shook her head.

Breathing heavily, Detective Rosato shouldered past me. "Go wait in the foyer."

She strode to where an EMT bent over a still form on the tile floor. The EMT stood to speak to Detective Rosato. The nurse we'd met earlier lay on her side, her eyes closed, her uniform skirt spattered with liquid. A delicate tea service was in disarray on the table, a cup broken on the floor near her hand.

"Is the nurse alive?" I whispered.

Verity wiped her eyes. "I don't know."

Chapter 48

After the EMTs left with the nurse, Verity and I met with Detective Rosato and Chief Brooks in the morning room of the Wells House. It was surreal to sit on the same sofa as the woman we thought was Juliet Wells, a woman who'd killed her sister and almost killed three other innocent people. My ankle throbbed. I trembled as I recounted what had happened on the widow's walk.

"First time I've had a case cracked by a dance-off." Detective Rosato rubbed her forehead. "Still, there's no way to prove what she told you was true—that she's the real Contessa Wells."

Ravings of a madwoman, the real Contessa'd said.

I was sure it was true. I'd seen her dance.

"We'd need to do DNA testing to confirm her identity," Detective Rosato continued.

"So what would you need for that? For DNA testing?" I asked.

"A sample we were certain identified each woman. Then we could test this sister who says she's Contessa Wells by matching to a sample we were certain was from Contessa Wells."

Verity and I looked at each other. The silhouettes.

"Look at these." I hobbled to the childhood portraits of Contessa and Juliet.

I took one down. On the back, in spidery handwriting, was a label. *"Contessa."* I handed it to Detective Rosato. She showed it to Chief Brooks.

"There's hair in them," Verity explained. "Hair braids."

I took down the other and turned it over, showing Detective Rosato the same spidery writing. *"Juliet."* I imagined a mother, preserving these precious reminders of her beloved daughters' youth. What would she think of the cruelty of one daughter, the insanity of the other?

I handed the frame to Verity and she replaced the two silhouettes. "Hair art was a thing a long time ago," Verity said. "Pretty old for the Wells family even, but the Wells family was pretty old-fashioned. I mean she, Juliet, I mean Contessa, had that lachrymatory—"

"I'm pretty sure she hid the monkshood in it." I eased back onto the couch.

"Lachrymatory? Monkshood?" Detective Rosato asked.

"Victorian vial, for collecting tears," Verity explained. Detective Rosato blinked.

I shook my head. "I'm pretty sure she tossed it into the grave with Fake Contessa, er, Juliet. At the burial ground."

"The lachrymatory that was buried had monkshood in it?" Detective Rosato's voice resumed its precise edge. "Do you have proof?"

"No proof, but I just bet that's where she stashed the grated monkshood root she used at the food festival. What a great hiding place. She told me she grew her own." I nodded toward the garden in the darkness outside the French doors.

"We'll conduct a search," Detective Rosato said.

"What happened to the nurse?" I asked. "Was she poisoned with monkshood, too?"

"We don't think so," Police Chief Brooks said. "Looks like an overdose of a sedative."

"There are a lot of pills in a drawer upstairs," I said. "A lot."

"Will she be okay?" Verity asked.

Chief Brooks nodded. "The EMT said yes."

I set my foot on the coffee table. I imagined the starched and proper nurse, trying to be professional, trying to be kind, sitting down to share tea with Miss Wells. Susan would never have done that.

Chapter 49

"You go ahead and cry, Allegra Larkin. You stubborn thing." Aunt Gully threw a look at me from the driver's seat of her van. I slouched in the passenger seat. The pain in my ankle was excruciating, but not as bad as the doctor's news. My ankle had to be reset. Months of therapy and treatment ruined.

We drove past Verity's Vintage and She Sells Chic. Finella stood in front of her store with a guy in a gray suit.

"Hmmm," Aunt Gully said.

I raised an eyebrow. "What does that 'hmmm' mean, Aunt Gully? Hmmm?"

"That man's a real estate agent."

"Is Finella selling?" I sat up. "That would be great for Verity. She wants to expand her shop."

"She might get her wish. Rumor has it Finella's looking at other opportunities." Aunt Gully started humming "Get Happy" from *Summer Stock*.

I turned to her. "Spill."

"Well, back at the shack, when you mentioned Finella." Aunt Gully pulled over and turned to me. "It made me think about the letters and the tires. Now, I try to think the best of people, but Finella." Aunt Gully shook her head. "Well, I decided, best to let the woman explain herself. So I went up to her shop.

"Of course she denied sending the letters and ruining my tires, but that night Leo Rodriguez was on the news asking her questions about the lobster libbers. The next day she sent me a check for the tires. More than enough to cover the whole thing, labor, parts."

"How nice," I said, careful to keep my voice neutral. I remembered what I'd written on the envelope holding the fancy lobster pick that I'd tossed into Leo's news van: "Lobster Liberation Group. 55 Harbor Street. Mystic Bay." The address of Finella's shop, She Sells Chic.

Finella's moving was all the proof I needed.

Aunt Gully's voice faded as my eyes closed. "Funny, I couldn't find that fancy lobster pick anywhere."

Maybe I'd confess to Aunt Gully after the lovely pain medication wore off.

Chapter 50

A few days later, Verity and I sat at a picnic table by the Lazy Mermaid's pier just before closing time.

"Why couldn't the murderer be Chick Costa?" I said. "Personally, I'd like him to go to jail forever."

"Assaulting Ernie?" Verity said. "Destroying Ernie's car? He's got to get some jail time out of that."

"You know what I mean. That business with Megan. Hiding her own child from her. Not that it's not awful, what he did to Ernie, but what he did to Megan." I took a bite of my lobster roll. "When it all comes out, I bet he's going to wish he went down with his friend's sailboat."

Chick had indeed hidden his sports car at a friend's house on Fox Point and taken his friend's sailboat, the perfectly named *Escape Hatch*. Unfortunately for Chick, the last time he'd sailed off Mystic Bay was years ago. He'd forgotten the rocks off Orion Point and ran *Escape Hatch* aground. The Coast Guard picked him up and escorted him to the police.

Verity and I clinked bottles of lemonade.

"We could spread rumors about him." Verity's eyes

glowed. "Something embarrassing so he never gets another date . . ."

"May we join you?" A man wearing a floppy hat and white windbreaker took off sunglasses.

"Rick! Of course."

Rick Lopez held a tray with two lobster rolls, two cups of chowder, and several slices of coffee cake. Rio, wearing a baseball cap and an oversized sweatshirt, slowly followed him, using a walker. She placed the walker to the side of the picnic table.

We scooted to make room.

Rick placed the tray in front of Rio. Almost all the tables and Adirondack chairs were taken by diners enjoying the glow of sunset on the Micasset River. Aunt Gully had added strings of lights above the dining area, and the colors danced in the breeze.

"Your ankle! Wasn't it in a walking boot?" Rio asked.

I grimaced and held out my foot in its hard cast. "I reinjured it."

"In a dance-off with a murderer," Verity breathed.

"What!" Rick exclaimed.

Verity launched into the story of my dance on the widow's walk of the Wells House.

"So that's how it went down," Rio said. "Juliet was Contessa, and Contessa was Juliet. Ouch, my head hurts. We'd never have guessed she was an imposter. You see people in movies or television and you just think that of course they look different in real life."

"A dance-off with a murderer." Rick shook his head.

"It wasn't a dance-off. It was just"—I exhaled—"the only thing I could think to do."

"Well, thank goodness it was you and not me," Verity said. "What would I have done? Shown her my vintage cameo?"

"You're absolutely amazing, Allie Larkin." Rick high-fived me. I blushed. I had told my story over and over to police, but had turned down interviews with the media. What had happened on the widow's walk still seemed so unreal. Dancing with a woman I'd watched on-screen. Worshiped. My feelings were so tangled I didn't even know myself how I felt about the woman who was Contessa Wells.

"Tragic, really," Rio said. "I wonder what'll happen to her?"

I shook my head. "Nobody's heard."

Aunt Gully hurried down to the pier. Rio and Rick rose to hug her. I scooted along the picnic bench to make room for her.

"How do you like your supper?" Aunt Gully asked.

Rick and Rio grinned. "Fantastic!"

A disbelieving smile broke across Aunt Gully's face. "Really? You're not just being nice because you remember me from Mystic Bay Elementary School?"

Rio's brow wrinkled. "Is that it? You think we picked the Lazy Mermaid for the contest only because I know you?"

"Never fear." Rick burped. "'Scuse me. Am I not the meanest man in network food? I've made grown men and women cry with my honest, perhaps too honest, reviews."

"For real," Rio said.

"When YUM decided to do the lobster roll contest," Rick said, "they asked us to do the legwork, visiting dozens of lobster shacks all over New England. Since we were also scouting for a spot for our new spa, we jumped at the chance."

Rick leaned back. "At first, Rio'd wanted to skip Mystic Bay, but Kahuna's is here so we had to come. We came to the Mermaid, yes, because Rio knew Aunt Gully a long time ago, but also we'd heard this newcomer to the food scene was fabulous."

Rick wolfed a bite of lobster roll. "Rio said that even with the disguise she wanted to be extra careful 'cause your aunt's so perceptive she would've recognized her in a second. So I took the lobster rolls out to Rio and we ate them in the rental car."

"Come on, tell us about your disguise," I said.

"No can do." Rio chuckled. "Top secret."

"When we had your aunt's lobster roll." Rick kissed his fingertips. "Awesome, the pure taste of summer, man. That secret sauce rocked our world."

"Bottom line is . . ." Rio took Aunt Gully's hand. "Aunt Gully, we think you're getting a raw deal from YUM on the lobster roll contest. We want to highlight what we think truly is the best lobster roll in New England. We'd love it if you'd let us do an episode on the Lazy Mermaid."

"Yes!" I said.

Verity gasped.

"A *Foodies on the Fly* episode on me?" Aunt Gully whispered. "You mean, park your trailer right here in the Lazy Mermaid parking lot?"

Rick laughed. "Right here."

"And join me in the kitchen?" Aunt Gully beamed.

"And pick lobster?" I said. "That calls for a celebration." I hobbled as quickly as I could to the shack to tell Hector and Hilda. Aunt Gully always kept a bottle of champagne in the refrigerator "for emergencies." I grabbed it and some paper cups and hurried back.

We cheered as Rick popped the cork and poured. Aunt Gully raised her cup. "First of all, here's to our brave Allie."

"Hear, hear!"

"You cracked the case, Allie," Verity said. "With your fancy footwork you brought a murderer to justice."

"When did you first suspect the imposter?" Rio asked.

I put down my cup. "It was a feeling I had when we went to the Wells House the first time. The way Juliet, well, Contessa turned and moved. But still that was just a feeling. And you should've seen all the locks on the doors at the Wells House. It seemed impossible that she could escape with a nurse on duty and all the locks to keep her in.

"Then I saw the walled garden outside the morning room. There was a bench, pulled up right next to the wall. When I looked over the wall, there was another bench directly on the other side. I thought how simple it would be to climb over, using the benches as steps. The wall wasn't high. Juliet, um, Contessa was in amazingly good shape. She didn't bother with the doors. She just went out through the garden and over the wall."

"She's the one who painted the X on the sign at Kahuna's," Verity said.

"She hated Ernie," I said. "She thought he was destroying the town."

"She put on a baseball cap as a disguise," Verity said. "Without movie star clothes, she just looked like an average person."

"Same thing at the food fest," Aunt Gully said. "I saw the cap, but just didn't notice her face."

"But you noticed her rings, Aunt Gully, subconsciously," I said. "She wore rings on every finger. When you ran down the church hallway after going back to get your apron, I remembered you were humming a nursery rhyme: 'Rings on her fingers and bells on her toes, she shall have music wherever she goes.'"

"I had no idea!" Aunt Gully breathed. "I don't even remember seeing her rings!"

"Thank goodness you're free, Gully!" Rick raised his glass. "To Aunt Gully!"

"To Aunt Gully!"

Rick whooped, pulled Aunt Gully to her feet, and swung her in a circle.

"I've got to tell Lorel." I dialed and stepped a few feet away from the table.

As I told Lorel the good news about the Lazy Mermaid and *Foodies on the Fly,* Rick's and Aunt Gully's voices rose in song. Rick's raspy baritone provided an antidote to the pain of Aunt Gully's screeching. Soon everyone at our table was singing. Some customers joined in.

"They're singing?" Lorel said. "Is Aunt Gully getting drunk?"

Aunt Gully's eyes were shining and her cheeks were pink as she swayed with Rick. "Nope, just happy," I said.

"I still cannot believe you were up on a roof with Juliet, I mean, Contessa Wells. You drive me crazy, sis." She exhaled. "But I'm glad you're okay."

"Thanks," I said. "I wish you were here for some champagne."

"I'll be home this weekend. Until then, keep an eye on things."

"You bet." My heart warmed as I watched Aunt Gully celebrate. "What could go wrong?"

Read on for a look ahead to the next
Lobster Shack Mystery

AGAINST THE CLAW

Coming in August 2018 from
St. Martin's Paperbacks!

CHAPTER ONE

Day One
Tuesday, June 30

For all her MBA, perfect French manicure, and fancy Boston job, my sister Lorel was still at the mercy of her passion for the bad boy of Mystic Bay, Connecticut, Patrick Yardley.

In the frame of the Lazy Mermaid's front window, Patrick and Lorel kissed, Patrick astride his Harley, totally ignoring the "get a room" looks from customers heading into my Aunt Gully's lobster shack.

"What's a guy got to do to get some chowder around here?" a customer at the counter said.

"Sorry." I served him a bowl. He added crackers and dropped his spoon in with a splash.

Lorel hurried in, the roar of Patrick's Harley following her as he gunned out of the parking lot.

Aunt Gully shot me a warning glance and grabbed a plate from the kitchen pass through.

"What?" Lorel smoothed her gold blond hair.

"I didn't say anything." I wiped drips of chowder spattered by the sloppy customer. He threw me a look. "No need to rub a hole in the counter, honey."

Lorel joined me behind the counter. "Patrick and I were talking about a new social media campaign for New Salt."

"Since last night when he picked you up for dinner?" I muttered.

She brushed past me into the kitchen.

Two men in Harbor Police polo shirts bellied up to the counter and scanned the chalkboard menu on the wall behind me.

"What can I get you, gentlemen?" I said, trying to swallow my irritation with Lorel.

Bertha Betancourt, Mystic Bay's Lobster Lady, shifted aside to let the two men get closer to the counter. Bertha's family had been lobstering in Mystic Bay since the town was founded and her Learn to Lobster cruises were a popular tourist attraction. She leaned toward Aunt Gully.

"Gully, when I pulled up those lobster pots, I had a feeling, you know how you get a feeling?" Bertha's round, sun-reddened face crinkled into a grin. "Well, I reached over and what do I see? Some joker's stuffed a wolf fish in one of my pots. Ugly monster nearly took my hand off!"

"God bless America!" Aunt Gully chuckled.

"That woke me up, let me tell you!" Bertha swigged her mug of coffee like it was a tankard of rum. "Shoulda been there, Gully. Ugliest thing you ever did see."

No. The ugliest thing ever was the thought of my sister rekindling her relationship with the guy who'd been breaking her heart since middle school.

The two men ordered lobster rolls with extra coleslaw. I clipped the order to a metal wheel and turned it into the kitchen.

Lorel frowned at me through the pass through window. "Don't look at me like that. I know what I'm doing."

I started after Lorel, but Aunt Gully pulled me back. "I don't like it either, Allie, but she's a grown woman. Opposites attract, right?" She picked up two plates of overflowing lobster rolls from the kitchen pass through and brought them to a couple seated at a counter by the front door. The shack's interior was tiny—just four tables, a counter by the kitchen and one by the front window. Most diners took their rolls to the picnic tables outside.

I sighed. "Everyone loves the bad boys."

Some people would say that Lorel was out of Patrick's league. Others would say Patrick was out of hers. The problem was that they were in different leagues. Patrick's bar/restaurant, New Salt, catered to Mystic Bay's yacht club set. Rumors, about drugs mostly, drifted around the club like tendrils of fog on the bay. Sure, Patrick looked like the cover of a romance novel come to life, but he'd had numerous brushes with the law. Was I the only woman in Mystic Bay who was immune to his charms?

The wall phone shrilled. I picked it up. "Lazy Mermaid Lobster Shack."

"This is Zoe Parker, personal assistant to Stellene Lupo. I'd like to speak to Gina Fontana about catering." The clipped voice made me feel like I was wasting her time.

"Gina Fontana?" For a second the name didn't register. My Aunt Gully was Gully to everyone from Mystic Bay. No one here called her by her given name, Gina.

Lorel came out of the kitchen's swinging door, tying an apron behind her back.

I caught Lorel's eye and enunciated clearly. "Sorry, we don't do catering."

"Who is it?" Lorel said.

I pressed the phone to my chest. "Somebody somebody, personal assistant to Stellene Lupo." As soon as I said the name it registered. Stellene Lupo.

Lorel yanked the phone from my hands.

"*The* Stellene Lupo?" Aunt Gully hurried back to the counter. "She owns that big modeling agency in New York."

Bertha turned. "And the Harmony Harbor estate!"

Lorel covered one ear and murmured on the phone, using her money voice, all modulated and clearly enunciated. "Catering? Of course."

Of course? "What?"

Lorel waved me off and turned her back.

Catering? We'd never done catering. My aunt's Lazy Mermaid Lobster Shack had just opened this past spring. Business wasn't just good. It was overwhelming. There was a line waiting to get in as soon as we opened the doors at 11. We'd talked about what my MBA sister called other "income streams" including catering, but we'd decided to just get through the busy summer tourist season first. Now she was talking about catering?

A group wearing neon green New England Lobster Trail t-shirts surged through the screen door into the shack. Aunt Gully turned to greet them. "Welcome, lobster lovers!"

"I'll have Mrs. Fontana get back to you," Lorel said. "She's in a meeting right now." Aunt Gully posed for a selfie with a stocky guy wearing a baseball hat decorated with red foam lobster claws.

"Thank you so much. Good bye." Lorel hung up and jotted notes on an order pad.

I put my hands on my hips. "I thought we didn't do catering."

Lorel's green eyes sparkled. "We do now."

Aunt Gully leaned over the counter. "You look like the cat that got the cream, Lorel."

"Our ship has just come in, Aunt Gully," Lorel said.

CHAPTER TWO

After the lunch rush, a couple of Aunt Gully's friends came in to help. Lorel, Aunt Gully, Aunt Gully's assistant manager, Hilda, and I gathered at our conference room: a wobbly picnic table on a patch of gravel behind the shed where we stored live lobsters.

Lorel sat at the very end of the table, as if she were leading a meeting at the big Boston social media company where she worked. She'd taken a week off to help with the Fourth of July rush, then she'd go back to managing accounts for Fortune 500 companies.

I adjusted the high tech, waterproof wrap on my left ankle. All I wanted was to get my almost-healed broken ankle completely healed so I could return to my soloist spot with New England Ballet Theater. In the meantime, I'd accepted a role with minimal dancing in a show at Mystic Bay's Jacob's Ladder Theater. I'd work with Aunt Gully until I got the all clear to dance again from our company doctor.

"Listen to this," Lorel's green eyes glittered. "Stellene Lupo's throwing her annual Fourth of July party. She wants us to serve our lobster rolls, chowder, and coleslaw to her guests. One hundred people. From 7 to 9 P.M. We've been talking about additional income streams—"

Aunt Gully's eyes took on a dreamy, faraway look.

Uh oh.

Aunt Gully squeezed Lorel's hand. "I have to admit, I'd love to see the inside of Harmony Harbor. Too bad you didn't see Stellene when she was here oh, maybe three, four weeks ago?"

"You never mentioned it!" Lorel exclaimed.

"I must have missed her, too," I said.

"Well, Hilda follows the society news and she said it was her."

Hilda Viera and her husband, Hector, were the shack's only other full-time employees—Hector cooking lobsters and Hilda managing the shack with Aunt Gully. Hilda and her husband, Hector, had both worked in the restaurant industry before retiring and sailing around the world. When their sailboat *Happy Place* docked in Mystic Bay, they'd decided to stay and take jobs at the Lazy Mermaid. "She was with her teenage daughter, Tinsley," Hilda said. Her big brown eyes radiated concern. "Tinsley has a reputation for being wild. In and out of rehab, poor thing."

"That's not important." Lorel took Aunt Gully's shoulders and turned her toward her van parked by the side of the shack. "This is important. With what Stellene will pay us, you could buy a new van."

I straightened. If Aunt Gully's van had been a cat, it would be on its seventh or eighth life. The rust-flecked Dodge had more than 200,000 miles on her, plus several scrapes from where I sideswiped our mailbox when I was learning to drive.

"One problem." One of us had to be sensible. "How will we be in two places at the same time? How do we keep the shack open and do Stellene's bash? The prep work alone for the party will take hours—"

Lorel cleared her throat. "We could just close the Mermaid early and do Stellene's party." She looked out over the river that flowed behind our shack, avoiding Aunt Gully's eyes.

Aunt Gully, too, looked out over the Lazy Mermaid parking lot to the river. A sailboat with all the time in the world slid past our dock. Aunt Gully straightened her pink Lazy Mermaid apron. "Well, the money is"—

"Crazy good," I sighed.

"Tempting," Aunt Gully said. "But I have to open the Mermaid on the Fourth. We're part of Mystic Bay. We'll have so many summer people here, and people coming after the parade. I want to be part of that."

"Stellene's party's at night." Lorel leaned forward. "We could call in reinforcements. Hector and Hilda can manage."

I was torn. On one hand, we said no catering! On the other hand, great money! Aunt Gully's face was even pinker than usual, matching the pink barrette holding back her silver hair. She was excited, sure, but was I the only one who cared about the woman's health? Aunt Gully's not old but does qualify for the senior center where she takes a Zumba class one day a week. She already worked long days, seven days a week at the shack.

"Did you say yes already, Lorel?" I asked.

Lorel shook her head.

"Good. Because if Stellene's willing to spend that much money, that means she really wants us." It was an insane amount of extra work, steaming the lobsters, picking the meat, toasting the rolls, making Aunt Gully's lobster love sauce, coleslaw, chowder.

"Tell Stellene we can do it if her staff can do all the

prep work." I held Lorel's eyes. "It's the only way it'll happen."

"Yes, yes. I can show them how to do it right." Aunt Gully tapped her lips with her forefinger, her thinking pose. Her cheeks pinked and her dangling lobster earrings caught the sunlight. She was getting into it.

What Stellene wants, Stellene gets. The words, unbidden, slid in my mind.

Lorel jotted notes. "I'm sure Stellene can afford plenty of kitchen staff at Harmony Harbor."

"Hilda, would you and Hector handle things here?" Aunt Gully squeezed Hilda's hand.

Hilda nodded. "Of course, we can handle things here. Though I'd much rather be there."

Aunt Gully hugged Hilda. "Me, too."

"You'll have to tell me every detail. And I mean every detail," Hilda said.

"Do you really think it can work?" Aunt Gully's brown eyes shone. We were all giddy with the thought of all the money Stellene would pay, giddy at the thought of getting behind the walls of Harmony Harbor, serving our lobster rolls to the rich and famous movie stars and models who would be there.

"If they give us the staff," I repeated.

"OK. I'll call Stellene's assistant." Lorel jogged back into the shack. Aunt Gully and Hilda, chatting excitedly, followed.

I stretched my arms over my head and turned my face to the sun. My red hair is the type that comes with sunburns and freckles, but I love the feel of the sun on my skin. Maybe if business slowed, I'd get away for a quick swim before rehearsal.

The blare of a car horn yanked me back into the real world. Voices rose. I hurried to the front of the shack. As usual for the summer, tourist traffic on Mystic Bay's narrow streets flowed like winter sap, slow and sticky. "Honking won't do you any good," I muttered.

Our parking lot was full. Customers streamed from the sidewalk to the door of the Mermaid. No time for a swim.

A lobster boat pulled up to our pier. The captain waved and I returned the greeting as I went to meet him.

"Hey, Allie." Ten-year-old Bit Markey brushed his floppy black hair out of his eyes and joined me on the pier. Together we hauled buckets of live lobsters into the storage shed.

Bit lived with his mom and dad in a pre-renovation 1840 house across Pearl Street from the Mermaid. A sagging front porch and a marijuana flag in the parlor window made it stand out from the other, more carefully restored buildings on the street. Bit spent several hours a day working at the Mermaid, ferrying live lobsters from the pier to the lobster storage shed, sweeping, and what he called "policing the grounds."

A car horn blared as a blue van with BEST OF NEW ENGLAND TOURS squeezed into the lot. Ever since the New England's Best Lobster Roll competition in May, the Mermaid had been visited by several tour groups a day.

"Here we go," I said.

Bit and I hurried into the kitchen. I slung a pink Lazy Mermaid apron over my head. Lorel emerged from Aunt Gully's tiny office. She pursed her lips, scribbling on the order pad.

"Well?" I asked.

Lorel hugged Aunt Gully. "It's a go! Stellene's assistant says they'll have her staff provide you with everything you need, Aunt Gully. Her daughter wants Lazy Mermaid lobster rolls and Stellene'll do whatever it takes to get them."

"Lorel, that's just grand. Grand!" Aunt Gully twirled me around and then strode out of the kitchen into the dining room. Lorel and I exchanged looks.

"Oh, God, here it comes." I peeked through the pass through window.

Aunt Gully started singing her victory song, "Get Happy" from *Summer Stock*, a song made famous by Judy Garland.

Aunt Gully's no Judy Garland.

Bit ran out the kitchen door, his hands over his ears.

As Aunt Gully squawked, conversation in the shack ceased. Customers caught each other's eyes and tried not to laugh. Then Aunt Gully hit a high note.

A man in a Red Sox t-shirt, broad and tall as a football linebacker, set down his lobster roll. Next thing I knew, he was dancing with Aunt Gully and singing along. The diners crowded into our tiny shack all started applauding and talking at once. The tour group stood at the screen door, holding cell phones high.

Next to me, Lorel was quiet. She scribbled on the order pad, avoiding my eyes. I took the pen from her hands. "OK, Lorel, spill. There's a catch, isn't there?"

Lorel tucked the pad in her pocket. "Nothing to worry about, Allie. Details, details. But Stellene asked for us, you and me, to help serve."

"You and me? Why?"

Lorel waved it away. "Who cares? Come on Allie, the people at Stellene's party are the type to throw huge parties. Rich movers and shakers. This is a golden opportunity. Stellene chose us because her daughter loved the lobster roll and Stellene likes Aunt Gully's," Lorel lowered her voice, "primitive, naïve aesthetic."

"Primitive aesthetic?" I folded my arms.

"Primitive. And naïve," Lorel said. "In the art world it means childlike."

"I know what it means." How could I argue? Most sea-side restaurants have that typical old-fashioned nautical look: fishing nets, antique wooden lobster traps, ships' wheels, little statues of lighthouses and pipe-smoking sea captains in yellow slickers and sou'westers.

Aunt Gully had that on steroids and sprinkled with glitter. Shelves that ran along the top of the wall of the shack were crowded with her mermaid collection, what she called her mermaidabilia. It was the kitschiest, tack-iest, tchotchke-est mermaid stuff ever—mermaids on dolphins, mermaids with hula skirts. Cowboy mermaids, mermaids with maracas. Customers had started bringing Aunt Gully mermaid tokens from their homes. We even had a life-sized wooden mermaid figurehead standing outside the door of the shack.

Just when I was sure I was getting a migraine, some-one dropped a coin in Aunt Gully's jukebox and Tom Jones was singing. I pulled my eyes away from the mermaidabilia. There wasn't an inch to spare in our tiny lobster shack, but now some teenage girls were dancing with Aunt Gully and the man in the Red Sox shirt. A little boy about three years old stood on a chair, marching in place, conducting the music with a plastic fork.

It's nuts. Absolutely nuts. The lobster shack had only been open a few months. We'd never gotten through a Fourth of July holiday. Now we had to get through Fourth of July and cater a party for one hundred one percenters at Harmony Harbor.

Still, excitement kindled in me. I couldn't wait to get behind the walls of Harmony Harbor.

That evening at Aunt Gully's cottage, Gull's Nest, Lorel, Aunt Gully, and I relaxed on the patio, taking advantage of the cool evening air. A storm two days earlier had left behind calm clear weather and a reprieve from the humidity that was typical of summer in Mystic Bay.

The old-fashioned wall phone in the kitchen shrilled. Aunt Gully went inside to answer it.

Music thumped as a car rolled down the street. The scent of charcoal, lighter fluid, and grilled hamburgers and hotdogs was in the air. Summer people were moving in for the holiday weekend. Down on the beach at the end of the street, fireworks crackled in a trial run for the Fourth. The sulfurous smell drifted on the breeze.

Strings of fairy lights strung over the patio mimicked the fireflies over Aunt Gully's garden. Lorel bent over her smartphone. Usually her texting was work-related, but tonight I wondered if she was texting with Patrick.

I tried to swallow my words but I couldn't help it. "Lorel, listen, I know your affairs are none of my business—"

Lorel didn't look up. "That's right, Allie, my affairs are none of your business."

I drank the last of my lemonade. Sweet and bitter.

"I—"

"Allie. I'm not discussing it. If Aunt Gully can stop nagging me about Patrick, so can you."

"I—"

Lorel raised her head, her look hard even under Aunt Gully's string of fairy lights. It was the same hard look she'd give when I wanted to tag along in middle school. The lights highlighted her high cheekbones, her sculpted chin, her strong jaw. She looked like the cool blond heroine of a Hitchcock movie.

I changed tack. "Well, I took your morning shift today. You owe me."

Lorel scrolled on her phone. "I already told Aunt Gully I'll take your morning shift tomorrow."

"Oh. Thanks." I stretched my legs on the chaise, inhaling the calming scent of Aunt Gully's basil plants. I could already imagine those wonderful extra hours in bed.

"A little something to celebrate our catering venture!" Aunt Gully set a tray with shortcakes, strawberries, and whipped cream on the table.

"My favorite!" I sat up. "Thanks!"

Lorel waved it away.

"Who was on the phone, Aunt Gully?" I heaped my shortcake with fresh strawberries and whipped cream.

"I've lined up helpers for the night we're working The Stellene Lupo Affair," Aunt Gully grinned. "Harmony Harbor, here we come."

When I finished my shortcake, I set my plate on the tray with a sigh.

Lorel's phone buzzed. "Gotta take this."

She went inside, no doubt heading to the small downstairs guest bedroom. Growing up we'd shared one of the bedrooms upstairs under the eaves but now she slept in the little room on the first floor that had been Uncle Rocco's study. Since our mother had died giving birth to me, Aunt Gully had been more than an aunt to us. When my dad was out lobstering, we lived with her and Uncle Rocco.

"Probably Patrick." Aunt Gully pressed her lips together in a little red lipsticked downward bow.

I frowned. "Aunt Gully, I can't help it. I know she's a grown woman and all, but her dating Patrick again makes me just furious."

Aunt Gully shook out the tablecloth. "Everyone has to make their own mistakes, Allie." Her eyes were worried. "Maybe she'll meet someone new in Boston. Take her mind off Patrick."

"Guys as hot as Patrick aren't exactly a dime a dozen." Though hotness alone didn't explain Patrick's allure, did it? Why did Lorel keep taking him back? He always hurt her. He always had another woman. It always ended in tears. My eyes met Aunt Gully's and I realized it was simple. For all his faults, despite them, Lorel loved Patrick.

"Oh, I forgot." Aunt Gully folded her tablecloth. "Bertha asked if one of you girls could help her on her boat tomorrow morning. Her sciatica's flaring up and her doctor told her to get some help with her lobster traps. Lorel said you needed a break from work and that she was taking your morning shift. So you wouldn't mind helping Bertha, would you?"

I let my spoon clatter onto the tray. *Thanks a lot, Lorel.*